"What's a wyvern? How did you get here? What do you want?"

With each question, the creature flinched.

Moira shut her mouth and waited.

The wyvern blinked. "Wyvern is drag...on."

Moira's eyes widened. That leap her mind hadn't wanted to take came back to her. Except it wasn't a leap anymore. It was a cliff. And her thoughts had just been pushed off into the abyss below. "There are no such things. Dragons don't exist." The words were out of her mouth before she could stop them.

The dragon's head ducked. At the same time, it lifted a shoulder as if to say, *Well, here I am.*

The door in Moira's head cracked open. Her breath started to come faster and faster, the muscles in her chest contracted, and all of a sudden it was too much. The walls of the cave pressed in on her. Head swimming, she knew she had to get out of there. She lowered the pick. "I can't—I have to go. It's—I have to get out of here."

"Wait."

She rushed to the fissure, crouched, and made her way through the rock wall to the outside, even as the voice of the dragon rose to reach her ears.

"Wait—drag...oneer!"

The Dragoneer

Amber Boudreau

DRAGON STREET PRESS

DSP

CINCINNATI OHIO

A Dragon Street Press Book

PRINTING HISTORY
Published July 2020.
2nd printing . . . March 2022

3 5 7 6 4 2

Trade Paperback
ISBN: 1-7331225-2-4 ISBN-13:
978-1-7331225-2-8

Printed in the United States of America

To my family,

in all the ways you define the word.

1

Moira Noble ran the back of her wrist across her forehead, wiping the sweat from her brow. The rock samples she'd collected that morning weighed more than the food she ate and the water she drank. The extra weight pulled at the straps of her backpack, making her shoulders ache, but it didn't slow her down. Her strides ate up the distance between where she was and where she wanted to be.

The briefest of rainstorms had blown through earlier, turning the hills a green so bright, her eyes hurt. Ahead, an overgrown trail came into view, leading upward. Her heart thrummed with exertion, but a pinch of sadness gave it an extra squeeze. Moira was prepared for the emotion. It came with the bittersweet memory of the last time she'd visited the top of the hill with her dad. They'd raced to the peak, laughing the whole way. She'd almost beat him, too, because she was tall, like him. At almost six feet—when not stooped under the weight of a bag full of rocks—people often asked her if she played basketball. Despite her father having played in college, she did not.

The toe of her boot caught on an angular stone and sent it flying, drawing her thoughts away from the past. She liked rocks. Identifying the ones on the other side of the hill would fill a void on the geologic map she was drawing up for her earth science class. The finished map would be a big part of the project. She had to do well on it.

Moira circled the base of the hill, tramping through the dirt and brush until she came to a clearing, thirty feet across and twenty feet deep. She crossed the grass to stand against the tree line and craned her neck. The rock wall rose straight up into the sky, the peak out of sight.

Her backpack slid to the ground with a thud, and she rolled back the sleeves of her khaki button-down shirt. Underneath, she wore a plain cotton tank. It stuck to her back. She tugged the fabric away from her sweat-slicked skin, sank down to sit in the shade, and grabbed her water bottle for a long drink. The grass tickled her legs, bare below the hem of her shorts. The summer temperatures were hanging on. That morning, she had added a floppy-brimmed sun hat to keep her curls from going every which way. They still went every which way. They were just out of sight.

Moira slipped her water bottle away, dug out the weatherproof journal she kept her notes in, flipping it open to where she had left off. She clicked her pen three times, climbing to her feet. Drawing a rough sketch of the cliff face, she noted any interesting contacts or faults while ignoring the graffiti. She silently wished Hoss and Joey luck, whoever they were. She hoped their love really was 4-EVA but didn't appreciate their need to spray paint it all over the cliff face. Finished with her sketch, she pulled out her borrowed digital SLR camera and snapped a few photos. She wrote the file numbers in her notes to match them up later because that was the level of attention to detail the project required. The same level she tried to apply to everything, not just projects that determined her grade.

The tinny sound of an 80's rock song reached her ears over the rustling of leaves, and she smiled. She knew the ringtone. The caller borrowed her phone one day, set it up, and Moira never bothered to change it. She pulled her phone from her pocket and swiped the screen to answer. "A-ha."

"Hey, Em, wh—" The wind snatched Ansel's words away. Their connection hummed with static.

She stepped in close to a tall oak. "What?"

"I said what are you doing? Where are you?"

"I'm in the woods working on something for school."

"Really?" Surprise made his voice raise half an octave.

"Yeah, why?"

"The woods are creepy. Aaron cut his run through there short the other day. Didn't say why—just kept looking over his shoulder for the rest of the day. Jumped at every little sound."

Moira lifted a brow, glad that her friend couldn't see her. Aaron and Ansel were twin brothers. On more than one occasion she'd witnessed a silent glance or nod from one to the other. These small exchanges often took the place of entire conversations. More than once she'd wondered if all siblings shared the ability to communicate in such a way, or if it had more to do with the fact that they were twins. She wasn't sure, not having any brothers or sisters herself.

"Are you okay out there? By yourself?"

"I'm fine, thanks." She appreciated his concern, but she was doing okay. She hadn't had an episode in forever.

"All right. I still owe you a movie. Ready to collect?"

Their plan to celebrate her birthday by sitting in the dark with a room full of strangers while sharing a bucket of popcorn had fallen through. Moira had been down with some twenty-four-hour bug her aunt said was going around at the time. The flu, or whatever it was, had come with a fever that knocked her out and she'd missed the entirety of her fifteenth birthday.

Moira glanced at her incomplete map. "I've still got some stuff to finish up out here. Call you later?"

"Yeah. Whenever. Don't do anything I wouldn't do."

"But then I would never get anything done."

"Har, har." Ansel's false laugh cut off as they disconnected.

Moira slipped her journal and camera away along with her hat and dug out the rock pick she'd found in her dad's things. At first glance, it looked like a hammer, but it had a flat, square face and a long, curved head that tapered back to a point. Squatting down with her head tilted in search of a spot where she might break off a piece of rock for a fresh surface, a particular section of the wall caught her interest. The pattern of weathering and lichen growth didn't quite fit. They didn't line up the way she expected them to. "Huh." Head tilted the other way, she chewed the inside of her lip, resting the pick against her shoulder.

Moira stood, taking one step into the clearing. The world went silent. She stopped. Both of her arms broke out in gooseflesh. All she could hear was the whooshing sound of blood through her ears, which was strange because there was always some kind of noise in the woods between the birds singing and the wind blowing. But not right then. In that instant, the world held its breath. It reminded her of a lull in a conversation, like a pause in the back and forth between Earth and all its inhabitants. The moment passed, and she heard a black-capped chickadee call its name, *chick-a-dee-dee-dee*.

Moira shook herself and strode forward. This would be her last stop for the day, she decided. She had other homework, and tomorrow was Monday. The map could wait. It wasn't due for a while. She headed straight to the section of the rock wall that interested her. The patterns there didn't line up because of a fault in the rock, which wasn't unexpected, but it wasn't just a crack. It was a fissure. She stepped in close to the rock face and peered into the dark crevice. There was no way to tell how deep it was. She switched on her phone's flashlight app and shined the light into the crack. The fissure bent back on itself, the grey stones folded over. It looked tight, which meant she had to crouch, knees out, and sidle in sideways, around the bend, into a cave.

Some indirect light made its way inside through the rock face, but the only other light came from her phone, which wasn't bright enough to reach the edges of the pitch-black interior. A musty scent invaded her nose, the cooler air making her shiver. She edged forward, sure that she would run into the back of the cave any second, but after ten feet she hadn't reached it. She shined the light upward, but couldn't make out any details of the ceiling above. Gravel crunched underfoot, but there weren't any animal droppings, which she took as a good sign.

A scraping noise made her jump. Her head whipped around, searching for the source.

There it was again, louder.

Whatever made the noise was getting closer.

Moira took a deep breath and blew it out slowly, trying to think. Bears were rarely seen this far south in Wisconsin, but today could be her lucky day. She remembered the rock pick and gripped the handle tight, raising it over her head.

"What's that?" she squeaked. She cleared her throat and tried again. "Who's there? I'm not scared of you."

The scraping noise stopped.

There was a pop as the light on her phone burst and went out. Moira swiped at the screen and held the dimmer light in front of her.

A voice reached her ears, breathy and soft. "What's…that…who's…there…"

That's not an echo, she thought.

The scraping noise was way too close this time. Moira spun to face the way she'd come in, and, to her knowledge, the only way out.

Movement—there at the edge of the light filtering in from outside.

Some kind of creature, low to the ground, with yellow eyes. The breathy voice came from the creature's mouth, her own words repeated back to her. "I'm not s-s-s-scared of you."

2

When Moira was eleven, her father died suddenly of an undiagnosed heart condition. His death broke something loose inside of her, leaving her unmoored. Her anxiety skyrocketed. She couldn't deal with ordinary, everyday tasks the way she did before. Her days often started well, but frequently ended with her in a heap on the floor, heart racing, gasping for air in a pool of sweat and tears. She fixated on situations or circumstances beyond her control, losing focus, falling into a tightening spiral from which she couldn't break free. It was like her world sharpened and imploded simultaneously.

She scraped by, managing to pass the sixth grade but didn't return for the seventh or eighth, instead opting for homeschooling. Regular therapy sessions taught her how to cope with the symptoms of her anxiety. She knew how to handle her physical responses and it gave her the confidence to deal with whatever life had to throw at her, but this—the yellow-eyed creature in the cave—this felt like a curveball.

Moira blinked in an attempt to calmly assimilate the information her eyes were sending her brain, trying to make sense of what she was seeing. The creature was backlit by the cave entrance. It moved with a deliberate sinuosity and suppleness, reminding Moira of a cat. Except that whatever it was, it was definitely not a cat. For one thing, it was as big as an Alaskan husky and twice as long when you considered the tail. And instead of fur, it was covered in scales so dark they soaked up the sliver of light from outside, making its yellow eyes, the pupils nothing but vertical slits, stand out all the more.

It reminded her of some kind of lizard. The fact that it could speak added a whole new dimension to her rapidly expanding reality. If she didn't know better, she would say the creature was a—*nope*. Her mind skidded to a halt unwilling to make the leap.

The creature glided forward.

Moira jerked back, adrenaline surging, and lifted the rock pick high. She could feel herself starting to panic, a sensation she knew well.

She forced herself to stop, and take a deep breath. The extra oxygen acted like a big stick. Moira used it to beat back the part of her that wanted to scream and run away. In her head, she put that scared part in a room and slammed the door shut. Then she could think. If the creature meant her harm, why step into the light, ruin the element of surprise? Why speak at all?

Still scared, but nonetheless intrigued, she kept the pick raised over her head. "What are you?"

"What..." it said before lifting its blunt nose in the air and tilting its head back. The creature stared for so long Moira stole a glance upward. The ceiling was dark. "...am I." It finished, lowering its head. The weight of its yellow gaze tried to pin her in place, but she was already growing accustomed to its odd-colored eyes.

She pocketed her phone, which was no help anyway, and took a step to the side, maintaining the distance between them.

At first, only the creature's eyes followed her, but soon its head turned on top of its long neck and it, too, took a step. It slipped away from the entrance, deeper into the cave opposite her. Moira could see an angular head with a long snout. The end of its nose was flat like it had run into a wall. Its elongated neck was thick and flared into a pair of broad shoulders. The scraping sound came again. Moira placed the noise as the creature's curved claws came into contact with the stone floor.

The creature came to a stop and settled back on its haunches, torso lifted upright. Despite moving around on all fours, Moira got the impression it could walk on its back legs with no trouble if it wanted. If the creature hadn't stopped, they might have continued circling each other.

"I am…"

Moira was so wrapped up in getting a good look at the thing she forgot she had asked it a question.

What is it?

She stopped, waiting for the answer, and watched the creature's head tilt one way and then the other as if struggling to find the word.

As it struggled, so did she.

Why am I still here?

She adjusted the pick in her grip and glanced at the light filtering into the cave through the fissure. The way out was clear. The creature and she were both about the same distance away from it now. She wasn't much of a runner, but her limbs twitched with the adrenaline pumping through her veins. If she gave in to the impulse, she could be out of there in a flash.

But how far would she have to run before she could forget what she'd seen? The edge of the forest? Her house? Judging by the pursing of the creature's mouth, the answer to her question was forthcoming. She could leave and know nothing, or stay and learn something.

Moira had always been an inquisitive person. She got a healthy dose of natural curiosity from her dad and she thought he'd be disappointed if she left now. She wanted to know more.

"Wy…vern. I am wyvern."

Her eyes slid shut for an instant. The danger in wanting to know more was the near painful guarantee that one answer wouldn't be enough. One answer could, and often did, lead to more questions. Her aunt had warned her that her curiosity would get her into trouble one day. This could be the day.

"What's a wyvern? How did you get here? What do you want?"

With each question, the creature flinched.

Moira shut her mouth and waited.

The wyvern blinked. "Wyvern is drag...on."

Moira's eyes widened. That leap her mind hadn't wanted to take came back to her. Except it wasn't a leap anymore. It was a cliff. And her thoughts had just been pushed off into the abyss below. "There are no such things. Dragons don't exist." The words were out of her mouth before she could stop them.

The dragon's head ducked. At the same time, it lifted a shoulder as if to say, *Well, here I am.*

The door in Moira's head cracked open. Her breath started to come faster and faster, the muscles in her chest contracted, and all of a sudden it was too much. The walls of the cave pressed in on her. Head swimming, she knew she had to get out of there. She lowered the pick. "I can't—I have to go. It's—I have to get out of here."

"Wait."

She rushed to the fissure, crouched, and made her way through the rock wall to the outside, even as the voice of the dragon rose to reach her ears.

"Wait—drag...oneer!"

Moira kept moving. Outside, she shook her head and then shook it again, almost as if she believed shaking it enough would make her forget about what she had seen and heard.

She scooped up her backpack. The clash of rocks bouncing against each other reminded her that she hadn't collected a fresh rock sample, and she didn't care. She had to get away from there, but couldn't stop herself from glancing over her shoulder to see if the dragon followed.

No sign of it.

She took off into the woods, her mind searching for a way to explain away what had just happened. When she'd stopped for a granola bar earlier, she decided she must have fallen asleep. That must be it. Finding the cave had been a dream. It never happened. In fact, she was still dreaming. She pinched the skin on her forearm between her thumb and index finger hard. It stung.

The musty smell of the cave still clung to her clothes. No way had she dreamt that. She sneezed.

Her steps slowed. A dragon. The word conjured up all sorts of images. The one that kept coming up had a knight in shining armor bearing a long sword, silhouetted against a wall of flame sprouting from the throat of a giant, winged beast. And then there were the myths. Weren't dragons supposed to fly around, setting fire to the countryside until someone chained a virgin to a rock? Didn't dragons hoard piles of gold and treasure that didn't belong to them and only speak in riddles, if they spoke at all? Dragons breathed fire first and asked questions later. They were the villains, meant to be slain by guys in suits of metal.

They didn't talk to teenage girls.

Did they?

Moira's footsteps slowed further. The more she thought about it, the slower she moved. By the time she admitted to herself that she might have let her anxiety get the better of her, she was at a near standstill.

The sun disappeared behind a cloud, and the abrupt lack of sunshine made Moira tilt her head back to see if another storm was brewing. The ground was shady under the trees, but the forest had taken on a darker, bluish tinge, which was surely caused by more than a single cloud.

A wet, snuffling sound reached her ears. Something snorted once, harsh and deep, far off into the woods. Moira drew in a deep breath, prepared to tell the wyvern what she thought about it following her. She spun, but there was nothing there.

"Shhh," hissed a voice above her.

She started and looked up.

Wrapped around a sturdy pine, some ten feet off the ground and four feet above the top of her head, was the dragon. It held up a single digit, facing the direction they had both come from. Its brows lowered, if she could call the spiny ridges over its eyes *brows*, the dragon watched, its head cocked to the side, eyes scanning.

Moira swallowed. Whatever she had been about to say was forgotten. She stayed where she was and strained to hear anything, but nothing reached her ears beyond the rustling of leaves and birdcalls. She stretched her neck, but couldn't see anything. Minutes passed and nothing stirred. She glanced upward. The dragon blinked, its neck relaxing. Still wound around the tree, it looked down at her, nodded once, bunched its lithe, reptilian body like a coiled spring, and jumped to a tree five feet away.

Moira didn't move. The dragon stared back at her and dipped its head, which suggested she should follow. She did so quietly, watching the wyvern leap time and again from one tree to the next. What little noise it made could have been confused with the scrabbling of a squirrel in search of a nut.

Her sense of direction told her they were traveling in a wide arc back toward the cave. She estimated they were halfway there when the dragon dropped to the ground and faced her.

The dark clouds had moved along, and the sun filtered down through waving branches burdened with their summer loads. Light flowed over the dragon and spilled onto the ground. Unimpeded by cave walls and darkness, Moira circled the creature. The dragon appeared to take her speculation in stride and used it as an opportunity to observe her, turning its head to follow her movements.

The dragon sat back. To observe her more comfortably, Moira presumed. Having now seen it in full sunlight, Moira breathed easier because she might have still been able to convince herself her mind was playing tricks on her. Sure, she'd pinched herself and she knew she wasn't dreaming, but she could imagine herself lying awake in the middle of the night, unable to sleep until she made peace with what she had seen. A trick of the mind was an excuse her hindbrain would have latched onto, but not now. Fancifulness didn't hold up to the strong light of day.

"You're real. You're a real dragon," Moira said.

"Yesss." It tended to hiss when speaking.

Her gaze darted to the trees around them. "What was that? What were we hiding from?"

Moira waited, certain the dragon was searching for the right word. Its speech had been mostly stilted as if it were having a problem with the language. Perhaps it didn't have a name for whatever it was.

While it struggled with the word, the dragon flexed its right hand. It had five digits, just like her. The movement caught her eye, but it was the blood that got her full attention. Ruby red droplets welled up from the base of one of the dragon's talons, glinting in the light.

Moira pointed with her chin at the injured digit. "You're hurt."

The dragon glanced down, head jerking closer to the injury. A drop of blood hit the dirt, and it hissed.

"May I see it?" Moira asked. The dragon's blood was as red as her own. She wanted to help.

The dragon cradled its right hand in its left. It had four fingers and an opposable thumb just like her, but its feet were long, with only three toes. For a second, she wasn't sure it would show her. Then it stretched out its right arm. She bent forward. The scales at the base of the talon weren't just broken, the inch-and-a-half long talon itself was split and oozing.

"I think I have something that'll help." Her voice trailed off as she shrugged off the straps of her backpack, setting the rock pick aside. "This is duct tape." Moira held up the small roll she carried with her when she was hiking. "I'm going to wrap this around here so it doesn't split anymore." She tore off a long strip and took a knee, putting her and the wyvern on the same level. Weren't dragons supposed to be bigger? And fly? She stole a peek over its shoulder. No wings. Moira tore the strip in half down the middle, then wound the tape around the root of the split at the base of the talon. She ignored the fact that the talon was longer than she'd initially thought, closer to two inches, and very pointy. As she worked, she snuck glances at the dragon.

Its attention remained fixed on what she was doing. Moira tugged, trying to keep the tape as taut as possible as she wrapped. When the piece ran out, she grabbed the other half. The entire time, the dragon watched. Moira focused on the task at hand, but as soon as she finished, she eased back and clapped her hands, rubbing them together to disguise their trembling.

"That should hold things for now." She gathered up her stuff.

The dragon inspected her work, giving his digits a waggle, flexing and making a fist before relaxing again.

Moira slipped the rock pick into her bag.

"Wait," it said.

"What?"

The dragon motioned to the pick, its gaze going from the rock pick back to her.

She suspected the dragon was telling her to keep the pick out, probably for protection. She hadn't seen anything earlier, but the dragon had had a better vantage point. She recalled its stillness and intensity. Both worried her. Then she remembered she was having a conversation with a dragon and decided that, yes, she would keep the pick handy.

"Okay," she agreed.

Bag over her shoulder and pick at her side, Moira stood. The wyvern's head didn't even come to her waist. She watched it open its mouth and snap it shut again. As close as she was, she heard its teeth click as they came together. She hadn't gotten a good look inside its mouth, but she imagined rows of pointed, serrated teeth. The dragon flexed the hand she had treated and raised its head to meet her gaze. "Help."

Moira shrugged, sending the pick into motion at her side. "With what? What can I do?"

A shudder ran through the dragon as it drew a breath. "Rrr...rocks."

"There are tons of rocks around here." She knew. She'd been collecting them all morning. She could have pulled some out right then.

The dragon shook its head. "Need...f-f-fire rocks."

Fire rocks? Did the dragon mean—

A twig snapped.

Both of them jumped, their heads whipping around.

3

Another twig cracked in the distance. The sound reverberated off of the trees around them.

"Go." The dragon turned to the nearest tree and climbed, putting Moira's tape job to the test.

"What—where are you going?"

More twigs snapped as a rhythmic pounding came closer, the sound of running feet. Moira turned to face the noise, standing her ground. She squeezed the handle of the rock pick tight, unsure of what good it would do her.

Aaron Idlewild ran straight and tall with his elbows tucked in.

Moira's breath rushed out of her, her body sagging with relief. Aaron pulled up short and jogged in place, knees high, staring at Moira.

He could stop running, she thought.

It took all of her might, but she did not glance around to see if the dragon was still there.

"Moira." That was it. Just her name. And a hint of surprise.

"Aaron. What are you doing here?"

He shrugged, as if the answer were obvious, which she guessed it was. "Out for a run. How about you?"

"Working on a project. For school."

He continued to jog in place. It continued to annoy her.

She glanced over her shoulder but didn't see the dragon anywhere.

"What's up?" Aaron followed her gaze and leaned to the side to see around her.

Moira sucked in a breath. "What? Nothing."

She couldn't risk looking for the wyvern with Aaron hanging around. He might see it and get the wrong idea, like he discovered it, and take all the credit, which was ridiculous because it wasn't like she was going to tell anyone. No one would believe her. If the dragon wanted someone else to see it, then it would show itself, as it did to her. She waited, but Aaron didn't yell out in terror and the dragon didn't reappear.

Moira knew exactly where the dragon had gone. But there was no reason to go back to the cave until she had the fire rocks. If the rocks around there weren't the fire kind, where would she find the right ones?

Moira squinted into the distance. "Got to go. Bye," she said. She turned on her heel and marched off in the direction that would take her to the main trail out of the woods and home. For a solid five seconds, she thought she'd gotten away without having to say more. She figured Aaron would continue with his run. And he did. He jogged behind her at a snail's pace.

She ignored him.

Aaron and she were friendly, but they weren't friends. They were polite acquaintances on a good day and rivals on a bad one because ever since he beat his brother out of the womb by fourteen minutes, Aaron had to be the first at everything. It didn't matter at whose expense. He had a competitive side a mile wide. It hadn't bothered her until sixth grade when he'd done something so sneaky and underhanded it still upset her to think about.

Later, after her dad died, Moira's own competitive nature sprouted, but she wasn't interested in competing against anyone but herself. The other kids in their class, Aaron included, didn't get that. Moira kept to herself and didn't waste energy on drama or games. It surprised her that Aaron had spoken to her in the first place. It wasn't like they ran in the same circles.

He jogged alongside her. "Everything okay?"

"Just great. I was working on something, and now I'm going home."

"Are you sure you're okay? You looked pretty spooked back there."

"I'm fine."

"You're positive?"

Moira spun to face the identical twin of her best friend, so alike, but so different. Aaron's hair was a touch shorter and less tousled. He also played more sports and had a deeper tan as a result, along with a few freckles his brother didn't.

"I'm absolutely certain. What about you? I thought the woods gave you the creeps."

He stopped jogging.

Finally.

"What makes you say that?"

Moira pressed her lips together. Had she betrayed Ansel's trust? She hoped not. Instead, she said nothing and shrugged, hoping Aaron wouldn't guess who she heard it from.

"Look, the woods aren't safe for people wandering around by themselves," Aaron said.

"You're by yourself."

"Yeah, but I'm a guy and I'm running."

She narrowed her eyes and spoke slowly. "So, the woods aren't safe for me because I'm a girl, and I'm not running."

She gave him the benefit of the doubt and waited for him to elaborate, but he didn't say he'd seen anything strange.

When he shrugged, she turned and started walking again.

"I didn't mean it like that," Aaron said, raising his voice.

"Like what?" Moira muttered to herself, refusing to turn around. She'd already walked away—twice. Her ears burned, listening to hear if he would follow her again. He didn't.

Who did he think he was? Moira had walked through the woods almost every day for over a year and more times than she could count before then. She wasn't afraid of them. The blunt head of the rock pick tapped against her thigh as she walked. She'd never had a reason to be afraid. Since she'd run into the dragon she might have to reevaluate.

Moira hit the main trail and took it out of the woods, crossing the street at the end of her block and heading down the alleyway until she came to her backyard. She used her key to let herself into the kitchen. Her backpack full of rocks hit the floor hard as she kicked off her shoes and set the pick on the counter.

"Aunt Paige! I'm home."

No answer.

But there was a note on the table. Her aunt had been called into work and wouldn't be back before dinner. The note asked Moira to check the mail since she was expecting a package.

There wasn't anything at the door, so Moira checked the mailbox. The glossy pages of the alumni newsletter addressed to her aunt for her and her father's alma mater caught her eye. The paper crinkled when she grabbed it. Continuing her education beyond high school hadn't always been her goal. Then after her father passed away, she'd applied herself to her studies and been rewarded with higher grades. Now her dream of going to the small liberal arts college her aunt had attended and where her parents met was within reach. All she had to do was keep her head down, nose clean, and act together for the next three years.

She'd also just agreed to help an honest-to-God fantastical creature.

Because it asked her to.

Again, the thought crossed her mind that finding a dragon could be considered an important scientific discovery. Maybe even the leg up she'd need on her future college application. Just as quickly, she dashed the thought away with a dose of reality. She wasn't going to tell anyone. If the dragon wanted someone else's help, even Aaron's, it would have shown itself. She would help it find some fire rocks, and that would be the end of it.

Upstairs, Moira pushed thoughts of her future aside to focus on what exactly a fire rock was and where she could find some. She consulted the internet, getting off track once when she searched for wyvern—not at all what she would describe having come into contact with. A short while later she thought she knew what a fire rock was, how they were made, and where to find them.

Afterward, she headed down to the basement to go through more of her dad's old things, finding what she needed in the same box where she'd discovered the rock pick. Then she called Ansel because she needed a set of wheels and someone to drive them.

"Can we go to Devil's Lake?" Moira asked when Ansel answered.

"Sure, but why the sudden desire to visit the largest state park in Wisconsin?"

"I'll explain when you get here."

Moira slipped her dad's detailed atlas and gazetteer into her backpack and took two minutes to scarf down a peanut butter and honey sandwich. She refilled her water bottle and grabbed a couple of protein bars for the road. The door banged shut behind her as an old pickup truck rolled to a stop behind her house. Ansel drove with his elbow stuck out the window of what he insisted was a classic automobile. He'd had the truck before he had a driver's license, and his plan for as long as she had known him was to restore it with help from his dad and Aaron. Between the three of them, they'd gotten it to run, but it was still three-toned and all dents where it wasn't curved.

"Ready to go places in style?" he asked as she rounded the grill.

Moira pulled hard on the passenger door and slid inside. "Absolutely." She yanked the door closed. "Too bad we'll be in your truck."

Ansel tsked in mock outrage.

She gave the dash an affectionate pat and buckled her seatbelt—a feature Ansel's parents had insisted he add before they let him drive anywhere.

"What do you need all the way out at Devil's Lake?"

"Rocks." The park was known for its 500-foot-high bluffs of purple quartzite. She had a very small sample of the metamorphosed sandstone upstairs in her room, but it wasn't what she was after.

When Ansel didn't respond, she glanced over. He arched a brow.

"They're for a project." A dragon she met in a cave in the woods asked her to find some fire rocks. Sounded like a project to her.

The truck shuddered as Ansel shifted into gear.

"We can go to a movie some other time. My treat," she said.

"Nope. No problem. It's your birthday. We can go to Devil's Lake if you want." Ansel slid a pair of dark sunglasses up his nose, covering his hazel eyes. "Your aunt's not going to be mad I'm taking you across county lines or anything, is she?"

"Nah, she got called into work. I left a note."

Ansel bobbed his head. A dark blonde lock of hair fell across his forehead. He shoved it back and tapped his fingers against the steering wheel before running his hands from top to bottom. A minute later, she caught him rubbing his jaw and checking his chin in the mirror. Did he think he'd missed a spot shaving? He pushed a hand through his hair again.

It was almost like he was nervous. "Do you have a hot date or something?" she asked. He hadn't mentioned seeing anyone, but it wasn't unheard of. His last two girlfriends had shared his interest in art. Moira lacked talent in that area herself, but she appreciated those who had an artistic gift, like Ansel.

"What? No. No, I'm not seeing anyone." He cleared his throat. "But I was thinking. Maybe—"

Something zoomed into Moira's peripheral vision. "Look out!"

Ansel stomped on the brakes and threw an arm in front of Moira as a sedan flew through the intersection. The truck ground to a reluctant halt, and they avoided hitting the car's rear quarter panel by a hairsbreadth.

"Idiot!" Ansel called after the driver, turning back to Moira. "You okay?"

Moira glanced down at the hand Ansel still held splayed across her sternum. He jerked it back as if scalded. Their eyes met, and a blush worked its way up his neck.

She huffed out a laugh. "Nice driving. My aunt does that, too."

"What?"

"Throws her arm up in front of me like it's the only thing that will save my life if we get in an accident."

Ansel laughed and flexed his hand before returning it to the steering wheel. "Driver's instinct," he said and faced forward. The truck rumbled forward. His elbow found the window again, and his hands settled at the bottom of the wheel. He had nice hands. The tips of his fingers were usually stained with ink when they weren't covered in paint, but they cleaned up well when he bothered to make an effort.

Moira had reconnected with Ansel when she'd returned to public school freshman year. After a couple of years of homeschooling, she'd been ready to get back, at least emotionally and academically. Socially, returning after a long absence had been hard. She kept to herself, and if there were no assigned seats, she sat in the back of the class with no one behind her. Her therapist called it a coping mechanism. Ansel sat in the back, too, so that he could draw without interruption. They were in algebra. One day after they'd both completed their assignments, Moira was staring off into space working through an equation in her head. To the outside observer, she guessed it might have looked like she was woolgathering.

"Are you finished?" Ansel had asked

Moira had started. She wasn't used to anyone speaking directly to her. What she was used to were lots of sympathetic looks and pitying glances. She didn't blame them. She'd cut herself off from everyone while she dealt with her issues, but the public school was where she was supposed to be. Everyone would get used to her being back sooner or later.

Moira recognized Ansel. They had never really spoken, but now he waited for a reply.

She nodded.

"You could work on tomorrow's assignment." He indicated the chalkboard with a tilt of his head. Their highly organized teacher had listed problem sets for the next two weeks.

"I did it already."

His eyebrows had gone up as he blinked. "You need a hobby." He pushed a blank piece of paper toward her. "Can you draw?"

Moira had picked up her pencil. She drew a quick sketch. When she was finished, he pulled the paperback and looked at it. "Okay. Well. It's a stick figure. Arms, legs, a head—everything. I can work with this."

The bell rang. Moira had gotten up and walked away without another word. She was not an artist. She knew that. It didn't bother her to have it pointed out, but she wasn't sure how to respond. Her social skills were still more than a little rusty.

The next day, she'd finished all of the assigned algebra homework and started on an essay for another class. In silence, Ansel slid a piece of paper to her. It was blank, but she could tell there was something on the other side. She flipped it over. Her sad drawing from the day before was now surrounded by a plethora of stick figures, each one doing something different. And, she realized, Ansel must be very talented if he could draw stick figures involved in any number of different activities including badminton, horse-back riding, and swimming. Her stick person continued to stand there, a quiet observer, not unlike Moira herself most of the time. She took her pencil and gave it a face; two dots for eyes and a curved line for a mouth. The drawing still hung over her desk at home.

The memory made Moira smile.

They drove for a few blocks in silence. Then Ansel asked, "When are you gonna start driving, anyway?"

Near-miss aside, at least he didn't seem to be nervous anymore. She wondered what he'd been about to say before the car had cut them off. He said he wasn't seeing anyone. Maybe he wasn't dating for a while. When he wanted a girlfriend, he could find one without trouble. Regardless of his relationship status, Ansel always made time for her. At least he had all through freshman year, and now, today, a fact which did not escape her. They never flirted and he'd never suggested they date. She wasn't sure what she would say if he did. She'd never thought of him that way before. Ansel was her best friend. She didn't want to mess it up.

Moira returned her focus to the road. "I just turned fifteen." Ansel was sixteen and already had the truck, but he couldn't park it at school until next year when they would be juniors. "Probably not until after I take driver's ed. Maybe in a couple of years."

"You mean next summer."

"Maybe. Driver's Ed costs money."

"You could get a job after school. Work weekends."

"Doing well in school is my job."

"That sounds like your aunt talking."

Moira tilted her head in agreement. "True, but money's tight. At least until I turn eighteen."

Ansel frowned. "And you get to vote?"

"Yes. That. And the trust my dad set up for me kicks in. It's not much, but it might be enough for driver's ed. Possibly a car." Moira had known about the trust before her dad's death, but she forgot about it all the time. Any amount of money was a poor substitute for a missing parent.

When Ansel didn't say anything more, Moira leaned over and switched the radio on, filling the cab of the truck with classic rock. Moira sang along loudly while Ansel sang off-key. He turned the radio down when they got close to the lake. "Where are we going exactly?"

"Keep heading this direction," Moira said and opened her bag. She took out the gazetteer and a geologic map of the area. Cross-referencing the two, she guided Ansel along in the direction she thought they needed to go. After a few minutes, she told him to pull over.

"What, here?"

"Stop or you'll pass it."

"Pass what? There's nothing here." Ansel pulled over, put the truck in park and flicked on his hazards.

Moira grabbed the pick out of her bag and jumped out of the cab. At the spot where the edge of the road cut through an outcrop of rock, she stood considering. Then she swung the square face of the pick, connecting with a *thunk*.

"Whoa," Ansel said, climbing from the truck. "What did it ever do to you?"

Another blow and a piece broke free. Moira bent to pick it up and examined the fresh surface where the rock had broken away from the wall. Exposed to light and air for the first time since having been formed, it gleamed under her eye. She tossed it aside. "This isn't the right stuff." She headed back to the truck.

"What are you looking for?" Ansel asked.

"Igneous rocks."

Two stops later, her head bent over another rock, Moira found what she was after. "Jackpot."

Ansel leaned against the side of his truck. "What is it?"

"Rhyolite."

"Rye-o-what?"

"Rhyolite. It's an igneous rock." Moira held the sample close to her eye. "I can make out individual crystals in a finer-grained matrix, which I think means it cooled slowly until some sort of event took place that made it cool off fast." She held the rock out for Ansel to take.

He shook his head. "You lost me at Rhyolite."

Moira pursed her lips, but she didn't get the chance to respond. A car pulled in behind Ansel's truck, lights flashing.

4

Moira's heart rate picked up a few beats per minute.

We're not doing anything wrong.

She held on to the thought tight, taking a deep breath and willing herself to remain calm.

"Uh-oh." Ansel straightened away from the side of his truck.

Moira couldn't tell if he was seriously worried or not. No one liked it when the police showed up with flashing lights unless they were needed and sometimes not even then. There was no siren and as soon as the vehicle came to a stop, the lights switched off. Moira wasn't sure why the lights were turning in the first place. Ansel's truck was parked completely out of the way on the shoulder of the road, hazards on. They weren't driving so they couldn't be pulled over.

Ansel shifted away from the truck so that he stood next to Moira. They watched the driver's side door open. A sheriff's deputy unfolded himself from inside the black and gold cruiser. The engine he left running filled the still air with a dull roar.

The deputy smoothed down his dark hair, settling his hat on top of his head. He moved stiffly at first but his gait loosened as he came forward. His mirrored sunglasses made it hard to read his expression, but his square jaw was clean-shaven and shut tight. He stopped and hooked his thumbs over his belt loops, elbows out, at ease.

"Good afternoon," Moira said as she sucked in a breath. What was wrong with her? She should let Ansel do the talking. It was his truck. "What seems to be the trouble?" She almost bit her tongue. She didn't know where she found the nerve to speak. Her hands curled into fists, fingernails digging into palms.

Stop talking.

"No trouble I know of. I'm Deputy Williamson with the Sherriff's department. Who does this truck belong to?" His head turned the slightest bit from side to side considering them both.

Ansel raised his hand, but no higher than his shoulder. "That would be me."

"Are you having car trouble?"

Ansel lowered his hand. "No, sir."

"You mind telling me what you're doing out here on the side of the road then?"

"We're looking for rocks—tell him, Moira." Ansel nudged her with his elbow.

Moira nudged him back. "We're looking for rocks."

The deputy remained silent.

"For school," Ansel said. "We're looking for rocks for school. Right?" At least he didn't elbow her again.

"Right. They're for a class. I need a few samples to take back with me so I can run some tests."

The deputy's head tilted to the side as if he were waiting. Moira had already said more than she meant to. Thankfully, Ansel didn't feel the need to add anything further either.

"What school?" The deputy asked, breaking the stalemate.

"North Wesley," Ansel said.

"Wesley? Bit of a drive, isn't it?"

Moira did bite her tongue this time, refraining from making a sound.

Why, yes, but this is where the rocks are so we didn't have much of a choice.

What was wrong with her? They didn't have time for this. Moira's breath came faster and faster, her mind turning. And then spinning.

Ansel said, "Yes, sir, but it was a nice drive even with all the construction."

The rock pick and sample slipped from her fingers as Moira bent over, hands on her knees.

"Miss, are you all right?"

"Moira?" Ansel stuck his head down next to hers.

Her heart pounded in her chest, trying to beat its way free of her ribcage. "I can't breathe."

"What did she say?" the deputy asked.

Ansel told him.

"Let's get this tailgate down."

Moira heard metal ring against metal before she was pressed to sit down.

"Has this ever happened before?" the deputy wanted to know.

Ansel answered for her. "Not for a long time."

"Stay here."

Over the pounding of her heart, Moira heard footsteps leave and return.

"Put this here." Moira felt something cool and moist press against the back of her neck. Her hand reached back to hold it in place.

The deputy grunted. "Now I'm a bit of a rock hound myself. Most people go up to Devil's Lake to see the rocks there. What did you all find out this way?"

"Uh, this." Ansel grabbed the sample she had dropped and handed it to the deputy.

"Miss, what can you tell me about this?" He placed the rock in her free hand.

What did she know about the rock? She knew there was a dragon in the woods waiting for it and she wasn't getting any closer to getting back, sitting there doing nothing. Moira sucked in a breath and tried to blow it out slowly. The negative self-talk was not helping. She needed to be kind to herself. She hadn't had an attack in a long time. Given what she'd been through that morning, and what was happening now, it wasn't that surprising she might be overwhelmed so far from home.

Moira focused on the rock in her hand, squeezing it. The rough edges dug into her palm. How long did it take the individual crystals to form? She could give herself a minute to rest. When she was ready, she began to speak. If she was speaking, then she was breathing. She told the deputy what she had told Ansel about the rock and how it formed.

The deputy listened, nodding along until she was done telling him everything she knew about rhyolite, which wasn't much but turned out to be more than she thought. He probably didn't want to hear about the whole rock cycle, but that was where her mind went.

He didn't say anything for a while. Instead, he took the rock, turning it over and over in his hands. He'd removed his sunglasses. When he looked at her, she saw his eyes were a tawny brown, a shade or two darker than his uniform. "Feel better?"

Moira dragged the compress from her neck. The folded piece of cloth had white markings against an inky blue background. The bandana was no longer cool. She held it out, but the deputy waved her away. "Keep it. Let me see some ID and you all can finish up here and be on your way."

Ansel's hand was already in his pocket. He fished out his wallet, opened it, and took out his driver's license.

Moira didn't move.

"Is there a problem, Miss?" the deputy asked.

Moira pointed. "My wallet is in my pocket."

"Go ahead and get it."

Moira stood up and retrieved her wallet. From inside she pulled out her school ID and handed it over.

"No driver's license?"

Moira caught the glance Ansel shot her from the corner of her eye but she didn't react. "No. I just turned fifteen and I don't drive, yet."

The deputy studied her ID. "North Wesley have a girl's basketball team?"

"Yes. But I'm not on it."

The deputy handed back their identification. "All right, then. Mr. Idlewild, let me see your registration, and I'll get you out of here."

"Sure thing."

The deputy turned away.

Ansel shrugged at Moira behind his back, climbed into the passenger side of the truck and took out some paperwork from the glove compartment. He handed it over. While the deputy checked it out on his computer in his car Ansel rejoined her.

"Should I be worried?" she asked.

Ansel shook his head. "Nope. He won't find anything." He turned toward her, eyes narrowed in scrutiny. "What about you? Do I need to be worried about you?"

"No. I'm okay. What do we do now?" she asked.

"We wait."

They probably shouldn't just stand there. Overcome with the sudden desire to be anywhere but there, Moira said, "Help me pick up some of these rocks." She started at the base of the outcrop picking up loose rocks and throwing them into the bed of the truck. Ansel helped. Together they cleared the roadside of rocks larger than a fist. Then she picked up her rock hammer and whacked off a few good chunks of the outcrop and threw those in the back of the truck too.

The dragon hadn't said how many fire rocks it needed or what it was going to do with them, just that it needed them. She wasn't sure how many she should collect.

A door slammed and the deputy came toward them with Ansel's paperwork. "Everything seems to be in order." He held the registration out to Ansel and peered into the truck bed, a frown forming between his brows. "Are you about finished up here?"

His expression told Moira they were done even if they weren't. If she didn't have enough rocks she could come back and get more.

At night, with no one around.

"We're all set."

They got in the truck. The deputy watched them put on their seatbelts and slipped back into his cruiser. Loose gravel crunched under the tires as the deputy made a U-turn from the shoulder of the road and took off.

Ansel turned to Moira, eyes wide. "What have you gotten me into? Is rock rustling illegal?"

"Not as far as I know. Picking up rocks from the side of a public road is not a crime. If we were on someone's private property it would be a different story."

Ansel nodded as he started the engine. He pulled back onto the road.

They drove for a minute before Moira said, "I think we need to go the other way."

"Not for at least five minutes we don't."

Moira checked the map and made a note of where they had found the rocks. Neither of them turned the radio on. The rocks boomed and clattered across the bed of the truck raising a racket whenever the road curved.

"Did I ever tell you my dad liked birds?" she asked.

Ansel glanced her way from across the cab. His brows drew together in a small frown, but he didn't say anything.

She didn't talk about her dad much. Maybe it was dealing with the deputy that made her think of him. The last officers she spoke with, besides the ones at her high school, were city cops, two of them. They'd come to the front door. Her aunt answered. Moira came running when she heard the first wrenching sob and got there in time to watch her aunt bury her face in her hands.

The memory made her chest tighten.

Moira nodded to herself and continued her story. "He did. My dad liked birds. I don't know why, but he did. And he liked to go birding. He'd come home all excited when he saw a bird he'd never seen before."

Ansel stared out the front window, eyes on the road, listening.

"He always took three things with him when he went birding." Moira held up her fingers as she counted them off, "a bird book, binoculars, and, most importantly, three forms of ID. I can't help but feel he'd be a little disappointed in me." She flicked her wrist and lowered her hand. She chewed on her bottom lip, caught up in her thoughts.

"Hey," Ansel said. When she didn't respond right away, he said it again, firmer. "Hey."

Moira turned. He watched her from across the cab of the truck.

"You didn't have anything to worry about back there. We didn't do anything wrong."

Moira huffed out a breath. "I know that. And I wasn't worried. I was with you." She faced forward.

A silent minute slipped away and she reached over to switch the radio back on. Ansel must have gotten the same idea because their hands collided and tangled. They laughed, and for a second Ansel's fingers squeezed hers. He smiled and said, "Thanks," before letting go and turning the radio on.

Moira knew she should be the one thanking him for driving her to the middle of nowhere to collect rocks. The moment passed as music filled the cab. By the time they pulled up behind her house, the day had grown later than she liked. She grabbed some crates from the basement and with Ansel's help got all the rocks unloaded and stored downstairs. About the time they closed the tailgate together, Moira's aunt came outside. She'd been home long enough to change out of her work scrubs into a pair of jeans and a plaid purple button-down she left untucked, covering the ensemble in a long hunter-green sweater. She leaned against the back-door jamb, a steaming mug of tea cupped in both hands, the tag flung over the side like a life preserver.

"Hey, Ansel. Would you like to stay for dinner?"

"Hi, Ms. Nobel. No, thank you. I'm helping my dad with the Chevelle tonight. Maybe another time?"

"Absolutely. Maybe by then, I'll have thought of something to cook." She sipped her tea.

"I hope that's decaf," Moira said.

Her aunt swallowed and pushed away from the door frame. "No way. You are not getting out of movie night again because I fall asleep on the couch."

"Is that tonight?"

"Yes, and it's my turn to pick." Her aunt's eyes narrowed. "Why?"

"I didn't finish a project I was working on today for school. I need to go back out to the woods."

"Can it wait till after school tomorrow? Or next weekend?"

Moira thought about it. She could try and wriggle out of movie night with her aunt, but not without having to answer a bunch of questions. "Tomorrow," Moira said. "It can wait till then."

The little dragon had been doing fine on its own before she showed up. One more night without fire rocks shouldn't make a difference.

I hope.

"Maybe we can catch a movie next Friday," Ansel said.

Moira nodded absently, thinking ahead, trying to work out how she could get the rocks to the cave tomorrow without hauling them to school with her.

Distracted, Moira asked, "At night?"

"Yeah."

Her aunt sputtered and coughed, patting her chest.

"Are you alright?" Moira asked.

She waved her away. "Fine. I'm fine. I swallowed a bug." She stepped inside, closing the door behind her.

Moira shook her head and turned back to Ansel. "I thought we only did matinees?"

Ansel shoved both hands deep into the front pockets of his paint-splattered jeans making his shoulders lift in a shrug. "I thought maybe we could try something different."

Moira's eyebrow went up. "Oh. Okay." Did he mean like a date? Dare she ask? What if he didn't and she asked and then it made things awkward? Okay. More awkward. "Don't movies cost more Friday night because, I don't know, it's date night or something?" He knew she didn't have a job and she knew his main source of income came from stuff he did around the house or in his neighborhood, like mowing lawns. He made enough to keep gas in his car and that was about it.

"Don't worry about it. It's your birthday," he said

"My birthday was like a month ago." Why was she pressing the issue? It was a gift. Why couldn't she say thank you and go to the movie with her friend like a normal human being? She couldn't because she wasn't sure if Ansel was asking her as her friend or something more. How did she feel about the more part?

"It'll be a belated birthday present," he said.

Moira let his answer convince her he was asking her out as a friend and nothing else. "Okay. Sounds good, but you're going to have to remind me because I haven't gone to a movie on a Friday night in—" she stopped. "I don't think I've ever gone to a movie on a Friday night."

Ansel grinned. "I'll remind you."

5

The next morning Moira pulled open her locker door. The hinges squealed. She would have to do something about that. The noise didn't usually bother her, but today she found it irksome. Her morning had not gone as planned and she couldn't stop thinking about the little wyvern out in the woods all alone, waiting for her to come back. It had to know that finding the fire rocks would take her a while. She would have gone to the cave before school, but she ran out of time.

Last night, she and her aunt watched a movie and had popcorn for dinner. Some nights were like that. Her aunt wasn't hungry and Moira's stomach was knotted with worry. She went to bed and tried to sleep, but couldn't. Alone, in her room, in the dark, the day's events kept running through her mind on a continuous loop. It wasn't until the small hours of the morning that she finally fell asleep.

She woke to find she'd slept through her alarm and rushed to get ready and out the door. In the basement, she stopped to fill her backpack with rocks. In the woods on the way to school, she found a safe spot to stash them, relying on the fact that they were rocks, thinking, and hoping no one would notice they were different from all the others lying around.

Now she grumbled to herself as she flung her backpack into her locker and set her camera case on the shelf inside.

"Is that locker taken?"

The voice sounded like Ansel's, so she attempted to smile before she turned around.

Too bad Aaron stood behind her, a messenger bag slung from shoulder to hip across his torso, a stack of books piled in his arms.

Her smile turned to a grimace. "What's wrong with yours?"

Moira peered over his shoulder back toward the middle of the bay. Not that she knew where his locker was or anything. She'd just seen him there between classes once or twice. Yellow triangle signs with a stick figure caught forever in mid-fall were standing near where his locker would be.

"There's a leak or something. I have to switch lockers. Is that one taken?" he asked.

Every student provided their own combination lock. He could see none of the locker doors surrounding hers had locks on them. She kind of liked it that way, but she couldn't deny that they weren't taken. At least he was asking first.

"Help yourself," she said.

To her dismay, he opened the locker right next to hers. The hinges wailed horribly. His eyebrows shot upward as he pushed the door closed again. "Wow." She thought he'd take another locker, but he didn't. Instead, he pushed the door back and forth, changing the duration and pitch of the wail.

Moira watched him from the corner of her eye.

He stopped fidgeting with the door.

Moira tried to finish getting ready for class, but Aaron's shoulder kept brushing hers as he put his books away. She gritted her teeth and ignored him.

Ansel whipped around the corner into the bay and came to a sudden halt. "Whoa. What's going on?"

Aaron slipped the rest of his books into his locker. "Some kind of leak. I have to switch."

"Huh. Why didn't you grab one at the other end?"

Aaron shut the locker door and put his lock on it. "This one's good."

Ansel frowned. "I thought you—"

Aaron faced his brother. "Look, bro, my locker wasn't the only one flooded. I'm sure the free ones at the other end have already been taken."

Ansel squinted at his twin. Aaron stared back. Eyes were narrowed. A brow was lifted. Something passing between them, but Moira didn't know what. For a second she thought Ansel would question Aaron further, but he tilted his head and shrugged. "Whatever. Did you guys hear about Mr. Bertram?"

Moira's ears perked up. Mr. Bertram was her favorite teacher. She'd had him last year for Chemistry.

"No. What's up?" Aaron asked.

"He's not teaching this year. He took a sabbatical or something all of a sudden, like in a hurry. No one knows when—or if—he's coming back."

Aaron leaned against his locker door. "Guess that's why we've had a sub so far."

Their talk turned to other classes and Moira tuned them out while she finished getting ready for class. She stared into her locker, thinking, wondering, and worrying.

"Moira." The way Ansel said her name made her think it wasn't for the first time.

"Hmmm?"

"You going to class?"

"Yeah."

"I'll walk with you."

The day dragged on, every class interminable. Moira's only recourse was to buckle down and focus on her work with laser-like intensity. Whenever thoughts of dragons arose, she pushed them from her mind. By last period she had no fingernails, each one chewed to the quick and two of them bleeding. Lucky for her there were lots of bandages where she was going. Paper cuts were a hazard of the job when you worked in the library.

She taped up her fingers and grabbed a cart full of books to be put back. Every volume had to be opened and paged through to make sure nothing was left behind. People would use anything as a bookmark, including pictures and money, but recently there had been a rash of notes all pleadeing for help. The books empty, she set off. She only had to get through the next thirty minutes or so and she could find out what happened to—Moira gritted her teeth and focused on finding where the book she held belonged on the shelf. She pushed the cart ahead of her, traversing time and space by call number.

At the end of one row, she heard a noise coming from the next one. She stopped to listen and could make out two distinct voices, one male and one female, but the words were muffled. The cart turned the corner ahead of her. She wasn't trying to sneak up on anyone but she had tightened the cart's wheels and oiled them so they no longer rattled and squeaked if you put more than two books on the thing.

She rounded the corner in time to hear the male voice say, "You know, I edit the sports page for the school newspaper."

Moira recognized Charlie Barrett, though he faced away from her. He stood with an elbow propped up on one of the shelves blocking the end of the row. She had to lean to the side to see whom he was talking to, but Moira didn't recognize the girl, who was likely a freshman. The petite brunette stood at a ninety-degree angle to Charlie, her back to the books, clutching a spiral-bound notebook to her chest, glancing everywhere but at him.

"Wow. I didn't know...um." Her gaze darted down and away to the free end of the aisle.

"Can I help you find something?" Moira asked.

They both jumped.

The girl started to speak, got a look at Charlie's face, and shook her head.

Charlie dropped his arm and glared at Moira over his shoulder. "No, we're good here."

The message was clear. She should back up and be on her way. She shouldn't have even stopped. But something held her in place, which wasn't like her. She knew it wasn't, but at the same time, it was like she couldn't help herself.

"Are you sure?" Moira's locked eyes with the girl when she asked. The other girl looked away first.

Charlie scowled and turned to face Moira, which put him square in front of her. She tilted her chin up and stared down her nose at him. Harder than it sounded as he was a junior varsity basketball player and taller than her.

"It's Moira, right?" he asked.

"Yes, Charles, we've been in the same class since sixth grade."

His frown faded into a smirk. "That's right," he said, "Moira Noble—daddy's girl." The words hung in the air as his gaze turned watchful, waiting to see how she would react to the taunt.

And to think, a moment before a part of her wanted to back up, crack a joke, and go back to putting books away as if nothing happened. That would have been the smart thing to do, and if there was one thing Moira prided herself on, it was doing the smart thing and staying out of trouble.

Moira didn't make waves. She was more like the beach. Waves crashed against her and flowed over her, but she remained solid and steadfast. Of course, given enough time and enough water, a beach would move. Maybe Moira's sands were shifting. Perhaps they were being washed away, and beneath the grains was something harder because she returned Charlie's stare with an icy glare of her own. She didn't budge. She didn't even blink. To an alpha-jerk like Charlie, reacting to his words would signal that she was beneath him. But Moira saw Charlie for what he was; a silly boy hitting on a silly girl and not doing a very good job of it. Bringing up her dead father was overkill.

Her feet rooted themselves in place. She wasn't going to turn and run away, but there was no need to otherwise react. Besides, after the way she'd seen the girl search for an escape like a cornered animal, she wasn't going anywhere.

"Kyna, you ready to go?" Another voice asked from the opposite end of the aisle.

Moira refused to break eye contact with Charlie, so she didn't see who it was.

"Um, I'll be right there," the girl, Kyna, said. "I've got to go. Bye."

Charlie tore his gaze from Moira's, twisting away. Not a moment too soon, either, as her eyes began to water. She blinked. If she was going to make a habit of staring people down, she would have to invest in eye drops.

"I'll catch you later, babe," Charlie said.

If that sounded as ominous to Kyna as it did to Moira, she didn't let on, just dashed away.

Charlie twisted back toward her. "What's your problem?"

Moira glared. "Not a thing. I'm having a great day."

She didn't ask him what his problem was. She had a pretty good idea.

His lip curled. With one swipe, he upset an entire shelf of books on human evolution. They clattered to the floor, pages fluttering and flapping like butterfly wings.

Charlie backed down the aisle with his arms raised knocking random books from their places. "How about now?" He glared at her the whole way. Moira didn't move a muscle. Then he was gone.

Once he was out of sight, Moira clenched her hands into fists, squeezed once, and relaxed. With a sigh she crouched down and closed books that had fallen open, smoothing out bent pages the best she could.

Maybe she'd misjudged the situation. Maybe Kyna wanted a Neanderthal-like Charlie drooling over her. Maybe not.

"Can I give you a hand?" a voice asked.

"Wha—" Moira rocked to the side, lost her balance, and ended up sprawled on the floor staring up at a stranger.

A man stood, arms crossed, leaning a shoulder against the end of the bookcase. Moira scrabbled backward and got to her feet. She wondered how long he'd been there. He was tall, even taller than Charlie, and dressed in a sharp black suit with a crisp white button-down shirt. No tie. The jacket color matched his dark hair and eyes and contrasted with the pale skin above his collar.

He stepped away from the bookcase and motioned with pale fingers at the literary carnage on the floor. "Sorry to startle you. Can I help you clean this up?" he asked again, one brow raised.

Moira squinted and tilted her head to one side. "Are you a substitute or something? I think I've seen you around." In truth, she didn't remember his features, but his suit was familiar. She was sure she'd seen him around the library since school started or at least caught a glimpse of him on more than one occasion as she passed through the aisles putting books away.

He didn't answer, but bent and picked up a book to set it on the shelf. He grabbed another and started arranging them.

"I can do that," Moira said. The books wouldn't be on the floor if she hadn't poked her nose where it didn't belong.

What was I thinking?

It didn't matter because as soon as she asked herself the question, she realized she would do it again.

What's wrong with me?

"I insist," the stranger said and continued putting the shelf of books Charlie had knocked down back to rights.

Moira picked up the other random books, replacing them on the shelves. Finished, she watched the stranger. The smell of books intensified as he worked. His motions were fluid with no hesitation. He slid each volume into place with conficence. When the shelf was almost full, he turned to face Moira and held out his hand for the last book which she still held. Moira's eyes met his jet-black gaze and she could have sworn the book in her hand twitched of its own accord as if it wanted to go to him.

Weird.

Then again, her weirdness scale had shot up a couple of orders of magnitude since yesterday. Perhaps this was no more than a blip.

Moira held out the book. When the stranger reached for it her stomach flipped, and she thought she might be ill. "Who are you?"

The stranger took the book and slipped it into place without bothering to watch what he was doing. One dark brow arched. "I'm the librarian." The tenor of his voice made the skin on Moira's arms crawl at the same time as the hair on the back of her neck stood on end.

"You're not the librarian. Ms. Haven's in her office."

He inclined his head, once. "You are correct. I'm not the librarian here. I'm visiting."

Moira frowned. Ms. Haven would have mentioned having a visitor.

A loud thump made Moira turn. A book had fallen off the shelf and hit the floor.

"Sorry!" a voice called from the next aisle. Some of the bookcases didn't have backs. You could see through them. Another student must have pushed too hard from the other side and knocked the book out of place. Moira snatched up the volume and put it back.

"Visiting from wh—"

He was gone.

Moira went to the end of the row, but there was no one there. She checked and there was no one in the other row either.

Out of curiosity, she double-checked the shelf of books Charlie had knocked down. They were in perfect order.

6

After school Moira huffed through the woods, her backpack crammed full of what she hoped were the kind of fire rocks the dragon needed. They were right where she'd left them that morning, along with her rock pick at the base of an unmarked tree. She palmed the handle of the pick and kept it out, swinging at her side. Had she brought enough rocks? The little dragon hadn't said how many it needed.

The sun was warm, but there was a near-constant breeze. She kept her eyes and ears open for signs of anything out of the ordinary. But there was nothing. She didn't head straight to the cave but took a roundabout way of getting there, similar to the path she took the day before. She also took her notebook out. If she ran into someone, she would say she was working on her class project. If they took the time to check her notes, they would see she hadn't written anything since yesterday, but she hoped it wouldn't come to that.

She worried for nothing. When she arrived at her destination, she scanned the rock face and her surroundings. From outside, everything looked the same as the day before. She loitered. When she was certain she was well and truly alone, she slipped her backpack from her shoulders, marching toward the rock wall.

She couldn't find the entrance. There was no rush of relief. She didn't take not being able to find a way into the cave as a sign that she should go home and forget everything that had happened. Her body went hot all over and she broke out in a sweat. Not because she was worried about seeing the dragon again, but because she was afraid she wouldn't. She could feel herself growing frantic.

Where is it?

She stopped, took a deep breath, backed away and tried again. There was a dragon on the other side of the cliff face that needed fire rocks. She was there to deliver.

This time she found the entrance and wiggled through.

Inside she dropped her heavy load and dug out her flashlight. She clicked it on and swept the beam one way and then the other. "Hello?" she called.

No answer.

"Don't tell me I made a trip to Sauk County and almost got arrested for nothing," she said.

She made another sweep with the light. And jumped. Where there had been nothing but empty space a moment before, the dragon now sat, not five feet away.

Its forked tongue flicked forth. "What is arrested?" A clawed hand came up to shield its eyes from her light.

Moira lowered the beam and turned it off. "Nothing. I was exaggerating. Nevermind. Here, I brought the fire rocks." She crouched down next to her bag and opened it. "I hope that's what these are."

The dragon stretched its neck forward before coming closer to sit next to the open bag. "Yesss." It picked up a rock about the size of a softball, turning it over, examining it from every angle.

"What do you need them for, anyway?"

A loud crack split the air, and where there had been one rock there were now two, one in each of the wyvern's hands.

"For food."

The wyvern's jaw opened wide, wider than Moira would have thought it could. Inside were rows of pointed white teeth. A pair of fangs protruded top and bottom near the front about twice as long as their serrated neighbors. As Moira watched, the smaller of the two rocks disappeared into its mouth. There was no chewing, but there was an awful lot of swallowing. Its throat stopped working and the dragon sighed

"You eat rocks. Of course, you do." Moira watched in horrified fascination as the wyvern repeated the process. Then she had a thought. "Are you hungry? For something besides rocks, I mean?" Moira searched through the front pocket of her backpack and came up with a vending-machine-sized bag of jalapeno-flavored chips she had bought by accident and a bar of chocolate. The bag was crushed, and the chips were broken, but they were still edible. Maybe they would make the rocks taste better. The chocolate could be dessert. "These are spicy and this is sweet." She set both items next to the backpack on the floor.

The wyvern's nostrils flared over the bag of chips, so Moira opened those first.

"So, what do I call you? Mr. Wyvern?" She hesitated. "Mr. Dragon?"

"Need name." It didn't say anything else, but stared up at her, waiting.

"Wait—you want me to give you a name?"

"Yes. A name..." It paused, perhaps trying to find the right words, "...is a gift." The wyvern blinked and sniffed at the chips, nose sinking into the package.

Moira wasn't sure she was qualified to name a dragon, but it had asked her to and it didn't seem right to refuse. "Okay. Are you a boy dragon or a girl wyvern?"

Do dragons even have gender identities?

"I am male."

"All right, give me a sec, I'll see if I can think of something." She was already running through a short list in her head and rejecting every name that came to mind. *Bob* just didn't cover all of what she had going on in front of her. She rubbed her forehead, searching for something suitable.

While she thought, the dragon picked up a chip and smelled it before popping it in his mouth. Crunching noises filled the air. She stood and walked to the entrance, leaning a shoulder against the wall next to the opening. A breeze wound its way into the cave spinning a few pine needles and other detritus into a small eddy. She watched the spinning and wondered if the wind was out of the west. Her mind seized on a name.

The crunching noises continued.

The more she thought about it, the more she liked it. "How about Zephyr?" she asked.

"Zephyr," he repeated the name. He said it out loud a few more times in between finishing off the bag of chips. Then he broke off another piece of igneous rock and swallowed that. "Why Zephyr?" he asked.

"I remembered the Greeks had a name for the God of the west wind—Zephyr."

"The wind," he said. It wasn't a question.

Moira pushed away from the rocks and stood, thinking it over. "It fits in a weird way. You can't fly, can you?" The question popped into her head and out of her mouth before she could stop it.

He turned on the spot and presented her with his back. He shrugged his shoulders and glanced at her over his left one. "No flying."

His back was completely wingless. There were only the slightest of protrusions over the points at the top of his shoulder blades where the scales built up into tiny mounds.

"Okay, well, I'm not the one who's going to be saddled with the name Zephyr. You are. What do you think?"

He didn't say anything, but his lids lowered at the same time as he displayed an alarming number of pointed teeth. Moira didn't so much recoil as lean back a fraction. It took her a second to realize he was smiling.

"I like it." An expression stole over his features. Happiness, with another emotion mixed in. She had a hard time recognizing it at first but then she realized it was pride. "I am Zephyr."

Moira relaxed enough to return his smile. "Nice to meet you Zephyr. I'm Moira."

Zephyr stepped forward and held out his right hand. "I am well met, dragoneer Moira."

She hesitated. His smile faded, but the pride remained in his eyes along with another emotion she couldn't quite pin down. Her gaze dropped to his hand. Every one of his five talons glinted in the light. She wasn't afraid, so she reached out, sliding her palm against his leathery one.

Moira gasped. Pain lanced through her ankle making her grip convulse around Zephyr's hand tighter than she intended. The skin on either side of her right Achilles tendon burned as if someone held a match to the flesh there. The burning rose, crawling up her leg. When it reached her stomach, it felt like she'd been punched. Her body curved over on itself.

Zephyr's hand continued to grip hers, not enough to hurt, but enough to ground her and keep her in the present.

She couldn't take this, whatever it was. When she tried, she couldn't let go of Zephyr's hand. "What's happening to me?"

"I am sorry," he said, still holding on.

His eyes never left her. He didn't even blink.

The pain spread up the back of her neck and into her head.

The edges of her vision dimmed. She slumped to the side and felt herself being lowered to the ground before the darkness engulfed her.

7

Not dead.

That was Moira's first thought as she stirred. The searing pain was gone, too. Whatever knocked her on her butt had passed.

Still, she kept her eyes closed and didn't move, staying on the cave floor where she had fallen.

I didn't fall.

If she remembered correctly, she would have hit the ground with much more force if Zephyr hadn't been there.

Now all was quiet. Perhaps too quiet.

Moira blinked her eyes open and sat up. She groaned and pressed the palms of both hands to her forehead. Mouth dry, she swallowed and tried to lick her lips. Her backpack sat next to her, hollowed out, the fire rocks gone, but her water bottle remained. She grabbed it, taking a long drink of water. Besides being dehydrated her elbow felt stiff, but otherwise, she felt okay. Not perfect, but not in pain either.

"Easy," a voice said from the shadows.

Moira jerked and spilled water down the front of her shirt. "Zephyr? Is that you?"

It sounded like him, sort of, but the voice was different, deeper.

"Yes."

Moira didn't see him, but next to her backpack was the empty bag of chips and the chocolate bar, the wrapper pulled back but only one corner nibbled on. She peered into the darkness but still couldn't see Zephyr.

"How long have I been out? And what happened?" she asked.

"Not long."

Moira's head swung toward the entrance. She couldn't remember the exact angle the sun had been at when she arrived, but there was still light filtering in from outside. She shook her head and turned back to face the dark interior of the cave. "What happened to me?"

"I can explain."

She frowned. "Okay. Go ahead and explain." Then she remembered the pain in her right ankle. Moira bent her knee, whipped off her shoe, and yanked the sock from her foot.

"Wait."

She glanced up, her ankle forgotten

A figure hesitated at the edge of the light before stepping into it. At the height Moira had expected to find the top of Zephyr's head, she found the top of a deep-green scaled kneecap. She tilted her head back, back, farther.

Gone was the little dragon.

Zephyr loomed over her, more than twice the size he had been before. If she had to guess, he was now taller than she was.

Her whole body went rigid at the same time as her jaw slid downward.

An x-ray image of *Tyrannosaurus rex* flashed across her mind's eye. She'd seen the dinosaur skeleton of Sue at the Field Museum in Chicago a couple of summers before. Zephyr reminded her of the Cretaceous period dinosaur, but as soon as she thought of it, she started comparing them and coming up with differences.

Zephyr wasn't as large, thank goodness, nor his neck as long. He stood more upright. Before, when he was smaller, he'd walked on all fours. He'd only just stepped into the light, but she could see he was meant to get around on two legs like Sue, his hindquarters and legs thick with muscle. His chest was not as broad as a T. rex, but he had thick, powerful arms that more than made up for it.

Moving upward her gaze met his and a sizzle of electricity shot up her spine, igniting the base of her skull.

Everything stopped.

A shiver raced through her and her vision went dark, but she didn't lose consciousness. Images flashed across the darkness in front of her as if projected onto a screen. The darkness had weight and it pressed in on her, making her skin warm and clammy. Moira glanced down and saw she no longer sat on the floor of the cave but stood in a field of tall grass. A rush of air blew past and the grass bent and parted in waves.

No moon showed overhead, but a light glowed ahead in the distance. The glow was weak and only emphasized the blackness around her. Unintelligible whispers slid past her ears and a heavy beat grew out of them accompanied by the clank of metal. Whipped into a frenzy the grass lashed at her with sharp edges. An unknown cry filled the air. The lonesome wail joined a chorus of others culminating in one giant, fear-inducing roar.

The cacophony coupled with a flash of late summer lightning sent Moira from standing in a field to standing in a room. The shift left her legs wobbly, and she threw up her hands to catch herself. She knew where she was, and the space was familiar. The room was hers, but different, the colors washed out. It was also tidy. Her desk hadn't been that clean since before school started. And the bed—

Moira's heart stopped a second before it began pounding anew. She was there, asleep in her bed, the sheets churned up and crumpled around her as if she'd had a bad dream. The curtain next to her open window twitched. Another flashbulb of light outlined a shape on the sill. There was something familiar about it. She watched as the shadowy figure flowed into the room and up onto the foot of her bed.

The sleeping Moira didn't stir as the shadow, silent, bent its head down close to her exposed right foot. She tried to shout a warning, but no sound escaped her. All she could do was watch. Seconds later the shadow slid from the bed, back to the window. It paused, twisting back to glance at the sleeping Moira on the bed. Another flash of light revealed a much smaller Zephyr than she had ever seen before, this version the size of a housecat, perched on the sill. The image faded, but the color yellow remained.

Moira stared into the same yellow eyes now. Her body tensed, ready to flee, but her mind kept her in place. If she didn't move, maybe she would go unnoticed. The place in her head where she tried to shove her fear and panic no longer had a door that she could keep closed. Every thought stuttered, stopped. The blood rushed in her ears with gale-force intensity.

No, not a gale. A breeze.

A Zephyr, in fact.

She came back to herself, sitting on the floor of the cave, the images fading from her vision. Or was it a memory? At first, it felt like a dream, but she'd seen herself asleep in bed before she saw the yellow eyes. The color of Zephyr's eyes remained the same, but the eyes themselves were bigger. She shuddered and blinked, dragging her gaze away from his. Instant relief. Her muscles relaxed and her heartbeat slowed. Her head swam and then it cleared.

Moira dragged air into her lungs for a solid minute before she tried meeting Zephyr's eyes again. Her legs twitched, ready to carry her away, but she must have been getting used to the sensation because she could still think. She wasn't sure she'd be able to find the headspace for her fear and anxiety again let alone a door big enough to fit it, but it didn't seem to matter anymore. The dragon was out of the bag and grown several times over and standing right in front of her. In passing, Moira noticed Zephyr's pupils were dilated and not the fierce black slits of a predator, which helped.

She swallowed. "What happened?"

"It had to be done."

"What? What had to be done?"

Zephyr's chin dipped and his gaze lowered. With both hands, she hauled her foot around and into the light. There, on either side, above her heel were two perfect circles, old and healed over, the puncture wounds a shade darker than the skin surrounding them. Moira wasn't sure she would have ever noticed the scars if she hadn't been looking for them.

She dropped her foot. "You bit me?" She recalled what she had seen in her vision/memory. "You crawled through my bedroom window and bit me on the ankle?"

"I had to."

"For what?"

Zephyr's hands came up, palms down.

"Do not tell me to calm down. You bit me. Did I taste good?" She leaned back. "Are you gonna do it again?" Moira thrust her foot back into her sock and jammed her shoe back on. She stood and discovered her estimate was correct. Zephyr was taller than her, by at least four inches. She gulped and continued. "I would like to know why."

Zephyr's entire being drooped. "For words. For knowledge."

Moira frowned. "You bit me so you could—speak with me?"

"Yes."

That didn't make any sense. Her throat tightened as a hysterical giggle threatened to escape her. She was in a cave, talking to a dragon. She closed her eyes and rubbed her forehead, pacing back and forth in front of the entrance. The way he explained it made it sound like biting her had unlocked some basic understanding of human speech and vocabulary which didn't sound possible. But whatever happened when he bit her must have worked if they were having this conversation.

The thought slid away as images from her vision/memory played through her mind and combined with everything that happened to her since she found the cave. Together it gave her enough information to piece it all together. "Let me see if I've got this right. A couple of weeks ago you climbed the tree outside my window, let yourself into my room, and bit me on the ankle so that you could have words and be able to speak to me when I showed up here yesterday?"

Zephyr winced and nodded.

She recalled watching him leap from tree to tree the day before. Climbing the tree outside her window wouldn't have given him any trouble.

"Did you know I was coming here? Because I sure didn't."

"No. I waited. I hoped."

For how long?

She already knew. Her feet came to a stop as she faced him. "I got sick before school started. My aunt thought it was some twenty-four-hour bug or something, but it wasn't, was it? Your bite made me sick."

Zephyr appeared to ponder her statement. "It could have. But you are better now."

"Not so fast. I missed my birthday because of you." Sure, she hadn't had any earth-shattering plans, but Zephyr didn't know that. He couldn't just go around biting people and not expect there to be some ramifications for his actions.

He lowered his huge head. "I am sorry, Moira. It was not my intention to bring you grief. I needed a dragoneer."

"You keep using that word. What does it mean?"

"Dragoneer. Someone to help me."

"Someone to fetch you fire rocks, you mean."

"That too."

"The fire rocks—they made you—" She waved a hand up and down in front of him.

Zephyr looked down at himself and raised his hands, gazing at their backs before flipping them over to see his palms, as if he were getting used to the sight. Come to think of it, he probably was. "Grow. Yes."

She thought for a second. "Are all dragoneers bitten?"

His gaze met hers as he shook his massive head. "No."

"Then why did you bite me?"

"I needed to."

"No." He had already explained about needing words. That she understood, or she thought she did anyway. "Why did you bite *me*? Why me, specifically?"

Zephyr frowned. "I am unsure of what you mean."

"You could have picked any window to climb in. Why pick mine?"

Zephyr sat back and gave her question careful consideration, or at least he didn't answer right away.

Moira waited. What he had to say was important. She wanted to know if there was some reason behind why she was bitten. As a rule, she didn't believe in fate or destiny, but she was curious why Zephyr had bitten her when perhaps someone else could do a better job.

Finally, he spoke. "When I hatched, instinct took over. It was beyond my ken. I do not recall much of what I did so soon after breaking out of my shell, only that there was no one here. I needed someone open to possibility. Not someone so set in their ways. Someone intelligent. And strong. Dragon venom is not for the weak. Those qualities drew me to you. And you answered."

Moira thought about what he said while she resumed her pacing. She had a few more questions. "I'm not going to turn into a dragon, am I? Start growing scales?"

"No. The bite will not make you a dragon. No scales."

"And it's not going to kill me?"

"No. You survived."

Moira's stomach turned over. Her body must have treated the venom like a virus, but that didn't make her feel any better. Peple who contracted the flu died every year. Getting bitten by a wyvern was no worse. Probably.

"What else do you need besides fire rocks?" He said he'd bitten her for words. His speech and vocabulary were fast improving, but there must be something more he needed.

"To go home. I do not belong here."

The fervent undertone to his words stopped her.

"Where's home?" she asked.

Zephyr shook his head and stepped to his right. "This is all I know." He bent down and reached behind a large boulder. Moira peeked over the top. The wall behind it was scooped out so there was more space available than one would think from the front. There might have been enough room there for Zephyr to curl up before he ate the fire rocks, but not now.

Zephyr stood. In his hand, he held a curved shard, stark white on one side, mottled black on the other.

"Is that what I think it is?" she asked.

He held out the shard to her. She took it. The piece of shell filled her palm. The outside wasn't smooth like she thought but covered in an irregular pattern of raised bumps. She ran the side of her thumb along the ragged edge where it was sharp and inflexible.

Moira held the piece of shell out to Zephyr, but he put up a hand. "Keep it," he said.

Since she wanted to take a closer look, she slipped the shell fragment into her empty backpack.

"Do you have any idea how you got here?" she asked.

Zephyr shook his head. "None."

Moira considered the situation, her gaze going from Zephyr to her backpack to the entrance of the cave and back again. Zephyr hatched, found her, bit her, and waited around for weeks hoping she would turn up. Now he'd consumed fire rocks, provided by her, more than doubled in size, and all he wanted to do was return to a home he didn't know anything about because he obviously didn't belong there.

Walking away wasn't really an option. She wanted to help.

She would have to start now. "Are you going to keep growing?"

Zephyr peered down at himself before he looked back up at Moira. "Yes."

"Then we're gonna need a bigger cave."

8

The problem was that while caves weren't unheard of in the area, Moira didn't know of one that was move-in ready and suitable for a dragon of Zephyr's size. There might be an as yet undiscovered cave out there suitable for his needs, but the probability was low. Moira dragged out her maps of the area, searching for an out-of-the-way place nearby where a dragon might lay low for a while.

Zephyr peered over her shoulder, his breath stirring her hair. Moira laid out her materials on the cave floor so they could both see. She pointed out where she found the fire rocks. Zephyr bent his head low and followed along.

"Can you read these?" she asked.

He raised his yellow eyes, pupils broad, without raising his head. "I can." The tip of one talon circled their current location as he asked questions about the area. Moira did her best to describe what was in their immediate vicinity and sent a text to her aunt saying she would be home later than she thought. She kept the details vague and didn't tell her aunt not to worry because doing so was a sure guarantee she would.

After studying the maps, they decided their best course of action would be to wait for dark and set out on their search. She sat back, frowning. "What happened after I left the cave yesterday? Was something following you?"

Zephyr's eyes narrowed and his lip curled. "I do not know. We shall see."

"Maybe we should wait—"

"No more waiting."

Outside the cave, Moira shifted her weight from one foot to the other. Behind her, trying to squeeze through the narrow exit, Zephyr grunted. She was glad he insisted on leaving, but she couldn't watch as he worked his way out from between the rocks. Maybe she should have stayed inside the cave to help push him out. *Too late now.* She waited in the gathering darkness with the rock pick at her side. Light from the moon would help guide them along when it rose above the treetops.

Another grunt.

Moira turned to the entrance. What were they going to do if he couldn't get out? She pulled in a deep breath, held it for a count of five and blew it out again. "Listen," she said, "you need to relax."

An irritated huff of breath came from the entrance.

"Close your eyes and take a deep breath," she mimed doing so by pulling herself up tall and raising both shoulders, "exhale all the way, visualize what you want to happen, and think fluid thoughts. Take your time. You can do it." And then, because she thought watching him might make him nervous, she turned her back to the entrance and faced the woods once more. It was a clear night and cool. The buzz of insects grew to replace the calls of birds. A rough scrabbling came from behind her and then silence.

Zephyr stepped up beside her. "Thank you for waiting," he said, his voice a deep rumble not much louder than a soft purr.

Moira lowered her voice to match his now that they were outside. "I wasn't going anywhere without you."

They agreed Moira would take point before they left the cave since she was more familiar with the area. Zephyr followed close behind.

More than once she caught herself checking to see if he was there. He moved so quietly she was afraid she had lost him. Every time she looked, he was there, less than three yards away, which was a little disconcerting if she stopped to think about it. She kept moving.

Moira headed deep into the woods away from the high school. They hiked for a half hour before she stopped, unsure of which way to continue. She kneeled on the dirt and pulled out the map. The moon still hadn't risen overhead. She warned Zephyr. "Watch your eyes."

He grunted.

Moira switched on her flashlight, oriented the map, marked their location, and decided what direction to head next. She faced that way and flicked the light off, stowing everything in her backpack before slipping it back on both shoulders.

A twig snapped, followed by a heavy thump.

Moira stayed low, her hand finding and gripping the handle of her rock pick. Her eyes were still adjusting to the dark, but she saw Zephyr crouch and face the trees behind them.

"Wha—"

"Shhh." Zephyr made a slashing motion. His tail stirred the air behind him as his empty hands opened and closed.

Moira's gaze dropped to the ground. There might not be enough light to read by, but she could make out a thick branch, some four feet long not far from where she kneeled. Without a sound, she got a grip on the branch and held it out to Zephyr. He took it by one end and brandished the improvised club.

Something growled, low and harsh.

Zephyr put himself square between her and whatever tracked them.

Moira gagged as an acrid stench rolled over her. It smelled like a sewer had backed up on a hot day. Her eyes watered, and she had to blink to keep the wetness from spilling over as she tried to breathe through her mouth.

A pile of leaves rustled and she jumped, every noise amplified. Her heart pounded, pushing the blood through her veins. The sound of an unmistakable footfall and a muffled snort came from her right.

"Move!" Zephyr roared.

Moira threw herself to the side as a towering figure burst through the trees. Leaves and branches rained down.

Zephyr swung the branch and connected with a solid *smack*.

From where she lay sprawled on the ground, she saw Zephyr swing again.

"Run!"

Moira scrambled away, putting distance between her and the fight. When she pulled herself to her feet the sensation to run swept over her, but she turned to watch Zephyr take another swing and couldn't make her feet move. The club gave a sickening crack and split into shards. Zephyr tossed the pieces aside as a square fist slammed into his side. He grunted and absorbed another blow, getting pummeled before her eyes. She had to do something.

"Hey! Ugly!" She waved her hands over her head and jumped. "Yeah, I'm talking to you!"

The thing was roughly humanoid with two legs and two arms and as big as Zephyr. It turned its head in her direction, and she got a good enough look at its face to make her wish she hadn't. Greasy black hair hung from its grey-skinned scalp past features that held only a passing acquaintance with symmetry. Everything about it was disjointed, including the broken, jagged teeth filling its sneering maw. Zephyr's fist connected with the jaw and the thing's mouth snapped shut. It shook off the blow and snorted, its soulless black gaze burning with renewed fury. The thing let out a terrible roar, latched onto Zephyr, and threw him to the ground with such force Moira felt the earth tremble. It raised a foot, poised to stomp on Zephyr, but the dragon grabbed his attacker by the leg, throwing the thing off balance and dragging it down to the ground with him.

They grappled, rolling around in the dirt and debris. Zephyr ended up beneath his foe, flailing, an arm pressed against his throat.

Her rock pick! Where was it? Moira bent and raked her hands through the dirt around her. A flash of metal. She dove for it and rolled to her feet, crossing to the fray and lifting the pick over her head. She intended to bring it down as hard as she could on the back of the thing's head, caving in its skull, but it shifted at the last moment and she struck it on the shoulder. The pick bounced back, not unlike striking a metal plate, but instead of a metal clang, there was the *thwap* of flesh being struck.

The thing jerked to a stop, shook its head, and growled, sitting up. She'd failed to crack its skull open, but she'd gotten its attention. An arm shot out and knocked the pick from her grasp before she could react. Zephyr remained on the ground, not moving. His attacker stood and faced her.

Moira backed away, but there was nowhere to go. Her insides heaved. The thing advanced. She had time to wonder if her death would be quick or not and the thought chilled her to the core.

The thing lunged.

At the last second, something slammed into her from the side and sent her flying. She landed hard and rolled to a stop several feet away. Ears ringing, she looked around for Zephyr but didn't see him.

Somebody else was there. Whoever pushed her out of the way lay next to her, holding their head in both hands.

The thing roared.

The other person moaned and asked, "Are you the dragoneer or aren't you?" An elbow pointed to the space between them.

At first, Moira didn't see anything, but then amongst the dirt and leaf litter, she made out something long, silver, and, most importantly, pointy. She scrambled to her knees and picked the sword up by the hilt with both hands. It was heavier than it looked. Still, she got the sharp end in the air as the thing took a step in her direction.

Moira climbed to her feet, stepping away from the mysterious stranger. She had no idea what she was doing, and she had a feeling her opponent knew it, too, because it didn't take any kind of defensive posture. Its lip lifted in a sneer and a guttural rumbling sound rolled from its throat.

It was laughing at her.

Moira lifted her arms higher and raised her chin in defiance.

Before it took a step, the bloodied tip of what was left of Zephyr's club erupted through the middle of its chest. Black gore gushed from the wound; its laughter cut off by a gurgle.

9

Moira stared, eyes wide as the thing dropped straight down to the ground and slumped to the side.

Zephyr stepped back, his shoulders heaving.

"Finish it," a voice said.

On the ground, the thing let out a shallow roar. Blood poured from its mouth but that didn't stop it from reaching for the wood protruding from its chest and attempting to pull it out or break it off. Its struggles grew weaker, but it wouldn't give up.

"Put it out of its misery," the voice said.

Moira started. She had the sword. She glanced at Zephyr. His massive head dipped, once. Without giving herself time to think about what she was about to do, she marched over to the thing that tried to kill Zephyr and stuck the silvery blade through its neck. Blood flowed from the wound as its last breath escaped in a wet rasp. As soon as it was done, Moira dropped the sword, turned, and puked.

A minute later the voice came again. "It's done. Good."

Moira dragged her attention away from the dead body.

Zephyr straightened up, rubbing at his neck. His shoulders were rising and falling with each breath, so she knew he could breathe all right.

"You okay?" she asked him.

He nodded as his gaze went from the sword on the ground to the other person before returning to meet her eyes, his brows raised in question. She picked up the sword by the handle. Zephyr stepped into deeper shadows, but remained within earshot. She let the point of the blade rest on the ground.

"I will be," the voice answered, unaware she was asking Zephyr.

Moira decided the voice belonged to a man after hearing it again. Whoever he was, he got to his hands and knees with a groan, holding his head like he was afraid it would roll off. When he let go and sat back on his heels, she got a good look at his features, though they were still screwed up tight in an expression of pain. Her eyes widened. "Mr. Bertram?"

One eye opened in a squint. "Ms. Noble?"

He *should* know who she was. She'd passed his freshman chemistry class with flying colors last year. His love and enthusiasm for chemistry made him her favorite teacher the year before, even if it didn't make chemistry her favorite subject.

The longer Moira stared at Mr. Bertram, the more his appearance troubled her. The Mr. Bertram she knew always kept a tidy, clean-shaven look, but the man on his knees in front of her had a face full of scruff and hair past his collar. His clothes looked like he slept in them, the t-shirt wrinkled under his dark blue pea coat, his jeans dirty and torn. She remembered him as slim, but now he was downright thin, his cheeks hollow beneath the new whiskers.

Hadn't Ansel told his brother Mr. Bertram wasn't teaching this year? Wasn't he supposed to be on vacation? No, sabbatical. That was it. No one knew when he was coming back. Moira hadn't paid attention because she didn't have any classes with him this year.

"What are you doing here? Are you lost?" she asked.

Mr. Bertram squeezed his eyes shut tight before he opened them again. "No. I'm looking for you, I think," he said. He blinked and rubbed his temples.

"What do you mean, looking for me? And what was that thing?" She motioned to the body with a flick of the sword tip.

He frowned and spared the body on the ground a glance, releasing his temples. "That was a troll. Ruthless, nasty creatures. They'll do any bit of dirty work that comes their way. You were very brave, taking care of it the way you did. That must have been hard."

Moira swallowed; the taste of bile still fresh in her throat.

"You are, aren't you?" he asked, "You're the dragoneer?"

Moira's eyes widened. She ducked her head to hide her surprise. That was what Zephyr called her. She still wasn't entirely sure what the job description included besides finding a bunch of rocks for him to eat, but the look Mr. Bertram was giving her made her think she should be more concerned with the fine print. His expression was a jumble of emotions, hunger, and hope mixed with sadness and suffering. She didn't know how to interpret any one of them, let alone all of them together.

Despite the troll and everything that had happened that evening, a part of Moira didn't think it was too late to deny everything. She could get Zephyr, skip off into the dark, and leave Mr. Bertram to his own devices. But if Mr. Bertram knew something about dragoneers, what else did he know? Could he help them find Zephyr a way home? She had to make a choice. Moira raised her head. "Yes. I am."

Mr. Bertram's head dropped forward and his shoulders sagged. "I knew it." He pressed his fingertips to his eyelids and sat down on the ground. "I knew it," he said again. Moira decided he was talking to himself and she might not be supposed to hear what he muttered.

"What do you know about Zephyr?" she asked.

Mr. Bertram's head jerked upward. His gaze met hers, a wrinkle of surprise creasing his forehead. "Zephyr?" A smile flashed across his face, there and gone so fast she wasn't sure she'd seen it after it fled.

"Yes. That's his name."

"It has a name," he said in a voice filled with wonder and despair at the same time. "Then you must be the dragoneer."

Moira shuffled from one foot to the other. "I am. What do you know about dragons, Mr. Bertram?"

"Only what I've read." He snorted as if he were laughing at a joke that wasn't very funny. "Please stop calling me Mr. Bertram. Call me Harold."

Moira grimaced. Not because she thought Harold was a terrible name. She just didn't feel comfortable being on a first-name basis with her teacher. It would have been like calling her dad by his first name when she'd always called him dad. It felt weird. "How about just Bertram? Maybe Mr. B?"

"Not Mr. B," he said. "Bertram will be fine." He started to say something and stopped. Then, "Would you mind sitting, Ms. Noble? My neck is beginning to ache from looking up at you."

Moira was too on edge to sit, but she squatted low so they were closer to being on the same level. The tip of the sword continued to rest in the dirt. If Bertram minded, he didn't say.

He rubbed the back of his neck. "How did you find it?" he asked.

A sound of exasperation flew out of Moira. "Stop calling him 'it'."

Bertram lowered his head, contrite, and held out a hand in apology. "I found him in a cave."

He frowned. "Do you do a lot of spelunking?"

"No. Geology. I was in the woods collecting rock samples for class."

Bertram scratched his chin. "Interesting."

"That's what happened," Moira said and wondered why she was defending herself.

"I believe you. I didn't mean to insinuate otherwise." He stroked his beard and stared off into space. "It's just...interesting." He gave his head a shake before his brows went up. "And you gave him a name."

At the time, Zephyr's request surprised her, but she had wanted to know what she could call him. "He asked for one. Why is that so important?"

Bertram met her gaze. "It's important, Ms. Noble because when you name something, you give it power."

Bertram had a way of explaining things in a way she could understand. That was one reason why he was her favorite teacher last year, but she wasn't sure she understood him now. If she was interpreting what he said correctly, then an amorphous something didn't have a lot of oomph, but the moment you gave it a name, it became something you could talk about, describe, share. There was something in being able to do that. A kind of power, as Bertram suggested.

Thinking back, she'd named Zephyr and nothing happened. It wasn't until after, when they shook hands that she was bowled over by whatever it was his bite did to her. Their formal meeting knocked the wind out of her and caused her to lose consciousness long enough for Zephyr to finish the fire rocks and grow to his new-found height. She wasn't so sure all of that came from a name.

"Who else knows about Zephyr?" Bertram asked.

"No one."

"Good. Very good. You should keep it that way. The fewer people who know about him the better. Likewise, for your new position."

"About that." Moira squinted. She could make out Zephyr in the shadows if she peered hard enough. His big head bobbed from time to time as he moved it from side to side while they spoke like he was watching a tennis match. "What does a dragoneer do?" The term sounded like it should apply to someone who knew a lot about dragons, which she didn't think fit her very well at the moment. But she did know a dragon, so perhaps it described her better than she thought.

"He hasn't told you?"

Moira's mouth curved down. She shook her head.

"You've taken on the position of Zephyr's squire and companion. One of your duties should be getting rid of that." Bertram pointed a thumb in the direction of the body without looking at it. "The world of dragons is very different from our own, Ms. Noble, and you must

be prepared for it. I can help train you, but we should begin at once."
He pushed himself to his feet. "I'd like to meet Zephyr."

Moira stood, sword in hand. "I don't think so."

10

Moira had admitted to being the dragoneer, but that didn't mean she was going to let Bertram anywhere near Zephyr. Not until she got some answers.

"You don't get to meet Zephyr until you tell me how you know so much about dragons."

It took some effort, but she did not glance over at the dragon in question. It was hard to believe Bertram hadn't seen him yet, but it was dark, the moon only now rising above the treetops. It helped that Zephyr stayed quiet and didn't make any sudden movements.

"Excuse me?" Bertram said.

Had he really not heard her? "How do you know so much about dragons?"

Bertram glanced down and away, frowning. "It's difficult to explain."

"You're a good teacher. I'm a good student. I think I can keep up."

Bertram stared into the dark and rubbed his palms together. "It's not an easy tale for me to tell."

"Please try," she said, voice firm.

Bertram pinched the bridge of his nose. He squeezed his eyes shut and took a deep breath before he blew it out slowly. "I read a book. Or maybe it read me."

"A book read you? What do you mean?"

"Just what I said."

Zephyr stepped forward. She waved him off. He stood within catching distance. His posture told her that he was content to let her ask the questions, but his forward movement let her know he didn't care for Bertram's tone.

Moira was willing to let Bertram's snapping at her slide. He wasn't acting like the teacher she knew from freshman chemistry. It looked like he was in pain, maybe some kind of headache. People didn't act like themselves when they were in pain.

Bertram massaged his temples before blinking his eyes open.

Moira waited.

"At the end of last school year, I found a book in the library. It was unmarked and obviously didn't belong there. Looking back, I wish I'd left the damn thing alone. But I didn't. I picked it up and took it home. I started to read it. I remember wanting to put it down, to get a drink of water, but I couldn't. The book wouldn't let me. I couldn't lay it aside no matter what I did. I just kept turning pages, one after another until I blacked out." Bertram ran a hand down the front of his face like he wished he could wipe the whole incident away. "When I woke up the next day, I could barely remember my name. The book was gone. I don't know what happened to it, but I remember things—sporadic bits and pieces of a bigger picture." He stared at Moira. "It was a book of wyverns or, as you know by now, dragons. Wyverns are what they call themselves. I think it must have been an important manuscript." He shook his head and shifted his gaze to the body on the ground. "I've remembered more and more the last couple of days for some reason." Bertram pointed with his chin. "I think that troll was sent to kill your dragon. The bad news is someone knows Zephyr is here. The good news is I don't think they know he has a dragoneer."

Moira's eyes narrowed. "How can you tell?"

"Because they would have sent more than one troll."

Moira digested that tidbit of information while she pondered what Bertram said. What he described made it sound as if he had a whole book squatting in his head that he couldn't evict. What was worse, he couldn't even recall the contents of the book at will. And he'd spent the summer like this? No wonder he wasn't teaching this year. How had he kept himself together? She took in his disheveled appearance once more. Maybe he hadn't.

"You think meeting Zephyr will help you—what? Remember more of this book?" Moira asked.

Bertram's shoulders came up in a shrug. "I don't know. But it can't hurt to try. Please."

He had a book about dragons stuck in his head. Moira just happened to know a dragon. If meeting Zephyr could help restore Bertram's memory, maybe whatever he remembered could help them find Zephyr a way home. A glance into the shadows told her the dragon waited for her decision. He did not wave her off or offer any other sort of action that would indicate his preference. She inferred from Zephyr's watchful state that the decision was up to her and he would go along with whatever she wanted to do. Despite Bertram's pitiable appearance, she had more questions.

"Where did you get this?" She levered the tip of the sword into the air between them. She didn't know anything about swords so she couldn't tell if it was a good one or not. The pointy bit at the end was sharp enough. Leather encased the unadorned handle.

"Ah, well." Bertram ducked his head. "I acquired it." He coughed into his fist. "I got the sense from the book that it would be a good thing to have around. And it was."

"And you just happened to be walking around in the woods with it?"

"Ha. No, I'm not in the habit of carrying a sword around in the woods after dark, but something told me tonight might be a good night to do so. Could have been the book stuck in my head."

Moira held the end of the sword aloft a moment more before she let it dip. "Okay."

"Okay? I can meet him?"

Zephyr stood not ten feet away.

"Sure."

Bertram searched the woods around them. Moira noticed he was looking in a downward direction as if he expected Zephyr to be the size he was when Moira first encountered him, which was a lot smaller than he was now.

He was in for a surprise.

"I assume he's somewhere nearby, probably listening," Bertram said.

Moira nodded. "Yep."

Zephyr drew himself up straight.

"Will he return?" Bertram asked.

"He doesn't have to." She tipped her head in Zephyr's direction. "He's right here." The trees rustled overhead as a slight breeze blew through. It was enough to send shadows dancing and tumbling over the dragon in the growing moonlight.

Bertram frowned into the night. "I don't—"

"He cannot see me," Zephyr said. He stepped forward.

Moira didn't understand.

Bertram gasped.

Moira twisted around to see Bertram standing stock still, mouth open. His eyes were so wide the whites showed all around the edges; his gaze locked on Zephyr. Moira understood the shock. She'd experienced it herself.

The funny thing was Bertram didn't seem to be breathing.

Moira rushed to his side and hesitated unsure of what to do. She settled for grabbing the sleeve of his coat and shaking him by the arm.

No change.

"Bertram? What's wrong?" Was he having some kind of seizure? She grabbed at his coat again, this time pinching his arm, hard. He wheezed, so at least he was breathing, but his gaze remained fixed on Zephyr.

"What's wrong with him?" Moira turned around. She had to look up at Zephyr, but he was just standing there, being a dragon. His big head turned and he blinked at her.

Moira swung back to face Bertram. She tapped him on the jaw.

No reaction.

She slapped him.

Nothing. He continued to stand without moving, his gaze unflinching.

She held up a hand in front of his eyes, blocking his line of sight. Moira couldn't see if he blinked, but his Adam's apple bobbed and he drew a ragged breath.

"Thank you," he said.

Moira dropped her hand. He doubled over taking deep breaths.

"Are you okay?"

"I think…I think so."

And he was—until he raised his head. He made a choking sound and went still all over again.

Moira followed his gaze straight to Zephyr. She muttered under her breath and set the sword aside. This time she hauled Bertram around by the lapels of his coat away from Zephyr, so the first thing he saw when he looked up wouldn't be a dragon.

Bertram buried his face in his hands.

"What was that? What just happened?" she asked.

Bertram uncovered his face and continued to blink. "Dragon freeze. I thought I could handle it, but apparently not."

"What's dragon freeze?"

Bertram shook himself. "If you haven't spent a lot of time around dragons, the first time you see one can send you into a state of immobility—all your instincts tell you to run, but the rest of you hasn't caught on yet."

Sounded familiar.

"And he came out of nowhere," Bertram said.

"No, he didn't. He was standing right there. He just wasn't moving."

Bertram frowned. "No. He appeared out of thin air." He squinted and started to get that pained expression again. "But you can see him?"

"Yes."

"All the time?"

Moira nodded.

"But that would mean—" He snapped upright, his head jerking. "Okay, then how—" He took a few steps, stopped and turned. He glanced in Zephyr's direction but avoided looking directly at him for longer than a fraction of a second. He paced back and forth, making excited noises, his hands moving as he spoke almost as if he was back in class, in the middle of a lecture, but she couldn't make sense of anything he was saying.

Moira slid over to stand beside Zephyr and together they watched Bertram pace back and forth, talking to himself.

"What did you mean when you said he couldn't see you?" Moira asked.

"You call it…camouflage."

"But I can see you. All the time." She paused. "Because you bit me."

"Yes."

Moira shook her head. What else could she do now that she couldn't do before because of Zephyr's bite?

Bertram wound to a halt with his back to them. Moira heard him draw a deep breath before he turned to face them. "Well, that took me by surprise." He risked a peek at Zephyr.

"Did you remember something?" Moira asked.

"Several somethings." Bertram gaze danced around them.

"Like what?"

"To be honest it's all a bit of a jumble. I'll make sense of most of it in time, but here's what I've deduced. When Zephyr revealed himself, I realized he was hidden in plain sight. That's not something every wyvern can do. They're all incredibly stealthy, but that particular trait is rare. Maybe one out of every three hundred or so wyverns can conceal themselves so. When you said you could see him all the time, I realized he must have bitten you."

Moira nodded.

Bertram drew a deep breath. "That doesn't happen often—oh!" He squeezed his eyes shut and pressed the heel of his palm to his forehead. "This really changes things." He dropped his hand but kept his eyes shut tight as his fingers began to drum a beat against his leg.

Zephyr caught Moira's eye. The pair exchanged a shrug.

"All right," Bertram said. His eyes sprang open and his hands clenched into fists at his sides before he released them. "I don't think you would have been able to find Zephyr if he hadn't bitten you. You were drawn to him." He made a motion with his hands starting far apart and meeting in the middle. It was like being back in class. "Then you went and named him and, I'm guessing, fed him a bunch of fire rocks. Now tell me if I'm wrong, but I bet Zephyr outgrew his current living situation and you're trying to find him a new place to stay?"

He wasn't wrong.

Moira glanced at Zephyr and nodded.

Bertram clapped his hands together and rubbed. "All right. I can help. Let's do this." He stopped and stared at Moira. "You should go home."

Moira's brows shot upward. A tiny laugh escaped her because she thought he was joking.

"I'm not kidding. You should go."

Moira felt the back of her neck grow hot as she drew herself up as tall as she could and faced Bertram. The old Moira, even the Moira from a few days ago, might have done what he said, but not the Moira he was talking to now. This was her business. She was supposed to be there.

"Find us tomorrow after school," Bertram said.

"I am not—"

"Don't you have someone who's going to be worried if you're not home soon?"

His question made her eyes narrow. "I'm not just going to leave you and Zephyr alone together."

Bertram frowned. "Why not?" He glanced all the way up at Zephyr before looking at Moira again. "Do you think I'm going to hurt him?"

He had a point.

"Truly, Ms. Noble, I only insist you go home because it's important to keep up appearances. If you deviate from your regular schedule any more than you already have, someone might notice. And then they might get curious. Secrecy is of the utmost importance. Isn't there someone waiting for you?"

Moira knew her aunt would not be happy when she got home, but if that were the case, then there was no reason to hurry. However, the longer she put off going home, the worse it would be.

Making up her mind, she strode over to where the sword still lay on the ground and snatched it up. She held the handle out to Zephyr. "You can be in charge of this," she told him, but she kept her gaze on Bertram and saw his throat work as he swallowed.

Zephyr accepted the sword, his jaw dropping open in a lazy grin, one that showed lots of fang and teeth.

Moira set off with a cheery wave. "See you tomorrow."

11

Moira eased the back door open. A light flickered in the family room. Her aunt lay curled on the sofa, asleep, her head on a throw pillow. Moira didn't recognize the station on the television. She dragged the blanket down from the back of the sofa and covered her aunt with it. Then she made herself a quick sandwich for dinner and scooted upstairs.

Weary to the marrow of her bones, Moira fell into bed without bothering to change or get under the covers. After a deep, dreamless night, her alarm woke her. She sat up with a groan. The sun shone bright and the skies were clear as she dragged herself out of bed and got ready. Her aunt was already gone, called in early, or so read the note she left.

Moira packed a lunch and took off for school. She paused in the woods, but she didn't leave the trail. If it was important to keep up appearances, she needed to get to school on time and do everything she would normally do. She couldn't worry about what Bertram and Zephyr were doing. More to the point, she could as much as she wanted. It just wouldn't help.

She sighed and kept walking.

At school, she wasn't expecting the crowd. She had to say "excuse me" more than once to reach her locker. Men in hardhats and school janitors raised yellow hazard signs and poked their flashlights into the drop ceiling in the middle of the locker bay. The leak appeared to have spread.

Students pulled books out of open lockers up and down the row on either side of Moira now. A few said, "Hey," and a couple of others nodded. She swung her locker door open.

Someone nudged her right shoulder. "Sorry. Oh, so sorry. Hey, how are you?"

She turned.

Natalia Oliver stood just behind her, grinning. She set down a tall stack of textbooks in front of the locker next to Moira's. Then she gathered her long auburn hair in one hand while she slid the backpack from her shoulder and set it on top of her books.

Moira tried to smile back. She could feel the corners of her mouth turn up, but her jaw still felt tight. "Okay. How about you?"

"Other than having to shuffle all my worldly belongings over here, not bad. I'm your new neighbor." She spun the dial of the lock on the door to the right of Moira's.

Aaron shouldered his way into the fray and spun the combination on the locker to her left. "Looks like someone wanted to be like the cool kids."

Moira did her best to ignore him and concentrated on getting what she needed for her morning classes.

Aaron's elbow nudged her and she jumped. "We're the cool kids in this scenario."

Natalia heard. "Right. I had the perfect locker and now I'm stuck in no man's land. No offense."

When Natalia said 'no offense,' she meant it. She and Aaron worked on the school newspaper together and before Moira had left school to concentrate on treating her anxiety, she would have counted Natalia as a friend. She was one of many friends Moira had failed to reconnect with upon returning the year before. Today was as good as any.

"It can't be no man's land because *we're* here," Aaron said.

Natalia laughed. "That's what you think," she said. "See you guys later." She closed her locker, made sure her lock was on, and waved goodbye.

Aaron grabbed his locker door and leaned on it facing Moira. "Do you have a minute?"

There were so many new people around Moira wasn't sure who he was talking to at first, but when nobody else answered, she looked up. He stared right at her. "I'm sorry, what?"

"Can we talk for a second?"

"We are talking." For longer than a second, though she didn't point it out.

He glanced around. "Somewhere else, maybe?"

The bell rang.

Moira shut her locker door. "Sorry. Maybe later. I gotta go." She was already turning away.

"Later," he called as she rushed out of the locker bay to first period. She wondered what he wanted to talk to her about. For about two seconds, it took her mind off of Zephyr and Bertram.

✂

The very best thing about having an independent study was getting out of the classroom and using the time where she needed to spend it most. For Moira, that was the library. She didn't have to worry about any of her regular duties until final period when she was scheduled as an aid, so she was free to work at her discretion on whatever she needed. At a small out-of-the-way table in the stacks, she sat down to work—except she couldn't concentrate. Her mind kept going over everything that had happened, trying to wrap her head around it all.

Dragons existed. Somewhere.

Somewhere dragons existed.

In an alternate universe was her working theory, perhaps one where dinosaurs never went extinct. Or only some of them. Zephyr had been brought, or sent, for some reason, found her, and bit her because she had—potential? She still wasn't super clear on what made Zephyr bite her instead of someone—*any*one—else, but he needed her help to find a way home. Enter Bertram, who happened to have a book stuck in his head about dragons, the details of which he couldn't recall at will. He said he would help with training, whatever that entailed. If there was a chance training her helped knock a vital piece of information free from Bertram's memory, Moira was willing to give it a try if it would help get Zephyr back home.

She read the same page in her world history text three times before she gave up and closed the cover, rubbing her eyes. As she reached for her backpack, she knocked another book to the floor. An irritated sigh escaped her and she squeezed her eyes shut. She opened them and leaned down to pick up the book, but a hand was there before her and she stopped. Pale tapered fingers flowed over the book's spine, lifting if from where it rested on the carpet. The hand was connected to an arm encased in the sleeve of a black suit connected to the stranger from the day before, the visiting librarian.

Moira's heart pounded and the bottom dropped out of her stomach. Sure, she was distracted but there was no way he could have snuck up on her without a sound. Who was this guy?

His suit matched the one he wore the day before.

The same suit?

She wasn't sure, but it was too crisp, too fresh, and his dark hair, though wavy, was perfect, without a strand out of place. His eyes were flat dark pools that didn't reflect the light.

She shivered.

He set the book down without a word and watched her, waiting.

"What do you want?" she asked.

One dark brow arched. "So many things." His voice was as deep and rich as the day before.

"What do you want from me?"

His eyes widened a fraction and he laughed.

It sounded wrong. Instead of wanting to join in, Moira wanted to find the nearest exit. The scent of old books grew and intensified as the noise filled the space.

His laughter faded and he wiped the corner of one eye.

"Who are you?" she asked.

"I'm the Librarian."

Moira squinted at him. The way he said it made it sound like there could be only one.

"Get away from her." The command came from the end of the row.

Moira's head snapped around.

Bertram stood at the end of the aisle. He wore the same clothes from last night, only dirtier. His hands clenched into fists at his sides.

"Bertram?"

He ignored her and kept his gaze locked on the Librarian.

"Leave this place," Bertram said, his voice quiet, but firm.

The Librarian, no longer smiling, tugged at the cuff of one sleeve and dipped his head a fraction of an inch in Bertram's direction. "As you wish," he said and evaporated into thin air. There one second, gone the next without so much as a puff of smoke.

Moira recoiled. From what she didn't know because there was nothing there. She blinked several times and stared at the spot where the stranger had stood. She pushed her chair back, got up, and waved her arm through the space. "What just happened?"

Bertram brushed up against the stacks. A visible tremor moved through him as he reached out to grab onto a shelf to steady himself. "You should forget about it."

She almost laughed, but at the last second thought better of it. There was no way to erase the last minutes from her memory any more than she could erase the past few days.

"He said he was the Librarian."

"Don't," Bertram said. "The less said the better."

Moira peered into the space around her table again, but whoever, or whatever it was, was truly gone. She had so many questions. She wanted to know more, but it was clear Bertram wasn't going to say anything else about it. Her shoulders rounded in disappointment. "Wait—why are you here? Shouldn't you be with Z—"

"Shhh."

Moira went still, listening, but there was no one around. "Don't shush me—you're not even supposed to be here. You're not teaching this year."

Her argument revived him. He stood up straight away for the stacks, no longer using the books to prop himself up. "Keep your voice down. Of course, I'm not teaching this year. Did you think I could with—" he made a circular motion around his head.

Moira lowered her voice. "I guess not. But why are you here? And where is—why aren't you in the woods?"

Bertram sighed. "I come to the library from time to time. It's not a crime." His gaze roamed the shelves of books around him, his brows arched in question. He brushed the backs of his fingers along the spines of the books next to him. "Tell me, can you hear them?" he asked.

There was no one else around. "Hear who?"

"Never mind," he lowered his hand. "I wasn't fired. I'm on sabbatical. I'm still allowed on school grounds. Being around so many books helps."

"But why aren't you with our mutual friend?"

"Well," he clasped his hand together, "believe it or not, after being up half the night wandering around in the dark, your friend and I found a place for him to reside for the time being."

"Okay. Let's go. The camera by the gym has a blind spot." Moira grabbed her books and tossed them into her backpack.

Bertram watched her, frowning. "It does? Wait—where are you going?"

Moira stopped. "You're kidding, right?"

"Ms. Noble, do you typically leave school early for no reason?"

"No, but—"

"Then you won't today, either. You should be sticking to your routine. We'll be waiting for you after school in the woods." Bertram turned to leave.

She stopped him before he reached the end of the row. "Wait—how will I find you?"

"That shouldn't be a problem for someone such as yourself."

He turned the corner out of sight leaving Moira to stew and count the minutes until the school day was over.

12

Finally—*finally*—the last bell rang.

Instead of rushing headlong into the woods like she wanted, Moira made her way toward the gym and out the double doors skirting past groups of students without a word, heading for the trail. In other words, she did everything she normally did at the pace she regularly did it.

"Hey, Moira—wait up!"

Not normal.

She was the only Moira she knew, so there was little hope that whoever shouted her name meant someone else. She stopped and turned. Aaron detached himself from a group of guys from their year and some upperclassmen. More than one glanced in her direction as Aaron slapped his friends on the shoulder and they slapped him on the back. Jaw clenched, she twisted around and started walking again. She did not have time for this. He jogged to catch up with her.

"Hey," Aaron said, falling into step beside her.

"What's up?"

"Not much. What's going on?"

"You tell me. You're the one who lives in the complete opposite direction."

"I know where I live, but thanks for worrying about me."

"I wasn't—I'm not." Moira struggled to retain a sense of calm. She had places to be, not that she knew where, and trading barbs with Aaron wasn't going to get her there any faster. "What do you want, Aaron?"

"I thought we could talk now. Can I walk you home?"

She didn't point out that he sort of already was. How was she going to get rid of him? "You can walk me to the fork in the trail. I haven't forgotten where I live, either." At the pace she was going, it wouldn't be long before they got there, so he'd better talk fast.

"What's that?" he asked.

She saw him point to the strap of the camera bag she'd slung over her shoulder. Her hand brushed against the bag and she patted it to make sure it was settled and secure. "Digital camera. Mr. Dee loaned it to me."

"Photography? Mr. Dee isn't teaching photography until next semester."

"That is correct."

"Then why did he loan you a digital camera?"

"I asked if I could borrow one to practice with."

"Smart. I never thought of that. Huh."

They walked another twenty feet or so in silence.

"Is that what you wanted to talk about?" Moira asked. She didn't mean to sound curt, but she couldn't very well go looking for Bertram and Zephyr with him beside her.

"I wanted to make sure you don't mind my having the locker next to yours."

She frowned. "No." *Is he serious?* She had better things to do than hang out at her locker. Before she could stop herself, she asked, "Why would I mind?"

"Because you haven't given me the time of day since sixth-grade Biology."

His words jolted her. She didn't know what to say. Sixth-grade Biology was where it started and ended for them.

They had a new teacher that year; a middle-aged dude with round, tortoise-shell spectacles and big ideas. One of his brainwaves was to divide the class into groups for a project about the human body or something, she didn't even remember. She thought she was lucky to be assigned to a group with Aaron and two others. They split the work amongst themselves, everyone doing their part. It worked well until she came down with a nasty cold virus and had to miss a couple of days of school. It didn't stop her from completing her assigned portion of the project, but it didn't matter. Their teacher decided to have the groups evaluate each other and let the points stand. Aaron and her project partners did fine. She'd given them all top marks because everyone completed their part of the assignment. They'd done well overall, just not on an individual basis.

As a result of how Aaron and the others graded her contribution to the project, Moira brought home the first and only failure notice she'd ever received in a class.

The disappointment on her father's face when she showed it to him stayed with her. It was an expression she never wanted to see on his features again, and as it turns out, she never did. Her dad passed away soon after and she'd barely scraped by. When she returned to public school last year it was with a single-minded purpose to do better, perhaps to the detriment of everything else.

"I'm sorry, you know. If that helps. The teacher gave us this speech when we were grading each other. You didn't hear it because you were out sick. I thought I was being fair, but I didn't mean to mess with your grade like that. If someone did that to me today—" he stopped with a shake of his head. "I hope there are no hard feelings. Again, I'm soryy."

Moira frowned. Sixth grade was a long time ago. So much had happened since then, and not just in the past couple of weeks or even days. They were different people now. The past was gone. They couldn't change it. Still, the apology was nice. And his acknowledgment of the part he played in what happened helped. Moira never thought Aaron set out to ruin her grade on purpose, but his confirming it helped her let go of a lot of anger. The other two people in the group had a hand in her failing marks as well, but she'd never held it against them the way she had Aaron.

"No, I don't mind. About the locker," she said.

They might never be the best of friends, but maybe she could try not going out of her way to avoid him. Considering their lockers were right next to each other now, maybe that was a good thing.

"Glad to hear it," Aaron said.

The split in the trail was around the next bend. "You could do something for me, though."

Aaron smiled. "You've never asked me for anything before." His eyes narrowed. "What is it?"

"Can you keep your buddy Charlie Barrett out of the library final period?" It was a long shot. Charlie and Aaron were friends and shared a lot of the same classes. And maybe it was selfish of her to have Aaron try and keep Charlie out of her way, but it couldn't hurt to ask.

"What's Charlie done now?"

"He likes to come to the library and check things out, but not the books, if you know what I mean. Don't you have a class together then?"

Aaron nodded. "We do. We work on the newspaper together. But I can't keep him from going to the library if he needs to."

Moira didn't say anything.

Aaron heaved a sigh. "I won't make any promises, but I'll do what I can." He smiled as they stopped at the fork in the trail sticking out his hand.

Moira thought it was silly to shake on it, but he did just agree to help her out if he could so she slid her palm into his.

Their hands connected thumb to thumb. Aaron's fingers wrapped around Moira's palm and squeezed. His grip was firm, but not too tight. The warmth from his touch spread up her arm. The handshake stretched on past the time when it should have ended, but Moira didn't let go. Their shared grip felt natural and comfortable.

Aaron's smile slipped a notch and he let go first. "I guess I'll see you around." He backed down the trail the way they had come.

"See you." Moira slipped her hand behind her back and flexed her fingers.

Aaron twisted around and Moira watched him until he was out of sight.

She backtracked down the trail a short time later. Two students passed her going the opposite direction. Moira stopped to tie her shoe and stayed, hunched over, fiddling with the laces. When she was sure there was no one around to see her, she stepped off the trail heading deeper into the woods. Nothing looked familiar for a long time until she reached a small clearing where she thought she may have parted ways with Bertram and Zephyr the night before, but there was no sign of them or the dead troll anywhere.

Now what? Bertram had said finding them shouldn't be a problem for someone such as herself, whatever that meant. Moira scrubbed at her face and turned on the spot trying to decide which way to go. She dropped her hands and stared at the sky through the trees overhead. Maybe she should go back to the cave—

No. Not there.

Moira's head whipped around. What the—where did that thought come from?

She thought about the cave. She knew where it was, but when she tried to imagine Zephyr in it, she got the same sensation. Something was telling her Zephyr wasn't there. Besides, she knew he was too big to get back inside.

So, where was he?

Moira's feet started moving. The course she trod changed every time she thought of Zephyr. Not by a lot, perhaps only a few degrees. It was an eerie sensation, almost as if someone had their hand on her shoulder steering her in the direction she needed to go. But no one was there. Moira checked. She didn't know where she was going, but she kept her ears open thinking she would hear something before she saw anything. She walked for five minutes. Then ten.

Moira saw a break in the trees ahead and the mysterious feeling that guided her along eased. With nothing urging her forward, she slowed until she came to a stop. Silence. The opening in front of her was a meadow. A lichen-covered wall of rock made up about a third of the clearing's perimeter. She stood amongst the trees opposite the wall of stone. A rockslide had left a pile of debris at the foot of it. Surrounding the rubble, the meadow was filled with a lush carpet of grass and wildflowers.

So where was Zephyr? He couldn't conceal himself from her, but what had Bertram said? Dragons were magnificently stealthy.

There, about half the distance between her and the rock wall, Zephyr sat with his back against a tree, eyelids lowered as if he were asleep sitting up.

She smiled and was about to call out when the scabbard-covered tip of a sword landed on her shoulder. Moira reeled, falling on her backside with a yelp.

Bertram held the end of the sheathed blade aloft. "Your training begins now, Ms. Noble."

Zephyr shot to her side so fast the air rushed around her. He dipped his head low and glared at Bertram, his tail slashing the air behind him as he edged between them.

Bertram dropped the sword's point so it rested on the ground and put his free hand in the air.

Moira stood, brushing at the seat of her pants. "What kind of training?"

Bertram didn't answer. His focus remained fixed on Zephyr who continued to glower at him. Bertram let the handle of the sword slip through his fingers so that it fell to the ground with a clatter and raised that hand as well in reaching for the sky. "My apologies, Ms. Noble, I didn't mean to startle you."

Moira laid a hand on Zephyr's arm. "I'm fine, Zeph. He just took me by surprise."

Zephyr glanced her way, his gaze giving her the once over, checking for himself before he settled back.

"What kind of training again?" Her gaze bounced from one to the other before settling on Bertram.

He lowered his hands. His Adam's apple bobbed once in his throat as he swallowed. "Defensive training. You should learn how to protect yourself and your wyvern." He squinted and blinked slowly, his eyes glazing over for a second before he blinked and focused once more. "You are connected now, for lack of a better term." He frowned and shook his head.

"I'm starting to get that," Moira muttered. There was no other way to explain how she found him. "What did you do with the troll?"

"Buried," Zephyr said.

"Near where it died. Zephyr helped, of course. I couldn't have done it without him. Thank you again Master Wyvern." Bertram dipped his head in Zephyr's direction. "But you both got lucky last night. I don't think the troll that attacked you was particularly skilled. Taking out an experienced troll is challenging enough for a full-size dragon, let alone a half-grown one."

Moira's brows shot up. "Half? *Half* grown?" She turned to Zephyr. He tilted his head to the side and shrugged. Zephyr was already taller than her. His head was massive and his mouth full of pointy teeth. His arms were muscular and thick as were his hindquarters. His entire body was about 12 feet long when you added in the tail that stretched out behind him and ended in a flexible, whip-like tip.

Zephyr peered down at himself, lifting a foot and putting it down again.

Moira turned back to Bertram who canted his head to the side as he squinted at Zephyr.

"I'm estimating," Bertram said.

Moira shook her head, glad they got out of the cave when they did, which reminded her, "You said you found a place for Zephyr to stay."

"Yes." Bertram threw out his arms. "This is it."

"What—here? Isn't it a little—" Moira gestured at the open expanse of rock, grass, and flowers that made up the clearing. It was no larger than twenty or so feet across and only half as wide, "—exposed?" Sunlight touched down and it was like someone turned a spotlight on.

"Follow me, please," Bertram bent down, snatched up the sword, and marched out into the open.

Moira caught Zephyr's eye.

He gave her a one-shoulder shrug.

Bertram walked straight to the pile of rocks and climbed up and over. Pebbles skittered in his wake and larger rocks knocked together with solid ringing *thuds*. Moira scrambled to follow. Zephyr kept pace with her. He had no problem with his footing.

On the other side, Moira could see where the bottom half of the wall had slumped away from the rest of it. This left a section of the face hollowed out. The rocks they climbed over had once been a part of the wall. The debris made a pile of rocks large enough for several people, or one dragon, to hide behind. Her mind skipped ahead, increasing the height of the rock wall, perhaps adding sight holes, but nothing too drastic. They didn't want to make it appear unnatural.

"Landslide?" she asked.

"That's what I was thinking," Bertram said.

Moira stepped inside spreading her arms. The space wasn't deep, but it was wide enough that she couldn't touch the sides. She dropped her arms. The overhang would keep the rain off.

"What do you think?" she asked.

Zephyr took in the hollowed-out wall, the pile of rocks, and the little space between them with a rove of his eyes. "It is no cave."

"I know. I don't like the idea of you being so out in the open either, but beggars can't be choosers."

Zephyr's eyes narrowed as his head turned to the side. "Why can I not both beg and choose?" he asked.

"Good question. I just know it doesn't usually work that way."

Zephyr tipped his head to the side as if he were considering it.

"I just hope no one decides to come this way," Moira said.

Bertram cleared his throat. "There might be something you can do about that."

"Like what?" Moira imagined hanging Keep Out signs.

"You could work some magic."

13

More than a little skeptical, Moira followed Bertram back over the pile of rocks away from Zephyr's shelter toward the tree line. Bertram went straight to a particular oak and whipped the cover off of an internal-framed backpack she hadn't noticed, the kind someone would use if they were backpacking for days on end. Bertram unclipped the top of the bag from the main compartment and rummaged through the contents. When he found what he was looking for, he straightened and turned handing her a metal plate and a bunch of thin green stems tied together.

Moira stared at what she thought were dried herbs. About six inches in length, they were silvery grey and green and smelled of sage, mint, and a few other scents she couldn't identify.

"We want to keep people away from here and the sooner the spell is in place the better," Bertram said. "The bundle of herbs gives you a focus. As we walk, you need to project your will to keep people away. Zephyr will follow us as we go."

Moira's gaze went from the bundle to Bertram and back.

"If you can do this, then there's no worrying that someone might stumble across Zephyr while they're out for a stroll," Bertram said.

She didn't know of many people who would go for a stroll in the woods, but she did know someone who ran through them on a regular basis. The thought worried her enough to know she had to try and do this.

Bertram was telling her she could do magic. All she had to do was take a walk and project her will at the same time. And Zephyr would come too.

"Wait, why does Zephyr need to come with us? Shouldn't he stay behind and out of sight?" she asked.

Bertram nodded. "I wish he could, but I have a theory. When Zephyr bit you, he injected you with his venom. It spread throughout your system and infected your cells, essentially altering them. Dragons don't perform magic on their own, but they are innately magical beings. Your ability to perform magic is what you might call a side effect. Truth be told, I think that's how you found him in the first place. Whatever it is you two share, it brought you together. However, I suspect you're not yet strong enough to do this on your own. We need Zephyr."

Moira opened her mouth and shut it again. Could what he was saying have happened without her knowing – had Zephyr's bite caused her to be drawn to him? She couldn't refute the theory. She remembered the eerie sensation from earlier of someone's hand on her shoulder guiding her to Zephyr, bringing her to the meadow they were standing in. There was definitely something there, a connection she was only now just becoming aware of. But Bertram was suggesting she do something completely different. To the best of her knowledge, she wasn't capable of doing magic, but he was telling her she could.

She would try for Zephyr's sake.

Bertram dug a lighter out of his jean's pocket. With a flick of his thumb, he brought up a flame and held it to the end of the bundle Moira held. It caught and flared before Bertram blew it out. The herbs continued to smoke and the scents she caught earlier intensified.

Moira positioned the metal plate under the smoking bundle. "Okay, so do I need to say some magic words or something?"

"Good question." Bertram stepped back. "But words are just another type of focus. The herbs you're holding will do it for now. You don't need to say anything. This isn't about words. This is about intent. What you must do is inject your will into the spell. Your purpose here is to keep people from stumbling through the woods and bumping into Zephyr. If it helps, imagine what chaos would ensue if they did." He pocketed the lighter and brushed off his hands. "We'll start with a turn about the clearing here and spiral out. We'll skirt the trails, but we won't cross them. People need to be able to come and go. We just don't want them to linger." His gaze rested on Zephyr for a moment before returning to her.

She arched a brow. Bertram didn't appear the least bit frozen by Zephyr's presence any longer. She took two steps, stopped and turned toward Zephyr. "Magic? Seriously?"

Zephyr shot Bertram a glare before his gaze landed on Moira and softened. "It is as he says. You have acquired some new abilities, but they require practice. You can do this. I will help." Zephyr spread an arm wide, indicating to her she should begin walking and he would follow.

Still unsure of what she should be doing, she paused at the edge of the meadow. "So, I should focus on turning away whoever might come this far out into the woods?"

Bertram stepped in front of her. "Don't forget to add a pinch of will and you have it. Now, if you please, follow me."

Bertram went first, holding branches out of the way and quietly pointing out obstacles to Moira as she followed, trailing smoke. Zephyr fell into line behind her, an oversized shadow.

The parade of man, teen-aged girl, and dragon marched on.

At first, all Moira could concentrate on was her own two feet as she tried not to trip over the uneven ground. She fumbled along holding the plate in front of her, unsure of what she was supposed to be doing. It would have been easier if Bertram had given her a few words or phrases to repeat over and over again, but this wasn't about words. Bertram said it was about intent, and she intended to keep people away from Zephyr for his safety and theirs. But how? And what about projecting her will? Did it have anything to do with willpower? If so, they were in real trouble.

The smoke coming from the bundle of herbs caught her attention. A thin grey line flowed straight upward before it caught the turbulent air and disappeared. Could she turn the smoke into some kind of invisible barrier, Zephyr on one side, everyone else on the other? Probably not. Moira sighed and focused on the smoke. She knew it was impossible to build an actual physical barrier with it, so she used her imagination.

She pictured the threads of smoke splitting and weaving together through the air to form an unseen tapestry. In her head, she reached out and flicked a trailing thread connected to the weave, not unlike flipping a switch. As she did, she pushed a simple thought down her arm and out the ends of her fingertips. Every time she 'flipped' a switch she thought, *turn away, there's nothing here*, or sometimes, *leave already*. After a while, Moira felt like she was getting the hang of it. It was like walking into an unfamiliar room and reaching out to turn on the lights, but the switch was in a weird spot, higher or lower than expected. In her head, she went along flipping on lights in one room after another, back to back to back. The switches got easier to find. She hoped whatever she was doing would make whoever came near uncomfortable enough to leave and not head deeper into the woods.

Zephyr followed Moira. Moira followed Bertram. They stuck to the plan and didn't cross any trails, but they came close to a few. Moira briefly worried about Zephyr being seen and hoped his camouflage would hold up in the afternoon light. Thankfully, they didn't run into anyone and arrived back at the clearing, sweaty and dirt-streaked.

"How do we know if it worked?" she asked.

"Unfortunately, there's no way for us to test it. We'll have to wait and see," Bertram said.

Zephyr sat with his back against a tree. Its leaves shuddered and quaked. He bent one knee and examined the bottom of his foot.

"You okay, Zeph?" Moira asked.

He grunted. "I am not used to walking for such long periods." He pressed his talon-tipped thumbs into the ball of his foot.

Bertram collected the plate and herbs from her. "Zephyr's feet will take time to toughen, in part because he grew so fast."

Moira checked the time. It was later than she thought. "I have to go."

"Already?" Bertram asked. "But we haven't gotten to any real training yet."

Moira grabbed her backpack and slipped her arms through the straps. "You said it was important to keep up appearances. I told my aunt I'd be home soon. I can stay later tomorrow."

Bertram nodded to himself, "Fine." He dowsed the herbs with water from a bottle and stuffed them back into his backpack. "Let's give you something to work on."

Moira stifled a groan.

Bertram picked up two pebbles the size of marbles and handed one to Moira. Zephyr kept his seat, massaging the bottom of his foot as he watched.

"Focus on the rock. Feel the weight of it in your palm." Bertram hefted his pebble. "Mass displaces space creating gravity, which is holding the rock in your hand. The magic you wield with your will warps space to create alternate forces, ones that can be exerted in any direction you like. Concentrate and release your will."

Moira stared at the rock resting in the palm of her hand.

Nothing happened.

She squinted at it and stood there for a full 30 seconds before tossing the rock in the air and catching it. Warping space to her will would have to wait. She needed to get home. "I'll work on it."

"Huh." Bertram frowned and dropped his rock. "I really thought—" He stopped. "Don't worry about it." He turned away, but Moira heard him say under his breath, "Maybe we should have started with fire."

Moira's brows shot up as she turned toward Zephyr. "You can't breathe fire? I'm sure that would have come in handy."

Zephyr moved his head from side to side with a slow smile. "No fire. Journey safe, Moira."

✂

She made it home in time for dinner with her aunt but then begged off doing anything together afterward with the age-old excuse of homework. Except it wasn't just an excuse. She had to study for her first Geometry test and start researching topics for an English paper. When she finished up, it was early enough to get to bed at a reasonable time, but she didn't let herself. She got up from her desk and stretched, turning her head from side-to-side to release the tension built up in her neck. Twisting around, she dropped to the foot of her bed and dug the rock out of her pocket. Palm flat, fingers splayed, she eyed the pebble.

It did what pebbles do and sat there.

Moira threw herself back against the covers. When she hadn't made the rock do whatever it was Bertram thought she should be able to do with it, she could see he was disappointed. He might have tried to hide it, but she could tell. Dragons were magic and Zephyr had bitten her, ergo she was magic now, too. Made sense, as much as anything made sense lately. If she thought about it too long, she got a headache.

She sat up. "Mass displaces space to create gravity," she said aloud. She opened her hand and stared at the pebble. Gravity held it in the palm of her hand. She intended to make it move; a little, a lot, she didn't care. She just wanted it to do something. After a minute, pins and needles raced up and down her arm. The sensation grew, but the rock didn't move. Moira took a deep breath, trying to ignore the growing sensation of white noise in her limb. Another minute passed and Moira's arm jerked with fatigue.

But the rock didn't move.

Moira no longer supported the pebble, but it stayed put suspended in midair without her palm supporting it. She stared, blinked once, and let out a whoop, bouncing up from the foot of her bed, arms raised in the air. The rock tumbled to the ground.

She gasped and snatched it back up to try again. The pins and needles returned, but they weren't as bad this time. And again, the rock defied gravity. From there it was a matter of tweaking her intentions and visualizing what she wanted to happen. She got the rock to move up and down and side to side. Satisfied with her attempts, she fell into bed and dropped off to sleep a moment later.

As exhausted as she was, she really thought she would have slept better, but she didn't. She dreamed. Her subconscious asserted itself and sorted through her day. Most of it she could ignore, but then she recognized Zephyr's meadow as she had never seen it, late at night and filled with moonlight. The dragon himself dropped into the scene, blurred and unfocused as he fought with a troll, hand-to-hand. They exchanged blows until Zephyr hit the troll with enough force to throw it back through the air. It hit the ground and disappeared into the roiling mist. Zephyr bent over with his hands on his knees, shoulders rising and falling as he sucked wind. An exact copy of the first troll materialized out of the shadows and the skirmish began anew.

Zephyr fought that one off too. The wisps of it hadn't even faded before another one popped up. Moira couldn't do anything in that frustrating way dreams have of not letting the dreamer interact with their surroundings. She shouted, but no noise came out. She ran forward, arms pumping, but she got nowhere. All she could do was watch Zephyr fight, again and again, growing weaker after each bout until the last one. Her dragon needed help and she couldn't do anything about it. The final troll knocked Zephyr to the ground, got on top of him, and didn't let him up.

Moira awoke tangled in the sheets, the sun peeking through her curtains. She rubbed her eyes and pushed the images from her mind, but the aftereffects of the dream stayed with her. Telling herself it was just a dream didn't help. She knew it wasn't real, but that didn't erase the feelings the dream brought forth. Her frustration and helplessness rose up like a wave threatening to capsize her. She sprang up and out of bed. Her feet planted on the floor she let the emotions roll over and through her, breathing the whole time, acknowledging the way she felt and letting herself experience the full weight of her emotions. Her shoulders rounded. Sweat bloomed across her forehead. She closed her eyes. A second later a new feeling coursed through her and her hands clenched at her sides. As soon as she acknowledged the anger inside of her, it too began to lose potency and fade.

Moira squared her shoulders and opened her eyes, ready to move on. It was time to get on with her day.

14

"Excuse me."

It was last period and Moira was behind the front desk in the library sorting through returns. A student she didn't know stood on the other side holding a book. He had a backpack hanging from one shoulder and dark hair combed forward, back to front and off to the side.

"Can I help you?" she asked.

He hesitated, glancing behind the desk, but there was no one else there. Ms. Haven was in her office and the other library aid was running an errand. He must have come to some decision because he lifted the book he held up by its spine. "This book had something funny in it."

"Some books are like that."

He frowned. "What do you mean?"

Moira smiled and shook her head. "Nothing. What was the matter with it?"

"This was stuck inside." He held up a scrap of paper. "It was jammed in the middle of it." The piece of unruled white paper had ragged edges all around it like it had been torn from the middle of a larger sheet. Written on it were two words in block letters: *HELP ME.*

"Oh. Another one," Moira said and opened a drawer. The bottom was littered with similar scraps of paper all bearing the same scrawled message. She took the piece of paper from him and added it to the pile. "Thanks for bringing it up to the desk. Did you want to check out the book?"

"Yeah." He handed over his school ID. Derek Mueller. Freshman.

"Are those like, a joke, or something?"

"Ms. Haven thinks so."

The notes defied any kind of pattern, popping up in books across every type of classification. Ms. Haven started finding them over the summer. The school librarian was sure someone was getting their kicks by sticking the messages into whatever book caught their eye. They always said the same thing. Whenever Ms. Haven or one of the aids found one, they added it to the drawer and forgot about it until the next one turned up.

"Sick," the Mueller kid said with a shake of his head and a weird little smile. She couldn't tell if he thought it was disturbing or cool.

Moira didn't know if the scraps of paper were a joke or not. She thought maybe someone needed help writing a paper and they stuck the messages in the library books like prayers. The more notes they left the more confident they felt their message was getting through.

Moira handed the book over.

Mueller left and Ms. Haven came out of her office with a stack of books that she asked Moira to put away. There were only five, so Moira scooped them up into her arms and left the cart behind. She worked through the stack until she had one left. The final book lived in the farthest reaches of the library. She sank into the stacks, turned a corner, stumbled, and caught herself. She'd tripped over a book lying on the floor across from an empty bookcase. It was empty because all of the books had been taken down, separated by color, and stacked into a tower, turning them into someone's personal building blocks. She might have been impressed if she wasn't so annoyed.

Moira made a frustrated noise and crouched down to start disassembling the structure, muttering to herself. "Jerks."

"Indeed," said a voice right behind her.

"Gaw—" Moira jumped and spun at the same time. The book she held slipped from her fingers and went flying.

The Librarian snagged it out of the air from where he stood without looking away from her. He wore the same dark suit and appeared altogether unchanged since she last saw him yesterday. She would expect some variation in his appearance if he were a regular person, but he was anything but normal. Not one hair was out of place on his dark head. Like a cartoon, he was too perfectly drawn, his edges sharp, never mussed.

Her heart hammered at her ribs. She hated being snuck up on and her anger moved her tongue before she could think better of it. "Maybe you should wear a bell."

The Librarian's dark eyes narrowed. He set the book he'd caught aside and undid the button of his coal-black suit jacket. He stretched his hands out, palms down, digits spread.

Moira pressed her back into the bookshelves behind her, alert and watchful. "What are you doing?"

The books on the floor quivered. The top book righted itself and flew back on to a shelf unassisted.

Moira gasped. One by one the rest of the books flew back on to the shelves. The last volume settled itself between two others. The smell of old books choked the air and did not dissipate. "Who are you?" Her voice only squeaked a little.

"I told you."

"You said you're a librarian."

His dark head jerked to the side. "Not *a* librarian—*the* Librarian."

"What does that mean?"

He dropped his hands. "I am the library. The books are me."

Moira shuddered and closed her eyes, focusing on what he said and trying to wrap her head around his meaning. "Are you trying to tell me you're some kind of amalgamation of all these books?" She waved a hand in the air at the shelves surrounding them.

The Librarian sighed and redid the button of his jacket.

Moira stretched out a hand, pleased when it didn't visibly tremble and poked him in the chest. Her finger did not go through him and he did not disappear like a burst soap bubble. She lowered her hand.

One brow arched. "No," he said.

"No?"

"I am not a construct limited to the books in this space." He took a moment to brush at the spot where she had touched him as if she had left an invisible wrinkle. "I am a projection incorporating all of the books in all of the libraries." He paused to tug both sleeves of his jacket down over the ends of his shirt cuffs. "Anywhere. Ever."

Moira could feel her jaw slide open, but she was powerless to close it. She had the insane urge to reach out and poke him again.

"Are you the one who's been leaving the notes?" she asked.

The Librarian's head jerked. He raised a hand and pressed his palm to the spine of one of the books he'd replaced. He stared at her, eyes wide. The pitch-black of his irises fountained upward and spilled over into the white sclera of his eyes.

Moira recoiled.

His blank gaze took in everything. He canted his head to the side as if listening before he closed his eyes. They opened a moment later and were back to normal; his irises a pair of intense dark pools and the rest, white. "There are sixty-three more such notes located in various texts throughout this library. I just checked."

"Did you put them there?" she asked again.

"No."

"Do you know who did?"

"Yes." One corner of his mouth curled up. She wouldn't call it a smile because it didn't reach his cold, dark eyes. It was more of a smirk than a smile. Like someone had given him a description of a smile and he was trying to do it half-way.

"Why are you here?" Her voice sounded plaintive to her own ears, but she couldn't take back the question.

His eyes blazed. They were deep in a corner of the library but the light faded further and the scent of old books took on a cloying musty sweetness that invaded her nose and filled her head. "I'm here to warn you of what will happen if you fail."

Moira breathed through her mouth. "Fail?"

"Fail to protect the dragon. You'll lose not only your life but the lives of countless others. Stop wasting your time with all of this," he raised a hand, fingers splayed wide in an all-encompassing gesture, which she took to mean school as a whole, "and get to work."

"I'm not dropping out of school." Bertram had said she needed to keep up appearances. If she stopped coming to school that would only draw attention to the fact that something wasn't right. And no way was she about to give up on school because some mysterious figure in a suit told her to quit. She had a dragon-free future to think about. "I will help Zephyr find his way back home and then—" she stopped.

Then what? Then her life would go back to normal. Why didn't that sound as appealing as she thought it would? She attempted to think in specifics. In her dragon-free future, she would finish the school year, find a summer job, do it all over again a couple more times and move on to higher education. After that, she would find a real job doing something she enjoyed, or at least something she tolerated so she could do the things she enjoyed.

"I'll show you," The Librarian said. If she stood close enough to reach out and poke him, he stood close enough to wrap cool fingers around her wrist. The contact jolted her. The lights dimmed. Moira blinked. She stood in the same field of tall grass as her vision before. A hot wind bent the tall blades turning them into an undulating sea. A light in the distance glowed and expanded, closer this time. An army of trolls marched forward. At their head was an armored man with a long cape. She was too far away to make out his features clearly, but he had dark hair cropped close to the scalp and an angry slash of a mouth. In the distance, the metal of armor clanked and clanged, but it was drowned out by the undecipherable murmuring sliding past her ears. She turned. The field behind her had been dug up and filled with bodies: dragons, trolls, and humans. All motionless. All dead. She gasped but didn't cry out because she knew it wasn't real.

A movement next to her made her look. Zephyr, his yellow gaze dull, shuddered and fell forward toward the pile of bodies at her feet. She reached out, toppling after him into a black abyss. Her whole being jerked and she stood on her own two feet again in the stacks.

The Librarian eyed her warily as he let go of her wrist. "I'm warning you. Protect the dragon. Or else."

"Moira?" A voice called.

She jumped. The lights grew brighter and the scent of old books receded to normal levels. She sneezed. The Librarian didn't move. He just disappeared. Right in front of her. Again.

She was beginning to hate that.

"Moira? You back here?"

She stepped away from the bookcase and gave herself a shake all over. "Here," she called.

Ansel stepped around the corner at the end of the aisle. "Hey—Ms. Haven said you were putting books away." He came down the aisle, stopping in front of her. "You okay? You don't look so good."

"Yeah. Yeah, just a little light-headed is all."

He frowned, stepping in close to her side, his fingertips brushing her arm. "Maybe you should sit down."

"I'm fine. I don't need to sit down."

Ansel blinked. "Are you sure you're okay?" He watched her as if he expected her to double over any second. Moira couldn't blame him. He hadn't seen her at her best, but not every odd little thing triggered an anxiety attack. She never really got to choose when, but she knew it wasn't going to happen this time.

Moira summoned up a smile. "I'm good. Thanks for asking."

He searched her face. He must have found whatever he was looking for because he dropped his hand. "Okay. Are you all done?"

"For now."

They walked back to the circulation desk in silence. Moira slipped behind it, while Ansel propped himself up on both elbows across from her.

"Was there a book you needed?" she asked.

"Nope. I just wanted to tell you I'll pick you up at six on Friday."

"Friday?"

"Yeah, for the movie."

Moira's eyes closed. Friday. "Yeah, about that—"

"You forgot, didn't you?"

"It's only Wednesday. I didn't forget—" she broke off. How could she explain what had been going on?

And then it hit her.

She couldn't.

There was no way to tell anyone what was going on without sounding crazy. She imagined saying, *Sorry, I got bit by a dragon and I'm kind of busy keeping him safe and trying to find him a way back home. Can we reschedule?* She should commit herself and save whoever she told the hassle. Her stomach churned and she worried her bottom lip.

"Are you sure you're okay?" Ansel asked.

"Yeah."

"Great. Then I'll see you on Friday."

Ansel left before she could gather her wits enough to tell him something had come up. Of course, she didn't know what she would have said if he asked her what that was, so perhaps it was for the best.

The final bell rang and Moira gathered her things, slower than usual.

15

Moira trudged through the woods after school pondering what truly bothered her. It wasn't that she couldn't tell anyone about Zephyr. She was fine with keeping him secret. She couldn't trust people not to overreact if they knew about him, never mind what they would do if they ever came face to face with him. Bertram had known about dragons before he'd met Zephyr and he'd just about keeled over.

What bothered her was the lying. It wasn't in her nature. Moira had told her aunt she was studying late so she wouldn't worry, but she had no idea what she was going to tell Ansel to get out of going to the movies. She'd never had to lie to anyone before. Sure, she'd spared people their feelings, and could dissemble when it came to hiding how she felt, but she'd never out-and-out lied to someone. Having to lie to Ansel was especially hard.

Sure no one was around, Moira stepped off the trail. She pushed thoughts of what to do about Ansel aside. It was time to keep her eyes sharp and her ears keen. The spell she'd put in place to keep people away seemed to be working. She followed her dragon-o-meter, what she'd come to think of as the guiding force that led her to Zephyr, deeper into the woods without incident.

Moira came to the edge of the clearing and froze in her tracks, mesmerized. In the meadow, Zephyr performed a series of intricate steps and jumps before he completed a graceful spin. Near the opposite side, he dropped, rolled, and came up holding the sword. He picked up his complex dance without missing a beat, adding the blade to the mix.

Her jaw dropped. Zephyr moved with a grace and agility that belied his size and proportions. He was large and solid, but his dimensions didn't detract from his fluid movements. One motion flowed into the next with no stuttering or jerking. In the middle of the clearing Zephyr flew into a flurry of complicated turns that ended when he thrust the blade forward, stabbing the air, holding his body in a straight line from nose to tail tip. The end of his sword pointed at Bertram who stood in the shade of a tree with his arms crossed.

Moira's knees wobbled.

Bertram stroked his chin and asked, "How did that feel?"

Zephyr relaxed his posture and stood up straight. He rolled his massive shoulders, his head tilting one way and then the other as he stretched his neck. "There is room for improvement."

Moira gulped.

As if he'd heard her hasty swallow, Zephyr turned to look at her. "What did Moira think?"

Bertram's head snapped around.

Nice to know she could surprise at least one of them.

What did she think? She took a breath to calm her sudden case of nerves. She'd gotten a look at what her dragon could do with a sword, and he thought there was room for improvement. Moira cleared her throat, but her voice still broke when she answered. "Looked great."

"Then I will continue." Zephyr faced Moira and saluted, raising the hilt of the sword to his opposite shoulder, the blade straight up and motionless a moment before he dropped the tip with a slash toward the ground and went to the middle of the clearing to begin again.

Moira scooted around the meadow, over to Bertram, still watching Zephyr. "Did you teach him that?"

He, too, looked on as Zephyr practiced. "Not at all."

Moira tore her gaze away from her dragon to peer at Bertram.

"I know. It's hard to believe, but wyverns have an inherited memory, much like elephants in some sense. He was born knowing how to fight, but he still needs to practice. And there's only so much of that he can do with the limited resources we have available to us here."

She turned back to Zephyr and they both watched him together in silence until Bertram cleared his throat and asked, "How was school?" He turned toward her. "What are you taking anyway?"

"The usual stuff. Honors classes. An independent study. Final period I work as an aid in the library."

"You spend a lot of time around those books."

Her lips compressed into a straight line as her brow furrowed.

Zephyr ended his practice and joined them.

"What happened?" Zephyr asked.

"I had a visit from the Li—"

"Don't say it." Bertram cut her off.

Moira threw up her hands. "What do you want me to call him—the Suit?"

Bertram made a slashing motion with his hand. "Don't call it anything."

Moira's mind stuttered like a needle skipping across vinyl, recalling what Bertram had said about names having power. That must be why he didn't want her calling him the Librarian. Calling him by the name he gave himself must give him some kind of power, or at least Bertram thought so. She thought of the Librarian as *him* because of the form he appeared to her in. Bertram refused to speak of it at all. Moira realized nothing was stopping the Librarian from taking whatever shape he wanted. Perhaps it chose the look of a man because that's what it thought she would expect. Her skin crawled with the thought.

"Wait," Zephyr held up a hand. "Who are you speaking of?" His gaze focused on Moira. "And why do they alarm you?"

"I wouldn't say alarm—" Moira stopped. Zephyr gave her a look. Like a knowing look. Except she didn't know how he could know. She told him about the mysterious figure, without calling it the Librarian, and his tendency to come and go in and out of thin air.

"Did it say anything?" Bertram asked.

Moira blinked, thinking over their brief conversation. "He wanted me to know who he is. What he is." *He wanted to tell me what'll happen if I don't keep Zephyr safe.*

Bertram shook his head. "That hollow creature is like a demon sent to confuse and torment everyone who comes into contact with it. I don't know why it showed itself to you, but best we forget it altogether. Let us speak no more of it. Please."

Moira didn't reply.

Zephyr continued to watch her. Did his dragon's gaze intensify? Was he trying to tell her something? Moira couldn't be sure. His scrutiny made her tense. When he turned away, she heard a rumble of breath escape him.

"Back to training—Zephyr will use the sword for today." Bertram turned away and headed toward a tent, which hadn't been there before, set up on the edge of the tree line. He unzipped the opening and bent to pull something out. "Your best defense is Zephyr. But to keep the wyvern safe, you need to attack from afar."

Moira recognized the curved limbs of a traditional bow as soon as she saw them. Bertram also brought out a quiver full of arrows with white feather fletching and a leather arm guard. He held them out for her to take.

She raised her hands. "I don't think this is such a good idea."

"I do. The bow is the most practical weapon for a dragoneer."

Moira backed away. "That's great, but I've tried archery before, and it did not go well. I'm legit terrible."

"That's the best part, Ms. Noble." One side of Bertram's mouth lifted in a smile, there and gone in a flash, but it had time to reach his eyes. "You don't have to be good."

Once they got a target set up, they went over the basics. What little she had learned at the one summer camp she went to all those years ago came back to her. She got the pointy end of the arrow going the right direction and started with a target at close range. After a couple of warm-up shots, Moira began trying to tap into her will and release it at the same time as she released an arrow. Visualization was key, as far as her will was concerned, but it was also a matter of strength and skill. A balance had to be struck. In her mind, she was back to flipping on light switches, but now she had to time the flip of the switch with the release of her arrow. And she understood what Bertram meant about her not having to be good.

The bow and her arm provided the impetus for the arrow while her will gave it the something extra it needed to hit the target with precision if not accuracy. However, as the distance between her and the target increased, so did the difficulty. Moira cleared her mind and focused. She pulled hard on the string. Her arm shook. She wasn't strong enough to pull the bowstring back as far as it needed before her fingers slipped. Whatever magic she scraped together and released at the same time overcompensated for her lack of strength and sent the arrow wide.

Bertram let out a shout. "Watch out!"

The arrow struck the tree Bertram's pea coat hung from; the tree two feet from where he stood. If she had been aiming for the coat, she couldn't have hit it better.

Moira grimaced.

Bertram jerked the arrow out of the tree with a grunt, his coat spilling over the projectile. He pulled the arrow out and stuck a finger through the hole left behind. He shook his head. "Let's take a break."

Just when she thought she was getting a handle on using her will and firing at the same time, something happened to remind her she needed more practice. She couldn't expect perfection, but she thought she would be doing better because of the whole dragon venom thing. Moira dropped to her knees, sat back with a groan, and removed the quiver from her back. She unfastened the leather bracer Bertram had given her to protect her left forearm and made a face as she shook away the moisture that had gathered beneath it. She set it aside and flexed her hands spreading her fingers and rotating her wrists.

Zephyr came and sat with her. Practicing with the sword made him perspire and he gently steamed from his exertions. He bent his head and thumbed the edge of the sword before he raised his gaze to hers. "You are doing well."

"You think so?"

He nodded.

"I'm not so sure."

He started to say something, stopped and then asked, "How passed your day?"

There was something about the way he said it that made Moira's eyes narrow, but she couldn't put her finger on it. Her mind skipped over her day landing on the Librarian and what he had shown her. She shuddered. "It had its moments."

Zephyr didn't say anything, but the spiny ridges over his eyes lifted in a way that let her know he was listening.

"That thing, the Lib—" Moira glanced in Bertram's direction, but he was busy fiddling with the tent. "The Librarian. He—it—whatever, keeps popping up and disappearing on a whim, whenever he wants."

Bertram wouldn't want to hear what the Librarian said about her failing and she didn't want to tell Zephyr about her vision because she didn't want to worry him. On top of her fear came a surge of anger. She let the emotion roll over her and away. There was nothing to be gained from getting upset. However, to her, getting angry was preferable to feeling scared.

Zephyr grunted. "Will he return?"

"I don't know. He tends to do what he wants."

"Did something else happen?" Zephyr asked.

Her eyes narrowed. "No. Why?"

Zephyr's big shoulders slid up and down. "No reason."

Moira lurched to her feet and went to her backpack. "Here, Zeph," she said and pulled out a full-size bag of spicy potato chips.

Zephyr's eyes lit up when he saw the bag.

"I got you this, too." She held up a small bottle.

"What is it?"

"Hot sauce. I thought you might like it." She'd guessed he would after the way he'd enjoyed the spicy chips.

Zephyr accepted both items like they were prized possessions and held them with care.

"You don't need any more fire rocks, do you?"

"No."

"What else have you been eating?" she asked.

"The tall white-tailed beasts."

"Deer?" She was glad to hear it. A bag of chips now and then would be a treat, but not enough to keep him full.

Zephyr grunted. "Yes. I do not like the tails, so I bury them with the bones to attract no other animals."

"Well, next time, you can sprinkle a little hot sauce on it. Careful, though. A little goes a long way."

"Thank you, Moira." He left to scale the rubble wall and stash the chips and bottle in his bolt-hole.

Across the clearing Bertram shrugged into his coat. Not only was there a hole in the back of the coat, but there was also one in the front right side. He poked a finger through the hole in the front and blew out a breath.

Moira wandered over. "Sorry."

Bertram collected arrows from the target. "It's fine."

Moira wasn't so sure. Winter was coming and she didn't know if he had another coat. She hoped so. His ratty jeans and t-shirts might be warm enough for now, but not much longer. "What do you do, Mr. Bertram? Now that you're on sabbatical."

He twisted around and peered at her, brows raised.

"When you're not teaching me how to use a bow, I mean. The rest of the time."

Bertram jerked the last arrow free. "I teach yoga at a studio downtown."

Moira didn't say anything.

He caught her stare and frowned. "What?"

"Nothing. I, uh, I just didn't know you were so—"

His brows went up. "Multi-faceted?"

"I was going to say flexible."

He laughed. "It pays the bills." He tapped the arrows down so all of the points were even with one another. "Mostly," he muttered under his breath. He didn't raise his eyes, so Moira decided he hadn't meant for her to hear that last part.

"At least people seem to be staying away. You haven't seen or heard anyone, have you?"

Bertram shook his head. "No."

"What about you, Zephyr?" Moira asked as the dragon rejoined them.

He shook his huge head. "No one."

Moira glanced at the tent. "Bertram, if you've left and come back to the clearing since I did what I did," she drew a circle in the air around them to indicate the barrier she'd set up, "how did you make it back through?"

Bertram's expression turned thoughtful and unfocused. "Probably because I was here when you put the spell in place." His eyes closed and he ran a hand through his hair leaving it as disheveled as ever.

Moira waited.

"Yes," Bertram opened his eyes and nodded. "I was here at the time. I'm aware of the spell so it doesn't affect me."

"Did you just remember something? From the book?" Moira asked.

He shrugged. "I remember lots of things all the time, Ms. Noble," he said. "Some of it useful. Some of it not. It's all minutiae. Nothing like what I really want to know."

"What do you really want to know?"

Bertram sighed. "What I've wanted to know since I woke up with this book in my head—how to get it out and get my life back."

He didn't sound angry, but there was a note of bitterness underlying his words. Her gaze sought out Zephyr. He stood steadfast and ready, watchful and alert. With him, at her side, Moira felt confidence she wasn't used to having. "I'll help you get it out if I can."

Zephyr's head jerked and he eyed her, but he didn't say anything. After a moment he dipped his head once in Bertram's direction to show he agreed.

Bertram's gaze went from Zephyr to Moira. A breath shuddered out of him. "Thank you. But I don't know what you can do to help me, besides this, besides what you're doing right now, which should be shooting arrows into your target."

Moira's shoulders slumped forward as her eyes rolled.

Bertram handed her the arrows. "Let's go again. Only this time, Zephyr will lend us his tail."

Moira and Zephyr looked at each other.

"Uh—what?" she asked.

"You'll naturally guard Zephyr from a flank position, a little behind and next to him, so you'll have to watch out for his tail while you shoot."

"Okay." Moira shifted over and took up a position behind Zephyr on his left side facing the target.

"Ready?" Bertram called from a safe distance.

"Not real—"

"Go!"

Zephyr's tail slammed into Moira, knocking her off her feet. The flexible end of his tail laid into the flesh around her middle like a lash. Pain blossomed at her waist spreading outwards. As quick as his tail wrapped around her, it was gone again.

She fell over gasping, the wind knocked out of her.

"Moira!" Zephyr spun around, at her side in an instant. Clawed hands, incredibly gentle for their size, and sharpness helped to roll her onto her back. "Are you okay?"

"Ms. Noble, what happened?" Bertram rushed over. "Why didn't you get out of the way?"

Moira didn't have the air to answer any of their questions. She laid there a moment and focused on getting her wind back. When she felt ready, she pushed herself up onto an elbow. With care, she lifted her shirt away from her waist to inspect the damage. She sucked in a breath through her teeth.

Zephyr hissed. "So sorry, Moira."

Bertram gulped.

A raised red welt ran around her with a line of blood cresting the center. As she watched more blood welled up. The pain drew through her, like a rubber band stretched too far, it snapped back and focused on the circle around her middle. The line where Zephyr's tail had laid into her felt like it was on fire.

"It could be worse," Bertram said.

Moira's eyelids fluttered shut, blocking the sight.

Zephyr emitted a soft rumble.

"You'll be fine." Bertram sounded so sure.

Moira hoped he was right.

16

The next afternoon, Moira stretched to replace a book on a high shelf in the library and winced at the pain in her side. No visible sign remained of the injury Zephyr's tail had inflicted. The broken skin healed and the welt faded overnight, but her flesh still zinged when she moved the wrong way. She gritted her teeth and grabbed another book off her cart.

The scuff of a shoe against the institutional carpet broke the silence. Moira jumped, turning to see behind her, but there was no one there. She sighed and relaxed. If it had been the Librarian, she imagined he would have appeared out of thin air without a sound, much the same way he tended to leave, only in reverse.

The rhythm of solid footfalls sounded from the main aisle. They stopped at the end of the row. She glanced over and did a double-take. Aaron stepped into the end of the aisle and smiled. "Hey, Moira."

They hadn't spoken since he tried to walk her home. She'd seen him at his locker in the morning and between classes, but they were always surrounded by a herd of other kids doing the same thing they were. They'd nodded to each other, but hadn't exchanged words.

Realizing a response might be required of her now, Moira said, "Hey." And there, her well of words ran dry. She went back to putting books away, assuming Aaron would move along.

She was wrong.

He stuffed his hands in the pockets of his khakis causing his shoulders to hunch in his navy polo and took another step down the aisle toward her.

She faced him. "Did you need something?"

Was that her voice? Why was it so breathy and high? It was just Aaron. She recalled his apology and their handshake from the other day and felt the blood rush to her cheeks. She'd disliked him for so long she wasn't sure how to act around him now. His being the twin brother of her best friend wasn't helping. His looks suggested her brain treat him with a certain level of familiarity, but they didn't know each other at all. Not really. They were closer to acquaintances than friends.

"I don't want to bother you if you're in the middle of something, but I need some help finding a couple of books. Shelly, behind the counter, said you were out here."

Moira's lips pursed in thought. "Shelly could have helped you."

"Ah, but these books are for Charlie. I talked him into letting me come to the library instead of him, so I thought maybe you could help me. If we get it right the first time he won't have to come back. In person." He raised his eyebrows.

Moira relaxed. Aaron was just trying to do what she'd asked of him. The least she could do was help him find what he needed. As he said, if they got it right, Charlie wouldn't have to come on his own until the books were due.

"All right, what can I help you find?"

Aaron told her. They left her cart of books behind in search of the materials he needed. She could have consulted the computer system, but Moira had a good idea of where the two books he wanted were located. The search was on. She didn't speak while she combed through the shelves, in part because she was focused on the task, but mainly because she wasn't sure what to say anyway.

Aaron didn't speak either. He followed close behind her up one row and down another keeping up with the pace she set. When she found the first book, she snatched it up and turned so quickly she ran into him. His hands grasped the top of her arms near her shoulders and steadied her, the book smashed between them. They stood that way a whole second, maybe a second and a half, but it could have been longer. She wouldn't have minded longer. Then Aaron took a step back and smiled. His hands went to the book, but he stared at her with a small smile curving his mouth.

"That was fast," he said.

Moira noticed how the dark blue of his shirt contrasted with his hazel eyes. Ansel's eyes had little flecks of gold in them. Aaron's were greener. They made her think of mint. Or maybe it was it his breath. She blinked and dropped her gaze to the book. "I wrote an essay. On Tennyson. Last year. I'm familiar with this section. But why does Charlie Barrett need a book on classical poetry?"

"You know, I'm not sure. I said I would come and get the books before he told me what he needed. He might just be giving me a hard time."

"Right. Okay. The second one should be around here somewhere. Not too far at all. Give me a minute." *Lord help me, why am I babbling?* She twisted away and searched for the next title in earnest. She found it on a lower shelf and made sure to stand up slowly and remain calm. Aaron seemed to have learned his lesson and hadn't followed her as closely as before. She slid forward and handed him the second book.

Aaron glanced at the cover of the book of poems and smiled. "That was quick. Thank you. Do you think you could check me out?"

I just did. She cleared her throat. "Sure." She led the way to the front.

Shelly stood behind the counter helping another student.

Moira slipped behind a second terminal. "Make sure Charlie takes care of these since you're checking them out under your name."

"Worried about my reputation?"

"No, just your good standing with the library."

Aaron laughed. "Thanks again," he said and turned to leave.

"No, thank you," she said.

He turned back, a question on his face.

"For trying to help with Charlie," she said, clarifying her appreciation.

He smiled and with a lift of the books, turned and walked away.

A deep sigh came from the other terminal. Shelly was finished helping the other student and was watching Aaron walk away. She noticed Moira watching her and shrugged. "What?"

Moira shook her head and went back to her cart. Thunder boomed in the distance as rain splashed the windows. Her final moments of the school day were spent deep in the stacks, putting away books and thinking about the human eye and how it detected more shades of the color green than any other.

The rain passed quickly. In the woods after school, Moira drew hard on her bowstring. Her thumb touched her lip as she concentrated on her target, visualizing what she wanted to happen. She exhaled and released her arrow as she imagined pushing her will down and out her fingertips at the same time. A split second later, she jumped, knees high in the air, avoiding the sweep of Zephyr's tail along the ground where she had been standing. As soon as her feet met the earth, she pulled another arrow from the quiver on her back and loaded it in the bow, her focus trained on the quivering end of her previous projectile sticking out of the target across the meadow.

She blew out her breath, ready to release the arrow, but her instincts told her to jump so she did. Zephyr's tail whipped through the air going the other direction. Moira landed, planted her feet and fired.

Bertram stood with his arms crossed where he could watch them without getting hit. "Let's take a break. I think you've got the idea."

Moira relaxed and let go of the arrow she'd reached for. It slid back into her quiver. Zephyr took off across the meadow to the target. Her last shot lined up right below the one before it in a cluster of hits near the upper right-hand quadrant. Her precision was good. Her accuracy could use some work. Zephyr examined the target and nodded before he removed the arrows and brought them back to her.

"Good shooting," he said.

She nodded her thanks and slipped the arrows into the quiver with the rest. Her hands found the tops of her knees and she bent over, breathing hard. Unlike yesterday, today all of her arrows found their target. Adding Zephyr's tail to the mix added an extra layer of difficulty. However, the more elements to keep track of, the better her concentration, contrary to what she thought. Sure, she was winded, but today had gone much better than yesterday. Not one arrow ended up piercing Bertram's coat, which was good because he was wearing it.

Moira stood tall and rolled her shoulders. "What now?"

"I think you've had enough for one day," Bertram said.

"Really?" Moira asked.

Zephyr continued to practice, whipping the blade through the air.

"Yes." Bertram took the bow and quiver from her. "Besides, I picked up a class I need to teach this evening."

Moira went to her bag and drew out an item she'd jammed into the bottom of it that morning. She crossed to Bertram and thrust the bundle at him.

"What's this?" he asked.

"A liner from a winter coat."

Bertram shook it out and held it up. A second later he shed the shabby pea coat and slipped into it. The sleeves were a tad long and it was loose around his middle, but he zipped it up without comment. He spread his hands, patting his chest and sides, sliding each hand down the opposite sleeve. "This is—I don't know what to say—thank you."

"You're welcome. Least I could do," she added, thinking about the hole she'd put in his coat.

Bertram didn't say anything, but picked up his pea coat and put it on over the liner.

"It used to be my dad's." She could have kicked herself. She hadn't meant to say that.

"He won't miss it?"

"No, he won't." She started packing up her things. "Hard to miss things when you're dead."

In her peripheral vision, Bertram went still.

"My condolences, Ms. Noble."

She scraped together the rest of her things, ready to depart.

"Was it sudden?" he asked

Moira couldn't stop a small laugh from escaping, another coping mechanism. "Yeah," she said. Heart-stoppingly so. They hadn't known her father had a heart condition until they found out in the worst possible way.

And just like that, it wasn't funny.

Moira heard her pulse thrumming through her ears; the beat steady, the rests between small, but not insignificant. One day they were a happy family, and the next it was just her and her aunt trying to make a go of it. The day her father died was the darkest in her memory. The weeks following it were a smear of black days, but that first one was like a black hole, no light escaped it. Then the black days turned into gray days, and the gray days lightened until they were color again. Not the same colors though. Everything would always be off, the colors muted, altered, not the same. Sometimes she hardly noticed and other times the after-colors were all she could see.

Moira swallowed and glanced at Zephyr. Her dragon wore a hangdog expression she might not have believed possible if she hadn't seen it for herself. "Are you okay?"

Her question seemed to snap him out of whatever funk he had descended into and he shook his big head. "Are you?"

Moira smiled. It was a reflex, but then she found she actually did feel like smiling. "Cheer up, Zeph. It happened a long time ago." She slipped her backpack straps onto her tired shoulders.

"I'll walk with you," he said and motioned with the sword for her to go ahead of him out of the meadow. Moira waved and turned to go.

"Careful, you two," Bertram called after them.

Girl and dragon walked close together in the gathering gloom. The distance between them grew every so often to make way for the occasional tree but shortened again so that they stayed within arm's reach of each other. Neither one spoke. The silence didn't bother Moira. She'd said too much about her dad and her staying quiet now almost made up for it.

Zephyr nudged a sapling aside with the flat of the sword and stepped around it. They had a quarter of a mile to go before they picked up the trail; the point at which she assumed Zephyr would turn and head back to the meadow. For being as large as he was, Zephyr moved lightly through the trees, hardly making a sound. Moira estimated his height to be at about six and a half feet. His head still reminded her of a dinosaur though his long snout ended in a broad, flat nose. Even with his mouth closed the tips of his fangs poked out. His neck was long but proportional to the rest of him. The muscles in his arms and trunk defined. He could get anywhere faster than her because his legs were longer. She knew he kept his pace slow to allow her to keep up. Zephyr ducked under a low-hanging limb. The leaves trailed across his shoulders and down his back. His scaled-reptilian hide was darker there than the rest of him. The interlocking scales on his chest and belly lightened to drab olive green. His eyes gleamed in the twilight when they glanced her way and saw her watching him. Moira turned her attention to the forest floor to avoid tripping. The silence stretched between them.

Moira opened her mouth to ask if there was anything he needed for his hideout, when Zephyr reared back and hissed, his head turned away from her. "What is it?"

"Stay here." He raised the sword.

Moira took a step in the direction he faced.

Zephyr stopped, lowering his head until his eyes were level with hers. "Stay. Here."

Moira raised her hands and held her ground.

Zephyr slipped away from her side, deeper into the woods. As she watched, his scales took on a mottled appearance. All too soon, he disappeared. Moira stretched her neck one way and then the other, but she couldn't see him. Darkness was coming on quick. Everything was quiet.

Moira dropped her backpack and paced. Where was he? What was going on?

A grunt. And then silence. It was probably nothing. He'd just stubbed his toe on a hidden root or something.

She paced faster.

What should she do? Zephyr told her to stay there. He had a sword. Her bow and arrows were back at the meadow. She was unarmed. There was nothing she could do. She should probably just go home. He would be fine without her.

Moira stopped pacing and bent down to grab her backpack.

Another grunt followed by more silence.

Moira stood up tall and took off running. She plunged through the underbrush, ducking branches while brambles clawed at her clothing. As she rushed forward, the smell of troll smacked her in the face. She bent to scoop up a rock the size of her fist. It was the best she could do. Breathing through her mouth she ran on. With no warning, she burst through a pair of bushes, startling a troll, its knife held overhead, ready to stab Zephyr in the back as he fought off another troll with his sword. Another troll already lay dead on the ground. The troll with the knife hesitated. Moira gathered her will, visualized what she wanted to happen, reared back, and threw the rock with all her strength, straight at the troll's forehead. The missile connected with a crack between its eyes. It wavered where it stood, the knife slipping from its fingers to drop to the ground.

Zephyr killed the troll he was fighting with an upward thrust of his sword, through its belly, into its heart. He stood up straight and turned in time to watch the troll she'd hit in the head fall to its knees, then slump to the side. Not waiting for it to wake up, Zephyr stabbed it where it landed.

Moira, breathing hard from the run, turned away from the sight. She bent at the waist, her stomach threatening to empty itself.

"I said to stay there."

Moira risked a peek over her shoulder. Zephyr pointed in the direction they had come. "You're welcome," she said.

"The situation was in hand."

Moira scoffed, "I could tell by the way that troll was about to stab you in the back."

"Bah," he said, ducking his head to clean the blood from the sword.

She wasn't sure how to interpret that. Her nausea passed. She stood up straight. "What happened?"

Zephyr nodded at the troll that was already dead by the time she got there. "That one carried a sword. I killed it first. The other two had only knives and charged me. I could have taken care of them both." He nudged the troll she hit in the head with his foot. "But thank you."

"What do we do now?"

"Bury them. Go home, Moira, I will see to it."

17

They told Bertram about the trolls the next day after school.

He insisted they take him to where the fight took place. There was nothing to see. Zephyr had buried the bodies with their weapons. After they showed him the spot, Bertram made them tell him what happened all over again, his gaze unfocused, darting from tree to tree as if expecting more trolls to appear.

"You could have been hurt." His gaze went from Moira to Zephyr. "Both of you."

"I told her to stay behind," Zephyr said.

"And I kept Zephyr from getting stabbed in the back."

"You got lucky. From what you described these trolls were more scouts. They weren't fully armed. You did right by taking out the one with the sword first." He raised a closed fist to his brow, eyes shut tight. "They weren't expecting trouble."

"But they were looking for Zephyr," Moira said.

Bertram blinked his eyes open. "Yes. They must have grown tired of waiting for their first scout to return, so they sent more. I suspect they still don't know Zephyr has a dragoneer otherwise they would have been better prepared."

Any more prepared and they might have been in serious trouble. Moira turned to Zephyr. He tilted his head to the side and shrugged.

"Enough, you two. Let's get back," Bertram said.

Moira led the way thinking over what Bertram had said. It felt as if they'd failed some kind of test they didn't know they were taking. But they couldn't have, because they were alive.

Back in the meadow, Bertram asked Zephyr for the sword. The dragon handed it over, scabbard and all. Bertram pulled the sword free and checked the edge of the blade with the side of his thumb. Satisfied, he slid the sword back into its sheath and offered the hilt to Moira.

She hesitated. "I thought a dragoneer's best defense was their dragon?"

"Indeed. But there may come a time when arrows are in short supply and you have to use a sword."

"What's Zephyr going to train with?"

He waved away her concern. "I'll think of something. With those things out there, I think it's best for Zephyr to stay close to the meadow and for you to be prepared."

Moira stepped forward and grasped the scabbard below the cross-guard.

She pulled back, but Bertram held fast. Moira's gaze came up to clash with his. Bertram's gaze met hers, his brow lowered, giving him a grave expression. His eyes shone brightly in the afternoon light.

Unnerved by Bertram's piercing gaze Moira's hand convulsed around the sword, jerking it toward her, but he still didn't let go.

"This is a brutal instrument for dealing out death and violence." Bertram's tone was flat, the words heavy. "It is not a toy. Do not let me catch you treating it as such."

Moira scoffed and then scowled. "Because the bow and arrows are just playthings, right?"

Bertram let go and she almost dropped the sword in the dirt. His voice lost its coolness. "Not at all, but there's a difference between taking life from a distance and taking one up close," he said.

Moira remembered sinking the tip of the blade into the flesh of the first troll's neck the night they'd met Bertram. Her stomach flipped over. For a second the weight of the sword pulled at her arm, heavier than it should be. "I remember."

Bertram bent and picked up a stick off the ground. He began his instruction by showing Moira how to engage an enemy and build a defense, stressing constant motion, encouraging her to be aggressive and take the initiative in any way she could. Then he sat on the sidelines and watched her practice, calling out to her on occasion.

"Faster!"

"Higher!"

"Again!"

Occasionally, he tossed out a "Good."

The times the end of the sword ran through the dirt or ended up on the ground altogether were met with silence. Each time, she picked up the sword and kept going. Her arms grew heavy, her shoulders tight. The back of her shirt clung to her sweat-slicked skin.

Soon it became clear that the problem with fighting off invisible assailants, besides not being remotely close to realistic, was that they were relentless and innumerable. Moira never thought it would happen, but she yearned to pick up the bow again.

Then he made her switch hands.

When she ceased showing improvement, which didn't happen as fast as she thought it would, Moira threw herself to the ground, arms and shoulders burning with exhaustion.

"Your stamina could use some work, but I'm otherwise pleased with your progress," Bertram said.

She didn't bother trying to summon up the energy to respond.

Everything ached. Her back and shoulders throbbed. Her arms refused to acknowledge the rest of her.

Zephyr lowered his massive head toward hers. "You will improve."

"Great." Moira rolled to her left and sat up with a groan. "You're on his side."

Zephyr huffed out a sharp breath and stood up straight.

Moira cupped her hand in front of her. "Why don't I just use magic to defend myself?" She focused on a pebble on the ground five feet away, gathered her will and thought about what Bertram had said concerning alternate forces. She visualized what she wanted to happen, released her will and watched the stone rise into the air. It hovered a foot above the earth. She'd been practicing. Her fingertips tingled, but the rock stayed aloft.

"Nice work," Bertram said. Then he knocked the pebble to the ground with a swipe of his foot. "Because magic alone is too costly a defense. I'm not saying don't use it at all, but you must remember where the energy required to use it comes from."

As far as she knew, her physical strength combined with her will gave her the ability to lift rocks and nudge arrows in the direction she wanted them to go. Magic wouldn't help her in a sword fight. In a real fight, she wouldn't have the time she needed to visualize anyway. It was simpler to strike with the blade than to summon the concentration and the will needed to perform a single sword thrust. Even if her aim wasn't perfect, firing off an arrow would beat wasting time between parries. Magic required energy. The energy used to direct arrows was slight and it didn't leave her fatigued. Like a muscle, the more she practiced, the less she felt the strain.

"We'll keep working with the sword, but not tonight. I think we've put you through enough for one day, Ms. Noble. Let's stretch."

Groaning, Moira got to her feet and followed Bertram through a series of yoga poses. Zephyr joined in. The dragon's downward-facing dog was impressive.

When they finished, the sun had set and she could move again. Not as fast as if she had never been flinging a heavy sword around, but well enough.

Beside the tent, Bertram cranked a hand-powered lantern to life.

Moira had a plan for the next time she ran into Ansel. Prepared to lay the groundwork for her plan, she practiced coughing and sneezing on cue. However, she didn't have to pretend she was coming down with something because she never saw him. Their paths didn't cross before Friday. It made what she did next that much easier. She sent him a text after school.

Hey. Under the weather. Can we reschedule?

His answer arrived less than a minute later. *Sure thing. Feel better.*

Moira went on her merry way and practiced with both the bow and the sword. She sensed improvement or, at least, she didn't feel like she was dying when they finished. Full dark fell and they made tentative plans to meet on Saturday morning. Bertram was pleased with her progress, but Moira could tell something was bothering him. He was a bit more distracted than usual but insisted he was well enough when she was leaving.

Zephyr walked her to the edge of the clearing.

Moira opened her bag and dug out a bag of spicy chips. "Here you go."

Zephyr took the chips with a rumble of thanks and peered into her backpack. "What is *To Kill A Mockingbird*?"

She snagged the novel from her bag. "It's a book I had to read for English. It's about a girl growing up in a different time. And you should never kill a mockingbird because," she stopped. "Never mind, I don't want to spoil it for you."

"May I?" Zephyr asked as he took the book and raised it to his nose. His nostrils flared as he sniffed the binding, his tongue, black and forked, making an appearance before he sent the pages fluttering with a flick of his thumb. Moira left him in Jean Louise's hands. He was already too busy reading to watch her go.

She went right in the back door when she got home and dropped her stuff. "Aunt Paige! I'm home!"

"We're in here!" a voice called from the front of the house.

We? Moira went straight through to the living room.

Her aunt sat on the sofa facing her as she walked in. Something wasn't right. She didn't smile and the skin around her eyes was tight with strain.

"What's up?" Moira asked.

Ansel stood up from the chair he'd been sitting in out of her direct line of sight. "Hey, Moira," he said.

She stopped.

"Glad you're feeling better." His gaze dropped to the floor. He raised his head again and turned away. "I'll head out now." He walked past her aunt to let himself out.

At the door, he turned around to step out backward. His features were clouded, but he mouthed the words, "Good luck," and shut the door behind him.

18

The door clicked shut behind Ansel.

Moira's stomach dropped and hovered somewhere around her knees.

The silence stretched until her aunt broke it with words clipped to precision. "Where were you?"

All her mind could come up with were all the things she couldn't say, like dragon, sword, and woods, so she went for simple. "Studying."

Her aunt recoiled. "Don't lie."

"I'm not lying."

"I don't believe you. You said you were going out with Ansel. Then he turns up here to bring you soup because you told him you weren't feeling well. I tried to reach you on your cell and you didn't answer. Where were you?" she asked again.

Moira frowned and spun around to go back into the kitchen.

"Do not walk away from me." Her aunt followed close behind.

"Geez—I'm not—just hold on." Moira bent to scoop up her backpack and pulled out her phone. Multiple missed calls from her aunt and Ansel. She checked the ringer. It was on the loudest setting. The thing hadn't made a peep all night. "I'm sorry. My phone's been acting up. Must need an update." She waved the offending piece of technology in the air and set it aside.

"Don't blame your phone. Where were you?"

"I told you. I was studying."

"With whom? Where? I was worried about you."

"Alone. Somewhere quiet. You don't have to worry about me."

The breath shuddered out of her aunt. "Don't tell me I don't have to worry. You are my responsibility. I thought I knew where you were and you were somewhere else." Her eyes started to well. "You could have been—"

"Don't say, 'dead in a ditch'," Moira muttered.

"Dead in a ditch somewhere and I would have had no idea. Do you know how that made me feel? After everything?" Her voice dropped to a whisper. "After your father?"

Moira flinched. "I'm sorry. I didn't mean to make you worry. It won't happen again." Her shoulders slumped.

"Damn right, it won't. From now on you go straight to school and you come straight home."

Moira cocked an ear forward. She must have misheard. "Excuse me?"

"You heard me." Her aunt crossed her arms, eyes dry.

"You're not seriously trying to ground me right now, are you?"

"I think I just did."

"I had to ask, because, you know, you've never done it before." Moira stared at her.

"You've never given me a reason to. And don't get cute."

"If I've never given you a reason to, it's because you've always trusted me."

"I have. Until now. I don't know what's going on with you. I've never had to worry about you like I did today. You were gone, God knows where, and you can't tell me all you've been doing is studying. You even lied to Ansel. You're too young to be out running the roads by yourself. You're fifteen. You need to start thinking about other people besides yourself. I expect more from you—"

"Whoa." Moira held up a hand. "I'm either too young to make decisions for myself or old enough for you to expect me to. You don't get to have it both ways. Which is it?"

"That's not what I'm saying."

"Yes, it is." Moira unclenched the fists her hands had curled into. "Just because the decisions I make for myself aren't the same you would make doesn't mean they're wrong. Do you think the grades I make happen by themselves? They don't. I have to study and I can't do it all under this roof, but I'll always come home or at least call if I don't. You can do what you've always done and trust me, or not. But I'm studying all this weekend, starting tomorrow morning." Her voice cracked. She picked up her things and left the kitchen.

"We're not done here," her aunt said to her back.

"I am."

Silence followed Moira upstairs to her room where she pushed her door shut, pressing her forehead into the wood. Hot all over, she stood up away from the door and threw her window open. She tumbled back onto her bed, pressing the palms of both hands into her eyes until her vision blurred. An ache settled in her chest, tucked up under her ribs. It hurt.

A skittering noise dragged her attention away from reliving every word she and her aunt said to each other. It happened two more times. She sat up, wiping her eyes and went to close the window.

"Wait! Moira!"

She let go of the sash and leaned outside.

"Down here!"

A hand waved at her from behind the oak tree.

Ansel.

"What are you doing?" she whisper-shouted.

"I didn't mean to get you in trouble!"

It wasn't his fault. "Don't worry about it."

"What happened?"

Moira's hands curled against the casing and she shook her head. "I'm sorry. I shouldn't have used you to cover for me like that."

"I don't care that you used me to cover for you! Just tell me what's going on!"

"I can't," she said, too quietly for him to hear.

"What?"

The outside light came on and the back door opened. Ansel ducked. Her aunt must have been taking out the trash or setting something on the back porch. Moira slid her window shut. When the door closed and Ansel looked up again, she pressed her open hand to the glass, backing away.

Something pinged against the house.

She ignored it.

❧

Moira studied at her desk until the lines of text blurred and sank out of sight. She vaguely recalled stumbling to bed, but in her dreams, she stayed where she was. Every book she opened had to be translated before she could read it and sometimes there weren't any words, just numbers. At one point she looked down and she was in the meadow. Zephyr stood next to her, silent and watchful. There was a *snick*, followed by a *pop* and they both turned to see the tent Bertram slept in burst into flames.

She awoke sprawled across her covers with a book open on her chest. It was early. She groaned when she sat up but decided that, as an object in motion, she should remain in motion. That's how she avoided her aunt. Moira was gone before she got up. Guilt pulled at her, making her stumble as she walked away from the house, but Moira kept going. She didn't want to talk; afraid she might end up saying something she really would regret. There were some things, once said, she didn't want to have to take back.

The woods waited, cheering her on with every step of the way. The branches of every tree were open waving arms, beckoning her forward. She inhaled the crisp morning air. It made her lungs burn at their fullest. It was going to be a lovely day. Perhaps one of the last nice days before the weather turned.

In the middle of the trail, she thought about Zephyr. Her pace slowed. She came to a complete stop, turning in a circle on the spot, trying to get a fix on which way she should go, except her dragon-o-meter wasn't sending her in any particular direction.

"Zephyrrrr?" She drew out his name, scanning the woods around her.

He had to be nearby. She might be able to see through his camouflage, but he could blend in with the scenery so well even she wouldn't notice him if she was just passing by.

A pair of yellow eyes popped open across the trail right in front of her.

Moira jumped.

"Boo," he said, followed by a rumble of laughter.

"What are you doing here? I thought you were supposed to stick to the clearing?" Moira threw glances up and down the path and started jogging in place, placing her fingers against the side of her neck. If someone came by maybe they would think she was out for a run and wanted to check her heart rate. It throbbed away under her fingertips now anyway.

"Race you." Zephyr's tail whipped through the air as he disappeared between the trees.

"Wait—what—hey, no fair." Moira took off after him. She didn't think she would be up for the chase, but one second she was running and the next she was flying. Not really, but she may have glanced down just to make sure her feet still touched the ground as she skimmed through the brush with ease. Zephyr bounded through the trees so fast he was a blur. Somehow, she managed to keep up. His rumble of laughter reverberated off sycamores and maples. Moira's face split into a grin from the sheer exhilaration of the race.

When they burst through the trees into Zephyr's meadow, he was ahead, but not by much.

Zephyr stooped, hands on knees. "I win."

Moira pressed a hand to a stitch in her side and grinned. She smiled so hard her face hurt. She felt good, but at the same time not quite right. Why was she smiling? Sure, the race had been a pleasant diversion, but it was done. She'd run away from her problems, literally, leaving her house early so she didn't have to see or talk to her aunt, doing the very thing they'd argued about. The thought caught her and brought her low, but there was another part of her that still felt light and energized, a mysterious feeling not entirely her own. The smile slid from her face millimeter by millimeter, the foreign happiness still there.

"Moira?" Zephyr studied her.

"This—something's not right," she patted her chest. Her heart raced, but it had nothing to do with the run. "What's going on?"

Zephyr frowned. "I am sorry. You were upset."

Moira felt the glowing radiance inside of her dim

"So what?" She couldn't deny she had been feeling a little down. "Why are you sorry?"

Zephyr ran the ball of one foot through the grass in front of him. "I felt it also."

"What do you mean you felt it? Like you can feel what I'm feeling?"

Zephyr nodded. "When it is strong."

"How—"

She shuddered. The happy, light feeling inside of her was still there, but the longer she noticed it, the more she was able to tell it didn't belong to her. "Can you stop this? Whatever it is?" The alien feeling sat like a cheerful lump inside of her, and she wanted it gone.

Zephyr's gaze intensified, his eyes flashing.

The little globe of artificial happy started to melt and run like ice cream in the hot sun, leaving sticky tracks across her psyche.

As it trickled away, Moira fell to her knees with a gasp.

19

Zephyr started toward her, but Moira put up a hand.

Her body curled over in a question mark a moment before she sat back on her heels, exhausted.

"I had an argument with my aunt last night," she said. "It was one for the books. We haven't argued like that in—I'm not sure how long."

Zephyr sat opposite her. "Ah."

Moira eased herself over onto the ground, weary. The run had felt good, but now that she'd stopped and Zephyr had quit whatever he was doing, she ached all over.

"Are you well?" he asked, his brows drawn down in concern.

"I'm okay."

Zephyr's frown deepened.

Moira sighed. "I'm tired, but it won't last forever." She ran a hand through her hair and twisted one of the more unruly curls around her finger, tugging at her scalp. "How do I keep you from feeling what I'm feeling?"

Zephyr tipped his head to the side. His frown lost some of its intensity. "I do not think you can. It is considered a great asset. Especially in a fight."

"This is because of the bite, isn't it?"

"Yes."

Everything came back to that moment when Zephyr sank his teeth into her flesh. There was a Moira before the bite and there was a Moira after the bite and the two were not entirely the same person. The marks had faded, but she was still learning about their consequences. She and Zephyr shared an emotional link she couldn't control. Maybe having to feel her strong emotions was the price Zephyr paid for having bitten her.

"I haven't felt any strong emotions coming from you." She didn't accuse him of not having any, but she hadn't felt anything foreign like that until today.

One corner of Zephyr's mouth lifted, but he still frowned. "I am better able to control our connection from my end, I believe."

"You're stuck feeling whatever strong emotions I have until I, what, learn not to overshare?"

"Something like that, I think."

"And I won't feel what you're feeling unless you project it, like this morning?"

Zephyr nodded.

"Okay. Well, don't do that again." She shuddered. "It was weird."

"I will not." He hung his head.

Moira could see he regretted doing it, but she could still feel the space the artificial glow that didn't belong to her had taken up in the middle of her chest. She could even understand why he did it, but still. "Oh, knock it off." She rolled her shoulders back and sat up tall. "I'm fine, Zeph." She thought about it. "I wonder if Bertram knows about this."

Zephyr frowned.

"Our—" Moira motioned between them, "—whatever this is. I wonder if we should tell him."

"No," Zephyr growled with an actual growl.

Moira leaned back and studied him. "I have bad news; he could already know and just not remember."

He shook his head. "We should not tell him."

She frowned. "You don't like Bertram." It wasn't a question.

Zephyr grunted. "I do not like the way he orders us about. He also claims to know more than he does and I do not trust him." He peered at Moira. "Do you?"

The question made her pause. She sucked in a breath and thought about it. "I don't *not* trust him."

He squinted. "Your use of the double negative confuses me. Speak clearly."

"How do you even know about double negatives? You know what—never mind." She explained. "Bertram hasn't given me a reason not to trust him. Until he does, I'm willing to give him the benefit of the doubt. He's got a book about dragons stuck in his head, which means he might have access to the information we need. Of course, he also wants it out. I'm willing to help him with that too if we can."

Zephyr grunted.

"We don't have to tell him about this thing we have. He knew I would find you that day after school when I had no idea where you were. So, as I said, he could already know about it and just not know he knows, you know?"

Zephyr's lip curled. "I fear there is much he does not know and will not remember."

"Well, unfortunately, we have no way of reading what was in the book."

His head came up. "What about the Librarian? He may know something about the book."

Her last visit with the Librarian had left her cold. She remembered it was Zephyr who had asked her what happened. Of course, it made sense now. He must have felt something amiss through their connection.

Something niggled at her, begging to be noticed, but she couldn't make it sit still long enough to figure out what it was. The wind blew making the leaves rustle in the trees, which wasn't unusual. It was the strident flapping of wings that had their heads whipping around. Something or someone had spooked the wildlife.

"Bertram?" Moira whispered.

Zephyr's nostrils flared. "No."

Moira regretted not picking up the sword as soon as they got to the meadow, sitting as she was now, weaponless. She wouldn't say defenseless though. Zephyr crouched, muscles taut, ready and waiting for whatever it was to show its face or pass them by. He could cover her while she went for the sword. She got her legs under her ready to run for it when they heard one footfall, and then another, closer. Her heart pounded, her adrenaline spiking. What else could it be but another search party of trolls? The spell she cast kept everyone else away.

Or, at least, it had.

"Moira?"

Her blood ran cold.

Ansel stepped out from behind a tree into the meadow. He came from the same direction she'd raced Zephyr earlier.

"There you are. I thought I lost you. What are you doing out here?"

Eyes wide, Moira glanced toward Zephyr to see he had gone stock still, eyes narrowed, and camouflage, presumably, engaged.

She jerked herself upright, feeling hot and cold all at the same time. Her limbs twitched with the wasted surge of adrenaline, and she brushed at the seat of her pants to disguise their trembling. "Me? What are you doing here?"

When in doubt, deflect.

"I was on my way to your place when I saw you take off into the woods. Did you get my text?"

"No. My phone's not working." Moira hadn't checked her cell that morning or even bothered to bring it with her when she left the house. She crossed her arms.

"Okay, well, I just wanted to check in with you after last night." He stepped farther into the meadow and stopped about the same distance from her as she was from Zephyr, drawing them into the points of an equilateral triangle. Ansel frowned and glanced around the meadow. "Who were you talking to?"

"Hmmm?" Moira's gaze darted to his face and then away.

"I heard you talking to someone. I thought you were on the phone, but if your cell isn't working—"

Moira uncrossed her arms and stuck her hands in her pockets. She opened her mouth and nothing came out. Nerves made her hands clench into fists within the cotton confines of her jeans.

Ansel took in the trees surrounding the meadow, unsettled. "I don't know if you've heard or not, but the other kids keep saying the woods are haunted and won't go in them anymore. What are you doing out here?"

"Working on something for school."

He raised a brow.

She really needed to come up with a better story.

Ansel shook his head. "If I didn't know better, I would swear you were hiding something."

"What?" Moira choked out the word with a chuckle.

He wasn't laughing. "You've been acting strange ever since school started. Your aunt doesn't know what's up. I don't either. Man, she was disappointed when I didn't have a clue."

Moira's neck grew warm as her temper started to burn. "You and my aunt talked about me?"

"Of course, we talked about you." He glared at her and Moira realized she wasn't the only one getting upset. "We would have talked *to* you if you were around. She's worried about you. So am I." He dropped his gaze. "How long have we been friends?"

She shrugged. "A while."

He snorted. "Sure. But you've never lied to me. Not once. Not even to spare my feelings." He inhaled sharply and held it before letting it out in a rush. "Whatever it is, it must be pretty important." Ansel's gaze settled on her once more. "You don't have to tell me what it is. Just tell me you're okay."

"I'm—" She wanted to say okay, but the word stuck in her throat.

Was she?

She was exhausted in every way possible, and the lying was making her more so. She could only bend and twist the truth so much before it wasn't the truth anymore. And lies of omission still felt like lies, even if she was doing it so people wouldn't worry.

Ansel hadn't asked her for the truth though. She knew he just wanted to know if she was okay, buried under whatever burden it was she carried. Her eyes burned, and she swallowed to try to dislodge the lump that rose in her throat.

She'd never wanted to spill her guts to someone as much as she wanted to right then.

From the corner of her eye, she glimpsed the tip of Zephyr's tail stir.

"What's that?" Ansel turned to look.

Zephyr's tail twitched again.

"Oh, no." The words fell from her mouth, though she couldn't be sure she said them out loud until her gaze flew to Ansel and she saw him frown.

"Moira, what is that?"

Ansel's gaze was glued to where the tip of Zephyr's tail had stirred before she watched his gaze move upward. Moira turned to watch also. It was a bright morning, but shadows from the trees dappled the ground all around. To Moira, the shadows appeared to shift over Zephyr's skin though there wasn't much of a breeze until they came to a stop. Ansel's breathing sped up. She turned back to see his eyes shoot wide open, his muscle tense, his jaw drop.

He could see Zephyr.

20

Even if he did look ready to bolt, Ansel wasn't going anywhere. She'd seen this before.

Moira turned to face Zephyr, palms up. "Why?"

"You did not wish to tell him about me?"

Moira squeezed her eyes shut tight. Yes, for a second there, she had wanted to tell Ansel everything, but she never would have done it. Now she didn't have a choice. She opened her eyes to stare at Zephyr.

He blinked and his tail swept the ground.

Ansel wheezed.

Moira rushed to her friend's side, skidding through the dew clinging to the grass. She grabbed him by the arm and spun him around. His gaze remained fixed on a point over her head. She called his name and then repeated it until he blinked and his eyes drifted down to meet hers. His arm shook where she had a hold of it. She said his name again.

His eyelids fluttered. "Moira! Get out of here, there's a—I don't know what it is." He tried to turn his head, but she caught his chin and held it. "Wait, what?" His voice dropped to a whisper. "Is it still there?"

"Okay. Deep breaths. Calm down." Moira let go of his face and took hold of his shoulders.

Ansel, in turn, gripped her arms. He continued in a whisper. "Can you make a run for it? If it tries to follow you, I—I don't know what I'll do—I'll think of something. Ready?" His knees bent, preparing to spring into action.

"Ansel, slow down. It's okay." She relaxed her hold on his shoulders and rephrased. "It's—it's going to be okay."

He squinted. "How come you're not freaking out right now?" He stood up straight and took Moira's advice to breathe deep, but his muscles remained bunched under her hands. "Maybe you didn't see what I saw, but it's about seven feet tall with hungry eyes. It didn't open its mouth, but I would bet it's full of razor-sharp teeth." He tried to turn his head, but she caught his chin again.

"Don't look. You'll freeze up again. Give it a few minutes."

"Give what a few minutes? Give whatever that monster was time to decide which one of us it wants to eat first?"

"Nothing is going to eat us." Moira's hand went to his shoulders again. She squeezed them and turned him loose. "Give your brain a second to catch up with what your eyes are telling you. And keep an open mind."

His eyes narrowed, but he didn't try to turn around again. "What did they see?"

"A wyvern."

"What's a wyvern?"

"It's a kind of—he's a dragon."

Ansel closed his eyes and swallowed.

Over his shoulder, Moira caught Zephyr's eye. She assumed she would get to do all the talking.

"His name is Zephyr."

Ansel's eyelids lifted. "It has a name?"

"I named him."

He stared at her. "After the Greek God of the west wind?"

A smile tugged at the corners of her mouth. Ansel put on a good show, but he was way smarter than most people gave him credit for. Just because he wasn't super-competitive like his brother didn't mean he didn't pay attention.

She nodded. "Yeah."

"Does it—he speak?" he asked.

"Very well."

"How—is that possible?"

"I don't know. But it is. He bit me and now we have this connection—"

"Hold on, he bit you?"

"Yes. When he was smaller. Before he ate the fire rocks."

A pained expression crossed Ansel's face. "Can we slow down? Maybe start over? At the beginning."

Once she started, she couldn't stop. It was such a relief to finally share what had happened. As she talked, she grew less tense. She told Ansel everything but kept the part about the emotional connection she and Zephyr shared to herself. It was still so new; she wasn't sure she understood it very well.

Ansel listened without comment, arms folded.

"I don't even know where to start, but—he's not done growing?" he asked when she finished.

"Nope."

"And he's standing right behind me?"

"Yep."

"Can I turn around?"

"Sure, but you might freeze up again."

He nodded. "I think I'll have to risk it." He started to turn and stopped. "If I do, snap me out of it?"

"You bet."

Ansel swiveled around on one heel, keeping his gaze lowered. His shoulders went up with the size of the breath he took. He let it out and gave his arms a shake. Moira watched as he raised his head inch by inch. His arms twitched and his whole body shuddered before his head came up all the way and tipped back. Zephyr's lids were half-lowered. Moira heard Ansel gasp and prepared herself to haul him around away from the sight, but then his whole body spasmed and he said in a rush, "NicetomeetyouZephyr."

Zephyr's nostrils flared once. "I am well met," he replied with a dip of his massive head.

Ansel's head tipped to one side. He stared, looking Zephyr down, then up again.

Zephyr took the scrutiny in stride, seizing the opportunity to look over Ansel in return. Moira saw him frown, a microexpression, there and gone so fast she wasn't sure she saw it.

"Can I...?" Ansel lifted his arm and took a tentative step to the side.

"Sure," Moira said. "I think he just wants the full picture, Zeph."

Ansel walked a complete circle around her dragon. Zephyr turned his head and followed his progress, but otherwise sat still. Ansel ended where he started.

"No wings," Ansel said. "I thought dragons had wings."

"Some do," Zephyr said.

Moira hadn't known that. She'd imagined dragons with wings, but Zephyr didn't have any. Of course, she'd never met an actual dragon before Zephyr, either.

"How did you appear out of thin air like that?" Ansel asked. "You weren't there and then, all of a sudden, you were."

"I did not want to be seen."

Turbid swirls of shadow began running over Zephyr's scales until they settled into a pattern Moira hadn't seen before.

Ansel turned. "Where did he go?"

Moira nodded to where Zephyr still stood and Ansel turned back. Zephyr dropped his camouflage.

"Whoa."

"Show-off," Moira muttered, catching her dragon's eye.

Zephyr smiled.

Ansel made a choking sound. "I was right about the teeth."

Zephyr's head whipped around to face the opposite end of the meadow. He'd heard something. He didn't go into a defensive crouch or use his camouflage, but he did go still.

Moira tensed.

"What?" Ansel's gaze darted between Zephyr and Moira, "What is it?"

Moira knew who it was. She did not relax. "Company."

Ansel followed her gaze to where a figure slid between the trees.

"Is that Mr. Bertram?"

The figure jerked to a halt before it came charging into the meadow. "What in the bluest of hells is going on? What is Mr. Idlewild doing here?" When no one answered fast enough, he turned to Moira. "Did you bring him here?"

"Unintentionally," Moira said.

"Explain."

"What's Mr. Bertram doing here?" Ansel asked.

"That is none of your business. None of this—" Bertram spread the fingers of one hand wide and made a circular motion that encompassed the entire meadow, "—is any of your business." He scowled. "Which one are you anyway?"

"This is Ansel. He followed me. He got past the barrier somehow."

"Got past the what? And how does he know about Zephyr?"

Bertram shut his eyes and rocked back. If there was any hope that Ansel didn't know about Zephyr, though he stood in plain sight of everyone, they were dashed in that instant. He asked again, "What is going on?"

"Ansel saw me hike into the woods this morning and followed me."

Bertram cupped an elbow in one hand and used the other to pinch the bridge of his nose. "Is that all?"

"Yes."

Bertram dropped his hand and glared at her. "Then how does he know about the great, big wyvern in the room?"

Zephyr stepped between them.

Moira hadn't heard a single footfall. One minute, Zephyr was a couple of yards away and the next he stood in front of her.

"I revealed myself." Zephyr let out a low growl.

Bertram's ire cooled rapidly to a wide-eyed stare before his gaze rose to meet Zephyr's, though his brows were still drawn together. "May I ask why?"

Zephyr closed his jaws with a snap, making all of them jump. Then he bent his head down close to Bertram, eyeing him. Moira was sure the dragon wouldn't hurt him. Seconds passed and she had to revise her thinking. As she watched, all of the anger went out of Bertram, but he stood his ground, face-to-face with a creature that could end him as soon as answer him. She didn't think Zephyr would hurt him though. Not really.

"I have my reasons. The boy is a friend and means us no harm." Zephyr turned his back on Bertram and swung around to stand next to her and Ansel.

"Fine," Bertram's voice shook at first but grew steady. "But I will not be responsible if anything happens to him on account of him knowing."

Moira glanced at her friend. "He's not going to tell anyone. Are you, Ansel?"

"Of course not."

Bertram's face crumpled. His eyes squeezed shut.

"Bertram?"

He swallowed before he blinked his eyes open and rolled his shoulder. "You say he followed you?" His voice sounded tired and scratchy all of a sudden. "That's how he got through. He saw you enter and knew you were here somewhere. All he had to do was stay focused on finding you." He ground out the last few words, exhausted.

Ansel's gaze flickered between them. "What? What did I do?"

"Nothing." Moira glanced down and away.

Bertram snorted.

"Just surprised us," Moira added. "Better you than someone else."

Bertram rubbed one temple. "You'll have to be more careful. If someone sees you come into the woods or even suspects you might be here, they'll be able to get through the spell you put in place."

"Spell?" Ansel's gaze shifted between Moira and Bertram. "Like Moira did some kind of magic or something?" He smiled.

Bertram stared at him.

Moira shifted her weight from one foot to the other.

Zephyr didn't so much as twitch.

Ansel's mouth fell open. "You're serious?"

Bertram shook his head. "Are you all caught up now? Can we get on with some training?"

Color crept up Ansel's neck but didn't make it to his face. "What kind of training?"

"I wish you'd asked this many questions when you were in my class, Mr. Idlewild."

Ansel turned to Moira. "Why is he here again?"

Before Bertram could respond, Moira answered. "He has his reasons. They're for him to say. Please, don't ask me again."

Only because they'd been friends so long did Moira see the flash of hurt that crossed Ansel's features. She couldn't help it. What happened to Bertram was for him to explain. Maybe he would if Ansel asked.

Instead, Ansel had something else on his mind. "This spell, or whatever, that you put up to keep people out, is that why everyone thinks the woods are haunted now?"

"I don't know. Maybe," Moira said. When she'd visualized erecting a barrier to keep people away, she'd been focused on discouraging people from heading deeper into the woods, not scaring them off.

"Did you say haunted?" Bertram asked. "That's something at least. Let them think it's bedeviled. It'll keep the brighter ones away and everyone else will be put off by the spell as long as they don't come looking for you."

Nobody said anything for a moment. Then Ansel caught her eye, "You've got bigger problems than that, you know."

Moira groaned.

"You have to tell your aunt something," Ansel said.

Bertram faced Moira. "What is he talking about Ms. Noble?"

The weariness she felt earlier came rushing back. She buried her head in her hands.

Zephyr grunted.

21

The next evening Moira lurked out of sight of the kitchen at the bottom of the stairs. The doorbell rang at six sharp. She answered it right away.

Bertram stood on the stoop fighting the cheap ribbon on a bouquet of fresh-cut flowers that had lost some of the fresh, but could still be considered flowers. In place of his tired t-shirt and jeans, he wore a pair of pressed trousers, a shirt, and a tie. He even wore a nicer jacket, though Moira could see the liner she'd given him, peeking out from underneath. It was a good thing he still had the beard, which he'd trimmed, or she might not have recognized him. She was glad to see he'd made an effort. Then she realized the clothes he wore reminded her of what he used to wear when he was teaching, and her smile dimmed.

Bertram glanced up and snapped to attention. When he saw it was Moira, he shook himself and peered around her into the house. "I hope you know what you're doing, Ms. Noble," he said, his voice no louder than needed to reach her ears and no farther.

"Trust me," she said just as loud. Then louder, "Mr. Bertram! What lovely flowers. You shouldn't have. Please come in. May I take your coat?"

Bertram handed her the flowers so he could shrug out of his things, then took them back so she could hang his jacket and liner on the coat tree.

Her aunt came down the hallway, slipping her apron over her head and giving her hair a quick fluff. She didn't typically wear an apron to cook. Then Moira saw the long-sleeved dark purple dress she wore, its hemline floating around her knees. They didn't usually dress for dinner either. Moira glanced down at her stretchy black athletic pants and her oldest, most comfortable sweatshirt. Had she missed something?

She and her aunt hadn't spoken much since the day before. Right after Moira returned home from "studying", she'd asked her aunt if Mr. Bertram could come to dinner. Her aunt had looked so confused, Moira thought she was going to say no, but she'd said yes. The brief exchange helped break the ice and Moira hadn't left the house since, studying in her room, only surfacing when needed. It was all part of the plan.

She couldn't figure out why her aunt was wearing a dress though.

Moira cleared her expression and made the introductions. "Mr. Bertram, this is my aunt, Paige Noble. Aunt Paige, this is Mr. Bertram, my chemistry teacher."

"It's nice to meet you, Mr. Bertram." She held out her hand.

"Aunt?" Bertram asked, switching the flowers to his other hand so he could slide his palm into her aunt's outstretched one.

"Yes. My brother was Moira's father."

Moira enlightened him further "My mom died a long time ago."

Bertram nodded. "The pleasure is mine, Ms. Noble. It's very kind of you to have me on such short notice. I hope I haven't put you through too much trouble." His tone was earnest, and he held her aunt's hand the entire time he spoke.

"No trouble." Her aunt's other hand came up to press against the back of Bertram's. "We're happy to have you. But you must call me Paige. No one calls me Ms. Noble."

"Ansel calls you Ms. Noble," Moira said.

"Paige," Bertram repeated. "Please, call me Harold."

Her aunt finally let go of his hand. "What beautiful flowers, Harold. Let me find a vase for these. Dinner's just about ready." She smiled at the bouquet and twirled away.

Bertram watched her go with a weird, little half-smile on his face until he caught Moira's stare.

"Remember why we're here?" she asked.

"How could I forget? And I'm sorry about your mother." The light left his eyes and his expression sobered.

Embarrassment made her cheeks burn. Bertram didn't deserve her snappishness. He didn't have to be there. The only reason he came was that she'd asked him to. She dropped her gaze before going the same way her aunt had gone.

Bertram waited a whole second before falling into step behind her.

Her aunt had the flowers tucked into a tall, square-cut vase and was setting them on the end of the table. "Sit wherever you like. I'll grab the roast, and we can eat." She turned to the stove.

Bertram started to reach for the chair at the end of the table, stilled, and looked at Moira.

Her aunt, busy with the oven, didn't see Moira gesturing to another seat. He'd been about to take the chair her aunt always sat in.

Bertram stepped around to stand behind another chair. "Is there anything I can do to help?"

"Thank you for asking, but no. If Moira will grab the rolls, we should be ready. Can I interest you in a glass of wine?"

"Yes, you may."

Moira got the rolls.

The table was covered in dishes, but there was a space in the middle for the roast her aunt carried, filling the air with aromas that signaled it was time to eat. She set it down and reached for the open bottle of wine on the counter, filling two glasses.

"Where's mine?" Moira asked, taking her seat.

One corner of her aunt's mouth curled up. "In the future." Before her aunt could reach for her chair, Bertram was there pulling it out for her.

"Thank you." Both corners of her aunt's mouth lifted in a smile now.

"My pleasure." Bertram slid the chair forward and she sat.

Moira had heard rumors of such manners, but she'd never seen them in person. Her aunt was still smiling. Moira tried not to roll her eyes.

Bertram finally sat down. Her aunt spoke a simple blessing as she did whenever they sat down at a meal together, and they started to pass dishes.

"This looks and smells wonderful, Paige."

"Thank you. Moira helped."

"Not really," Moira said.

"She was my sous-chef."

"That means I cut up the vegetables without hurting myself."

"One must take care when wielding sharp instruments," Bertram said.

"Hmmm, so I've heard," Moira said.

Moira's aunt passed her the mashed potatoes, flavored with dill and garlic. "And you did very well."

"Thanks."

The conversation paused as the first bites were savored. Then her aunt took a sip of wine. "I was surprised when Moira told me she asked you to dinner. You're not one of her current teachers, even though she introduced you as her chemistry teacher. That was last year. In fact, I heard you weren't teaching this year?" Her voice rose at the end, suggesting it was a question, but it had the finality of a statement.

Moira kept her eyes glued to her plate. How did her aunt know that?

Bertram cleared his throat before he answered. "I'm taking some time off to pursue other interests at the moment, though I still do some instruction on the side."

"Tutoring?"

"Not exactly."

"Mr. Bertram teaches yoga," Moira said.

A frown furrowed her aunt's brow, there and gone in a second. "Do you like it?"

"I enjoy it very much." He smiled. "It's a good deal different from teaching high-school students, that's for certain, but rewarding in its own way."

Moira stopped chewing and stared. Bertram's smile was so natural, so easygoing, and relaxed it was disconcerting. When they were training, he appeared to always be under the strain of having a book stuck in his head, but not tonight.

"What do you do when you're not teaching yoga then?"

Bertram stalled, picking up his wine glass and giving it a swirl before he took a sip.

Here we go. Moira put her fork down.

"I've always been interested in the Renaissance, especially archery and sword fighting. Moira expressed a desire to learn such skills when she was in my class and now that I've taken the time off, I've been training her." Bertram took another sip of wine, quick as if he were afraid he'd said too much and would say more.

Moira waited.

Her aunt's eyes widened before her gaze came to rest on Moira.

She forced a smile. "Surprise?"

Her aunt's eyes narrowed. "How long has this been going on?"

"Not long. I ran into Mr. Bertram in the library, found out he was taking some time off and asked if he would be willing to teach me what he knows."

As far as lies went, it was as close as Moira could get to the truth without mentioning dragons.

"Why didn't you say anything before?"

Moira lifted one shoulder. "I wanted it to be a surprise."

"Mission accomplished." Her aunt's mouth was a flat line as she sat back in her chair. "And you agreed?" She pivoted toward Bertram.

"Yes." He put his glass down. "I have a keen interest in the period. I always thought I was born at the wrong time. In another time and place, I would have been an alchemist. No surprise I got into Chemistry. When Moira asked me to share what I know, I was happy to do so." He stopped and frowned. "It was never my intention for Moira to keep her training from you."

He was good. Even Moira almost believed him.

Her aunt didn't say anything right away. Instead, she picked up her glass and took a large drink.

Moira picked up her fork and scraped it through the potatoes on her plate, the tines squeaking against the porcelain. She took a bite without tasting them.

"Why did you want it to be a surprise?" her aunt asked.

Moira swallowed. "Huh?"

"You said you wanted it to be a surprise. Why?"

Moira stammered, her mind blank.

"There's a Renaissance Faire not far from here this summer," Bertram answered for her. "Moira wanted to join the archery competition and win."

Her aunt turned to her.

Moira nodded and smiled in agreement.

"That sounds—" her aunt frowned "—dramatic. Why archery?"

"Well," Moira ate a mouthful of roast, stalling, hoping her aunt or Bertram would say something to break the silence and give her something to build an idea off of.

Neither one spoke.

Moira dug deep into her own sordid past. "I mean, you know organized sports were never my thing. Remember when I tried peewee soccer?" She didn't remember the specifics herself, but she recalled the tears and the blood. Not all of it hers.

Her aunt winced.

"I'm never going to earn a letterman's jacket playing a team sport, not that I want one, but archery is something I can do on my own and I like it." And she was enjoying it. Then again, she had an advantage. She wasn't sure how much she would enjoy it if she didn't have the magic to help her out.

Her aunt started eating again.

Moira took it as a good sign. The tension in her neck and shoulders eased for the first time since they sat down to eat.

"If Mr. Bertram truly doesn't mind teaching you what he knows, then I guess you can continue. As long as it doesn't interfere with your schoolwork."

"It won't. I promise."

"Good, because I look forward to seeing your progress report when it comes home."

Moira toasted her aunt—with ice water—and smiled.

"I wish you'd told me about all of this sooner. The Renaissance happens to be one of my favorite periods."

"Why?" Moira asked.

Her aunt took a second to answer. "I guess I find it all a bit romantic."

Moira snorted.

Her aunt lifted a brow.

"It's one of my favorite periods as well for similar reasons," Bertram said.

They began discussing poetry and theater and Moira tried to follow, she really did, but the more obscure their references became, the more she tuned them out. She ate her supper, smiling and nodding, but on the whole, keeping her mouth shut, unless she was sticking a fork in it.

Moira felt lighter than she had since entering the cave. The burden of lying to her aunt was significantly less than it had been at the beginning of the meal, though it still existed. But no way was she telling her about Zephyr. Her aunt did not need to know about dragons, or magic, or spooky librarians. It was too much to hope she wouldn't worry, but at least now she knew if Moira didn't come home after school right way it was because she was training with Bertram.

She refocused and checked in on the adults. They were smiling and chatting, so she figured things were going well.

A little too well, it turned out.

She tuned in with half an ear to hear Bertram ask, "Would you care to see it with me this Friday?"

Moira's head swiveled toward her aunt. She hoped she would let him down gently. She'd never seen her aunt go on a date. Like ever. Something about her being too busy working full time and being a single guardian to a gifted niece, blah, blah, blah. Moira blinked when she saw her aunt smiling.

"I would like that."

22

"You are not dating my aunt," Moira told Bertram as soon as she saw him the next day after school.

Zephyr paced the perimeter of the meadow. Was he picking up on her feelings of irritation? They were certainly strong at the moment.

"Is that what I'm doing?" Bertram had the nerve to grin. "I guess I am."

"No. You're not."

"Please, Ms. Noble. Your aunt is a grown woman. I asked her out and she said yes. You don't have a say in whether she goes out with me or not."

"Yes, I do."

"No, y—"

A rustling in the underbrush cut him off.

Moira's head swung toward the sound. From the corner of her eye, she saw Zephyr stop pacing, but otherwise remain unalarmed. She was sure no one had seen her leave the trail and certain Bertram took the same precaution.

"Expecting someone?" Bertram asked.

Moira spread her hands open. "I told him not to come."

Bertram grunted.

Ansel sidled into the meadow, backpack over one shoulder, large sketch pad tucked under the other arm. He saw Moira and smiled, raising a hand in greeting. He saw Bertram and put his hand back down.

"I don't think he got the message," Bertram said.

"Ansel, we talked about this. We decided it wouldn't be a good idea for you to come back here. Remember?" she asked.

"I remember you talked and I listened, but we never came to a decision. Not really. I made sure no one followed me. I'll just sit out of the way and sketch." He lifted the pad under his arm.

Moira glanced at Bertram, who rolled his eyes. "Fine."

Ansel grinned. "How did dinner go? You're here, so it must have gone all right."

Moira glowered as she turned back to Bertram.

He held up both hands in front of him. "If the idea of my taking your aunt out concerns you so greatly, why didn't you speak up at dinner last night?"

Ansel let out a low whistle as he crossed the meadow. "That well, huh?"

Moira glared at Bertram. "She'd just agreed to let me keep training. It didn't seem like the time to bring up the fact that I don't like the idea of you going out with her."

Zephyr emitted a low rumble.

Ansel started as if he'd forgotten the dragon, but he didn't freeze up.

"Your aunt will allow you to train? You do not have to hide it from her?" Zephyr asked.

Moira shifted her weight from foot to foot. "We can train."

"This is good news."

"Yes. It is," Bertram said.

"Why is Moira upset?" Zephyr asked.

"Why, indeed?" Bertram shrugged.

Moira's brow knit together. She had her aunt's permission to keep training, which is what she wanted, but at what cost?

"What if something happens?" she asked.

"We're going to see a play, Ms. Noble. I think your aunt and I can handle a little Shakespeare without going mad."

"What if something happens *here*?" Moira motioned to Zephyr. "What if someone else barges through the barrier and runs into Zephyr?"

"Is that what I did?" Ansel asked from the top of his rock perch. His sketch pad lay open on his lap as he sharpened a pencil.

"Yes," Zephyr said.

Ansel pocketed the sharpener and started making light strokes against his paper.

"I see what you're doing." Bertram crossed his arms. "I don't think anyone is going to happen across Zephyr, and before you ask, no, I can't be sure. All I know is that I'm going to go see a play with another adult who happens to enjoy that sort of thing. We don't need to borrow any more trouble than we've already had. As long as Zephyr sticks close to the clearing there shouldn't be any problems. What's the real issue here? Is it me? Do you think I'm going to do something unseemly?" He shook his head. "Ms. Noble, I'm about to hand you a sword and instruct you on how to use it effectively. Never mind, you could have Zephyr remove my head from my shoulders with little more than a word."

Moira perked up at the thought. "Could I?"

Zephyr lifted one shoulder and nodded.

Bertram pinched the bridge of his nose. "I get it. As difficult as it may be to believe, I get it. She's your aunt. It doesn't matter who she goes out with, no one will ever be good enough for her. Or for you, for that matter."

Would she feel any different if her aunt was going out with someone Moira didn't know? The answer surprised her. "You're right. She's my aunt. No one will ever be good enough for her."

Bertram dropped his hand and blinked his eyes open, staring at the ground. He didn't try to convince her otherwise because he knew there was no point. He just stood there and kept his mouth shut, refusing to look at her.

And Moira got it.

He didn't think he was good enough, either. Not for her aunt, maybe not for anyone as he was, a broken man with a book stuck in his head.

But did she get to decide that?

"Fine," Moira said. Then she raised her chin. "But don't even think about setting up a second date."

Bertram's gaze snapped to hers, eyes wide. "Wouldn't dream of it." He smiled and clapped his hands together. "Now can we get to some training?" He was still smiling as he turned toward Zephyr to discuss what he had in mind. He continued to smile. Moira could tell he was still thinking about going out with her aunt. Thank goodness, his grin faded before too long, otherwise, she thought she was going to have to do something about it.

Bertram handed her the sword and watched as she hefted it to get a more comfortable grip. He had her start off practicing moves he'd already shown her. Her muscles recognized the motions, but in the middle of running a drill, the sword slipped through her fingers and ended up on the ground.

"Enough," Bertram said. "Let's try something else." He went to the tent on the edge of the meadow and brought out two swords fashioned out of what looked like single pieces of wood.

"Neat." Moira wrapped her hand around the nearest hilt. It was thick but covered in a rough hide to give it some traction in her grip. This sword was lighter than the metal one, obviously, and, she grabbed the point, it had more flex to it as well. It didn't fool her though. It was still dangerous. Getting hit with the flat of a sword, metal or wood, would hurt either way.

"I was making one for Zephyr. Thought I might as well make a couple more for you to practice with." Bertram brought out a third sword that made the other two look like toothpicks. The wooden shaft of the larger practice sword was about nine feet long, or at least twice the size of the smaller versions.

Zephyr came forward and picked it up. He tested the weight, switching it from one hand to the other before grabbing the tip and giving it a good bend. It flexed without splintering in two and he grunted. He brought it up to his eye and gazed down its length. The sword might have been a little too long, but it didn't bother him. He crossed to the middle of the meadow and slashed the sword one way and then the other. The air parted around the wooden blade with a whistling noise.

"And now Mr. Idlewild can start earning his keep," Bertram said.

Ansel glanced up from his sketch pad with a frown. "Huh—what?"

"Mr. Idlewild can be your sparring partner while he's here." Bertram indicated the other sword with a nod.

"I'm—I'm drawing."

"I see that. But now you need to come and help your friend."

"Help Moira? By fighting with her?" He didn't budge.

"Sparring. You'll be giving her the opportunity to learn and grow by letting her practice her skills."

Ansel's fingers ran around the edge of his paper. "Why don't you spar with her?"

Bertram sighed. "It will be easier for me to correct mistakes if I'm watching."

"I'm not sure this is such a great idea," Moira said.

"It's a brilliant idea. It's my idea. Come on down Mr. Idlewild." Bertram held out the sword.

Ansel flipped the pad of paper closed and slid it from his lap. "You do realize I don't know anything about fighting with a sword, right?"

"Neither does she."

Moira scoffed as Ansel slid down from his rock and came forward to take the sword. He stared at the thing tracing its length with his gaze from one end to the other. "What am I supposed to do with it?" he asked.

"The objective will be to make contact with your sparring partner. Here, I'll show you."

Moira stepped to the side and watched Bertram go through the very same motions he'd shown her.

Silent as a shadow, Zephyr stepped up beside her and observed the pair. "It will be good for you to have someone to spar with."

"Yes. It's very sensible."

"Indeed. But you are worried." He crossed his arms. "Do not be. I like Ansel. I will not kill him if he hurts you."

Moira's brows went up, and she turned to look up at him. "You're kidding, right?"

The spiny ridges above Zephyr's eyes went up in response. "Of course." On a more somber note, he added, "I save death for our enemies." His voice was little more than a rumble, but his words were solid, weighty things. Moira felt their heft more through their bond than she heard them with her ears. Since she'd learned of it, she'd come to think of their connection as an invisible cable stretched between them, capable of sending and receiving information. She still hadn't figured out how to control the flow of information from her end, but Zephyr was good about not broadcasting what he was feeling. Just now it felt like the cable strung between them got heavier. She doubted she would have noticed if she weren't standing right next to him. Zephyr was serious about protecting her. She didn't know what he saw in her expression or felt on his end of their connection, but he went back to watching Bertram work with Ansel.

"Did you make contact with the Librarian?" Zephyr asked.

"Not yet. I'll try soon. I'm not sure what he'll be able to tell us. We shouldn't get our hopes up." She wasn't sure how to go about getting hold of the Librarian either. Whatever he was, he didn't strike her as the sort to turn up when summoned.

Ansel finished the drill he was working on.

Bertram motioned her forward but spoke to Ansel. "Now, engage Ms. Noble."

The tip of Ansel's training sword hit the dirt. "Whoa. I don't know what you think is going on, but Moira and I aren't even dating."

Bertram's hand flew to his forehead before sliding down his face. "I meant, begin sparring."

Moira shook her head. Ansel could have just said they were friends. Dating wasn't an option for them. *Was it?* She frowned. Now was not the time to redefine their relationship.

Across the way, Ansel hesitated. "I'm not sure about this."

"What's the matter?" Bertram asked.

"Moira's my friend, and, you know—" Ansel broke off, glancing at Moira and then away.

"No, I don't know. Tell me," Bertram said.

"She's a girl."

Moira exchanged glances with Bertram. "All I heard was you don't want to fight with me because I'm a girl. Is that what you heard, Bertram?"

"That's what I heard." He clasped his hands behind his back. "Ms. Noble, if you would, please engage Mr. Idlewild."

23

The next day Moira plodded into Mr. Dee's world history class because when she moved too fast her back twanged like a plucked guitar string. The twang had a name. It sounded something like, "Mr. Idlewild's Windmill of Fury." Not a particularly skilled move, but effective, nonetheless, when it took Moira by surprise the afternoon before.

Ansel might be used to wielding pencils instead of swords, but he held his own. She got a few good touches in herself. If anyone asked Ansel why he was limping today, she was sure her name wouldn't come up. He might have a thing about not starting fights, or sparring matches, with girls, but he didn't have a problem defending himself once they began—which was a good thing because, otherwise, Moira might have actually hurt him. She hoped he would stay out of the woods now like she'd asked him to before. It would be a shame to keep beating up her best friend.

There was one other reason she dragged her feet. She stopped in front of Mr. Dee's desk. When he glanced up at her she hung her head, holding the digital camera he had let her borrow.

Mr. Dee saw her and thrust his head forward in disbelief. "Again?"

She grimaced and nodded.

"It was working fine when I gave it back to you." He took the camera from her and toggled the power switch to the on position, punching buttons and scrutinizing the display. "I called the company, returned it to factory settings, updated the OS and everything, and it's still giving you trouble?" The question was rhetorical as Mr. Dee could see the digital SLR wasn't working properly. She appreciated the fact that he didn't suggest it was her fault or imply she did something wrong.

Mr. Dee shook his mop of dark hair. "This just won't do." He set the camera aside. "I'll take a look at it later. In the meantime, I have an idea." He stood up and spun toward the cabinets behind his desk. He opened one and then another, searching.

"Eureka," he said and turned around. He held another camera, similar in size and shape to the digital model, but not in any way automated. "Gather 'round, you all. This is what we used before fancy digital cameras became all the rage." Technically they were in the middle of world history class, but Mr. Dee also taught photography. The rest of the class came up and crowded around the desk as Mr. Dee gave them a brief introduction to the ins and outs of the manual camera including how to load the film.

At the end of the discussion, Mr. Dee let Moira take the older model with her. He would help her set up what she needed to develop the film later.

For the first half of last period that afternoon, Moira did nothing but check books out for students. Then she put a cart full of returns away. After she slid the last volume into place, she slipped to the end of the aisle and checked to make sure no one was around. She strained to hear if anyone was close by, convincing herself she would hear someone if they walked past. Then she went to the middle of the aisle and pressed her back against a bookcase. She was tired of being snuck up on.

"Librarian? Hello?" she called, sotto voce. Being overheard talking to herself was one thing, but being overheard trying to talk to someone who wasn't there? She didn't want to think about it.

The Librarian never told her how to get a hold of him, possibly because he wasn't the type of being you got a hold of. He got in touch with you. She hoped this worked.

"I've got a question about a book and I'd like to speak with the Librarian." She watched one end of the aisle and then the other. Maybe she needed to dim the lights and burn some candles.

She heard footsteps approach one end of the row and held her breath. A student walked by, there and gone in a flash. He didn't even raise his head. His muffled footsteps faded.

Moira stared at the row of books opposite her. She had an idea. She didn't like it, but she didn't know what else to do. She stepped across the aisle, reached up and slid her arm behind the volumes. The first book hit the floor and bounced. She sighed and kept going. The second landed with a plop. The rest did a variation of swan dives until the shelf was clear. She waited a minute, marched to the end of the aisle. Nothing. She stomped to the other end. More nothing. She turned back to face the books. The urge to put them back was surpassed only by her desire to speak with the Librarian. She didn't turn her back on the pile of books until they were out of sight. Then she snagged her cart and pushed it back to the front desk.

Someone was waiting for her, but they didn't want to check out a book.

"Do you have a couple of minutes?" Natalia grinned and gripped her backpack straps. One jostled the press badge she wore clipped to the front pocket of her light blue button-down blouse.

"Let me check."

Shelly waved her away when she asked if she needed a hand behind the desk.

"I guess so. What's up?"

Natalia motioned to a spot in the middle of the library away from the other occupied tables. They sat down across from each other. Natalia took out a yellow legal pad and a pen. "I was hoping I could ask you some questions and get a quote for the story I'm writing." She flipped a page up and over the top, still smiling.

"Why would you want a quote from me for your story?"

Natalia went still. "Because you are the story."

"Excuse me?"

"A different student from each class is being featured in every issue of the paper this year. Your name came up, and here I am."

Moira's eyes widened.

Natalia dropped the top page back down on her legal pad, her smile fading. "Let me guess, nobody told you about the story?"

"No."

"And I'm getting the feeling you don't want to be the featured sophomore in the next issue." She pushed the legal pad aside.

Moira remained silent.

"For what it's worth, it would be a good article. I would be the one writing it after all." She grinned and braced her forearms on the table.

Moira's gaze tangled with hers, but she didn't say anything.

Natalia put up her hands. "Okay, I can see I'm not going to change your mind. There's a whole class of sophomores to choose from. Aaron can find someone else. The story's for his page anyway."

Moira's eyebrows went up. "Did—did Aaron put my name out there?"

Natalia stuffed her note pad back into her bag. "I don't recall. Someone on the paper must have come up with it though." Her head tipped to the side. "You know, we should hang out." She spoke as if she was talking to herself and Moira just happened to be sitting across from her.

Moira's gaze collided with Natalia's and got stuck.

Natalia grinned and nodded her head. "Yep. We're gonna hang out." She reached into her bag and tore off a piece of paper, wrote down a series of digits and slid it across the table to Moira before she stood up. "I'd love to stay and chat, but I've got some hard news to cover."

Moira picked up the piece of paper, staring at the numbers. "Hard news?"

Natalia's voice lowered from library-approved to conspiratorial. "There was a break-in on school grounds. Okay, it was the concession stand down by the football field, but that's still school property."

Her manner suggested there was more to the story. Moira asked what happened.

"Last Friday, someone jimmied the lock and broke in. I heard it could have been a lot worse. Whoever did it could have done some serious damage, but all they did was eat a whole bunch of potato chips."

Moira guffawed. "A potato chip bandit?"

"That's not even the weirdest part. They only ate the jalapeno-flavored ones and left everything else." She squinted into the distance. "I'm going to have to work 'spicy' into the headline somehow."

Moira's eyes widened and her mouth dropped open in dismay. Thank goodness Natalia was too busy imagining her story in print to notice. Moira cleared her expression and they said their goodbyes.

The final bell tolled for the day, but Moira stayed behind, saying she left something in the stacks. She retraced her steps to the aisle from earlier. The books she'd left scattered across the floor were back on the shelf in order. A slip of paper sprouted from the middle of one. She tugged the piece of paper free and read it.

On one side was the *HELP ME* message.

On the other, someone had written in black ink, 57 REMAINING.

24

In the woods, Moira kicked a clump of dirt, making it fly apart. How was she supposed to get answers out of the Librarian if she couldn't even ask him questions in the first place? She kicked a rock. It bounced off a tree with a satisfying *whack*. Maybe the Librarian was too busy for a face-to-face and that was why he left the note on the back of the *HELP ME* message. Before, he had said there were sixty-three messages left. Now there were fifty-seven. Did he want her to find them all? Was it some kind of test? Or was he taunting her? If he didn't want to meet with her, why leave a message? Then again, perhaps she was better off dealing with a passive-aggressive note than she was an aggressive Librarian. She shuddered and kicked a pine cone, sending it skipping.

A few students rushed past and ran ahead of her down the trail. Maybe they were in a hurry to get home. Or maybe they were in a hurry to get out of the woods. Ansel had said people thought they were haunted.

No one lingered.

Not anymore.

Moira didn't notice anything out of the ordinary when she left the trail. Then she caught herself. She'd left ordinary behind when she stepped into Zephyr's cave. She trundled along wondering if she would be able to tell when she ran into her spell turning people away from heading deeper into the woods. If she hadn't been making a conscious effort to notice it, she would have missed the subtle change from one footfall to the next. The air become charged and the hair on her arms stood up. Once she noticed it, she couldn't stop noticing it. She kept walking, but each step came slower and slower. She reached out with a sense she didn't know she had. It was a little bit like discovering the tip of an iceberg in the woods. Once she realized there was a presence there, she understood that what she'd noticed was only part of a being so large and so imposing she didn't know how she could have missed it.

It was huge.

She stopped and pressed her back to a tree. Her chest felt constricted no matter how deep a breath she took. She wasn't afraid so much as she was overwhelmed. Wide-eyed, she stared through the branches to the sky overhead. What she felt was alive. It was behind her back, over her head, below her feet, everywhere. The forest was alive—silly, because, of course, the forest was alive. It teemed with life. But this was more. She was witnessing another level for the first time.

The forest was awake.

And because it was so vast, the largeness of it meant only a limited amount of its consciousness was brought to focus on the woods there. Her little corner of the woods wasn't enough to trouble it, but it was enough to notice.

But what could have woken it? What could have roused something so large? Moira chewed the inside of her lip, afraid that she knew. The barrier to keep people from discovering Zephyr didn't just protect her dragon. It protected parts of the woods at the same time. The area she'd enclosed was empowered by magic; the trees, plants, maybe even the fauna, holding onto it and passing it amongst themselves.

Calmer, Moira took a tentative step into the open, patting the tree she'd rested against.

She hadn't intended to make the forest haunted, but now it was aware, and while it was an awesome presence, large and lumbering, it wasn't hostile. Its awareness was enough to freak people out, though. Moira reasoned it had to be this spirit of the woods that was making people uneasy and not just her spell to keep people away. The two worked together, feeding off of each other.

Bertram hadn't said anything about this new presence. Neither had Ansel. Perhaps, like her, they hadn't been paying attention. She hadn't noticed until she'd taken a moment to stop and tune into it. Moira shook herself and kept going. Now that she knew it was there, the feeling settled itself into the background with a low hum, like white noise.

She wafted into the meadow to discover that not only was Ansel willing to get himself beat up again, but he had gotten there ahead of her and was already practicing with Bertram. "Wait a second, how did you get here before me? I thought you could only get through because you knew I was out here, but I wasn't here yet."

"Hey, Moira." Ansel didn't take his eyes off of Bertram, who was advancing on him.

"Ms. Noble." Bertram didn't look up either. "I surmise Mr. Idlewild knew Zephyr or myself were in place here, and that's how he got through." He lunged.

Ansel parried.

Bertram regrouped. "As long as Mr. Idlewild consents to be your sparring partner, he can stay. Is that all right with you?" He attacked, not waiting for her answer.

She wasn't going to be able to keep Ansel away. He knew too much. Besides, it was good to have someone else to talk to besides Bertram.

They continued to practice. Moira stepped back and watched. To be a good sparring partner, Ansel had to know what he was doing.

Probably for the best that he got in some extra practice. If he got better, so would she.

Moira scanned the meadow and noticed a distinct lack of dragon. She dumped her stuff and went up and over the rubble pile. Zephyr sat under the overhang of his hollow, reading, his dragon-sized practice sword set to one side.

"Moira." He tipped his head.

She sat on a rock and waited.

Zephyr glanced up from his book.

"Anything you want to tell me?" she asked.

"Ansel has returned."

"I saw."

"Surprised?"

"No. I wish he'd at least consider staying away, but never coming back was too much to ask."

Zephyr set the book aside. "Anything you want to tell me?"

She gave him her best blank look because she didn't know what he was talking about.

He sighed. "What happened before you reached the meadow? I felt your unease."

She rocked back. How could she forget? "Unease? You could call it that. Where were you?"

"You were not in danger."

She considered the statement.

"What happened?" he asked.

"Nothing happened." She shrugged. "But I think that spell Bertram had me do to keep people away did something to the trees. They're not dangerous, but they're not the same. I think whatever I did is working, but it's like the trees have taken advantage of the magic somehow and spread it around. Not in a bad way, but the message is sort of shared now. I think that's why people have been staying out of the woods and saying they're haunted."

Zephyr made a noise in the back of his throat. "And what of the Librarian?"

She told him what happened.

"Curious," was his only comment.

"More annoying than anything, I think."

Zephyr tipped his head to the side before picking up his book again.

"Did you finish *To Kill a Mockingbird*?" she asked.

He grunted.

"What did you think?"

"Interesting. Sad. There is right and there is wrong. Opinions often differ. Also, I am Boo Radley."

She didn't laugh. She had to think about that one. "Huh. Okay. What are you reading now?"

He held up the book so she could see the cover: *Jane Eyre*.

"Okay, I haven't even read that." She dangled her hands between my knees. "When were you going to tell me about the chips?"

Zephyr grunted. He kept the book between them.

"Why'd you do it, Zeph?"

He let out a rumble as he lowered the book and closed it. Then he stood up and set the book on a rock ledge, under an overhang, out of the way. She caught a glimpse of the bottle of hot sauce she'd given him. Empty. He grabbed her copy of *To Kill a Mockingbird* and handed it to her.

She took the book but didn't say anything.

"I am sorry. I could not resist."

"I don't understand. Are you not getting enough to eat? You said you were hunting. Do I need to get you more rocks?"

"No. No more rocks. They will not help. It is not a matter of quantity." He shook his head. "Hunting is plentiful. The food is fine. It is filling. But it tastes like nothing. Like air."

She squinted, thinking hard. "Do you mean it's bland?"

"Yes. It is bland. I need something to wake my mouth. After I have eaten something with flavor, then I feel like I have eaten."

"I think I understand. But why break into the concession stand?"

"The food was just lying there, unguarded—"

"There was a lock on the door."

"And it gave me something to do after."

"After what?"

His gaze wouldn't meet hers. "After the argument with your aunt."

Her brows shot up. "Zeph, you cannot go binge eating a bunch of chips, particularly ones that aren't yours, every time I disagree with someone. It's not healthy. On so many levels."

"It will not happen again." Chastened, his tail drooped.

"Good. If you want more chips or hot sauce, all you have to do is say something."

He waited for a whole beat. "Something."

She fought a smile and lost. "Okay. More chips or hot sauce?"

His eyes went wide before he blinked. "Yes."

"Hey, Moira, you ready for a rematch?" Ansel called from the other side of the rock pile.

"Coming!" She stood and brushed off the seat of her pants. "I'll try to pick you up a few things, but it might have to wait until I see you on Saturday. Can you wait until Saturday?"

Zephyr's head jerked in a quick nod. "I will wait."

25

After school on Friday, Ansel drove Moira home following a quick stop at the grocery store. He didn't ask her what the food was for. She thought he might be looking forward to a relaxing evening spent with his sketch pad. They'd spent the last week trying to do each other harm and, in some cases, succeeding. Their limbs and torsos sported a variety of bruises, though Moira noticed hers faded faster than his. Bertram suggested they take a break since her aunt would be going out with him and if he wasn't training her, she didn't need to be out in the woods by herself. Moira argued that she wouldn't be by herself because Zephyr would be there. To keep up appearances, however, she knew her aunt would expect her to be home.

Moira thanked Ansel for the ride and went inside. Her aunt came down the stairs in a dress she hadn't seen her wear for a long time. The black and white print stopped right above her knees.

Moira frowned. "I thought you were going to a play."

"I am. We are. People dress up to go to plays." She carried a black cardigan. "What's in the bags?"

"Chips and stuff—study group sustenance." Moira took off her coat and tossed it on the rack leaving her in a long-sleeved green t-shirt and jeans. Since she'd started training with Bertram and Zephyr, she carried extra layers of clothing with her and kept another set in her locker at school.

Her aunt nodded, her hair swinging free. She'd left it down. Her hand flew up and tugged at one of her earlobes. "Do I need earrings? I need earrings." She turned and went back up the stairs calling over her shoulder, "And Ansel's waiting for you in the kitchen."

"What?"

Her aunt was already out of sight.

Confused, Moira headed to the kitchen.

Aaron stood next to the counter with a glass of water clutched in one hand. He smiled when he saw her. "She assumed. I didn't want to correct her. She seemed a little distracted."

How could her aunt have mistaken Aaron for Ansel? Aaron wore a white button-down with tan vertical stripes, open at the collar, over a blue undershirt. Both were tucked into khaki trousers belted at the waist with a worn strip of dark leather.

If Ansel wore clothes like that, Moira knew he'd be tugging at his collar, even if it was open.

The white of Aaron's shirt set off the tanned skin of his wrists where he'd rolled up the sleeves. She had the insane urge to run her fingertips over the peaks and valleys of the muscles and veins that ran the length of his forearms.

Moira gave her head a tiny shake. "What's going on?"

"I haven't seen you around lately."

Moira laughed. Aaron was the one who took the locker next to hers, tracked her down to make sure it wouldn't be a problem, came to the library to check out books from her and then proceeded to completely ignore her. She hadn't gone out of her way to avoid him. She just hadn't run into him, or the entourage that typically accompanied him, at their lockers. Now here he was, in her kitchen, because he hadn't seen her lately.

"I've been busy. What's up?" she asked.

"I heard you don't want to be the featured sophomore in the next issue. Is there anything I can do to change your mind?"

Moira shook her head. "Not one thing. And I'm doing you a favor. No one wants to read an article about me. I'm not that interesting."

"Respectfully, I think you're wrong about that." Aaron set his glass on the counter.

Moira didn't know what to say. All she kept thinking was, *Aaron thinks I'm interesting.* She set her bags down.

"Another page editor mentioned you and I thought you'd make a great subject," he said.

Something clicked into place and her eyes narrowed. "And what did Charlie have to say about me?"

Aaron lifted a brow but otherwise appeared unfazed by her powers of deduction. "Nothing specific."

"I haven't seen him around the library, so thank you for that."

"That might have been what started it. Charlie wondered—" Aaron coughed into a fist, "—quite loudly and with some vehemence—what you were doing in the library. And it got me thinking as well. Why did you want to be an aid in the library?"

She considered not just his question, but the way he asked it. "I think you equate working in the library with volunteer work, but it isn't. This might surprise you, but I actually enjoy it."

"I didn't think you were being charitable. I guess I just didn't know why you would work there instead of taking another independent study or something."

"Maybe because I didn't want to?"

His head tipped forward in acknowledgment. "Right."

They stood there a second.

"Can you find someone else to be the subject of your article?"

Aaron's smile broadened. "Ansel agreed to do it."

"No way. He never said anything."

Aaron rubbed the back of his neck. "Yeah, well, little brother owed me one. And his stuff is fantastic. I know people only think I say that because he's my brother, but it's not true. He's super talented. I can't wait for people to see what he's been working on."

"Isn't that a conflict of interest? You're editing the page where a story will run about your brother."

He held up his index finger. "The editor-in-chief already brought that up, but I'm not writing the story myself, so it shouldn't be a problem."

"Well, if you didn't need to convince me to be the subject of the article, then why are you here?"

The smile slid from Aaron's face. He pushed his hands into his pockets, took them out again and settled them on the counter. "I wanted to ask you something."

His statement hung in the air, pinned in place by Moira's blank stare.

"Okay. What?"

Aaron's jaw worked. A quick grin flashed across his face. She felt it in her solar plexus more than she saw it. "I'm on the Homecoming court, but I was hoping—" he stopped and ran a hand down his face, all of a sudden very serious.

As a sophomore, he was nominated for Homecoming Duke. She'd heard the news as well as read a flyer about it, but that didn't explain why he was telling her.

"Moira, will you go to Homecoming with me?"

The question replayed in her head so many times, she didn't answer right away, during which time Aaron stared at her, an expectant look on his face. By comparison, Moira's face went slack with surprise before it went taut with shock. "Me? You want to go to Homecoming with me? Next week?"

Aaron cleared his throat. "Yes, you. Yes. And yes."

"Why?"

He shook his head. "Do you want a list?"

"No. But answer the question."

"I asked you first."

"I asked you second."

He laughed. "Okay. Here it is. I like you. Even when I'm arguing with you." He stared at her. "I like you." He shook his head. "I know we haven't hung out a lot lately, but when I ran into you in the woods, I remembered we used to get along pretty well. There's something—I like you, Moira." He shrugged. "A lot." His hand clenched into a fist like he wished he could take his last words back. He cleared his throat and backed away from the counter. "I should be going. I'm sorry I bothered you at home."

Stunned, her breath caught before she spoke. "Pick me up at six?"

Aaron stuttered to a stop.

"Is that too late—you said you're on the court—do you need to be there earlier?"

"No. Six is good." A smile spread across his face and stayed there. "Six is great. I'll see you next Friday. Goodnight." He left the kitchen. The front door slammed.

The breath shuddered out of her. She gripped the counter with both hands needing to hold on to something solid as her world tipped off-kilter.

She was going to Homecoming.

With Aaron Idlewild.

In a week.

How was she going to explain that to her best friend?

Moira buried her face in her hands and let out a groan.

26

Moira's aunt found her at the counter in the kitchen when she came down a few minutes later. She pulled at an earlobe. Not only had she added gold hoop earrings but she'd changed. Now she wore an all-black, wrap dress, with a deep V neck.

"Did Ansel leave?"

"That was Aaron."

"Really? Sorry, I'm a little distracted." She got a good look at Moira. "What's the matter?"

Moira faced her aunt. "I'm going to Homecoming." And then she made herself say it out loud. "With Aaron Idlewild."

"Aaron. Not Ansel?" She peered over her shoulder in the direction Aaron had gone.

"No. Not Ansel. Aaron."

"Huh." Her aunt draped her sweater over one arm, holding her purse, a small black clutch. She stepped around the end of the counter to stand next to Moira. "Do you want to talk about it?"

"Not really. I have to find a dress," Moira placed her head on her aunt's shoulder. She smelled citrusy and pleasant. She always smelled nice, but she could tell her aunt had spritzed on a touch of perfume. Not too much.

"You'll find a dress." She patted Moira on the back. "Are you sure that's what you want to do? Go to Homecoming with Aaron?"

Moira raised her head, started to speak, stopped, and put her head back down.

"Oh, dear." The patting turned to rubbing.

Moira didn't like to think flattery could turn her head. Presuming it wasn't a joke of some kind and no one had put him up to it, Aaron Idlewild wanted to go to Homecoming with her. And she was flattered. Way back in sixth grade before things had gone awry, there had been a tentative friendship between her and Aaron. Moira and he were like two magnets of a similar charge. They could be pushed toward one another, perhaps even held together, but not without force, and only for a short time. They had always been at their most comfortable with some distance between them and she'd just agreed to spend the whole evening with him.

And he was attractive.

Just like his brother.

Moira wasn't blind. Aaron and Ansel were identical twins, but the past affected how she viewed them in the present. Ansel had never messed with her grades the way Aaron did. But Aaron had apologized. And she'd accepted it. Ansel had always been a friend. He'd never come out and told her he liked her, not in that way. But Aaron had.

What was she going to tell Ansel?

Moira squeezed her eyes shut tight and pushed the thought away.

Her aunt went back to patting her on the back. "Well, this is exciting," her aunt said, "your first formal dance." She tucked a curl behind Moira's ear. "Is this going to become a recurring thing? Should we plan ahead for Winter Solstice?"

Moira opened her eyes and raised her head off her shoulder. Before she could answer, the doorbell rang.

Her aunt jumped. "That must be Harold." Her expression sobered an instant later. "Do you want me to stay?"

Moira recognized the opportunity wrapped up in those six little words. All she had to do was say yes and her aunt would send Bertram packing. Then the two of them could sit on the couch and eat ice cream right out of the container and watch overrated reality television together all night long.

Her aunt would do it, too.

Moira couldn't let her.

"No. No way. Go to your play." Next Friday might be a miserable experience for all involved, but that was next Friday. Tonight was her aunt's night. It might still be a miserable experience, but who knew? She could have a good time. Not too good, of course, but not awful. Plus, her aunt had gone through the trouble of getting ready, twice. Moira didn't want to make her miss out on her date, even if it was with Bertram.

Moira turned her aunt around by the shoulders and frog-marched her forward saying, "Go and have a good time." She pulled the front door open.

Bertram stood at attention on the other side. "Good evening." He blinked as if growing accustomed to the light after being in the dark too long. He carried a small bouquet, fresher than the last, every bloom a variation of the color purple.

"They're beautiful. For me?" Her aunt asked.

Bertram blinked down at the flowers like he'd forgotten he was holding them. "Yes. They are. You look lovely." He smiled and gave her aunt a glance from head to toe while she accepted the flowers and stopped to smell them. The glance was quick enough that Moira didn't have to use him for target practice, but if he did it again, she might reconsider.

When her aunt swung the flowers toward her, Moira made sure she was smiling.

"Moira, can you—"

"Yes, I can put these in water. Do you have everything? Should I wait up? What time is your curfew anyway?"

Her aunt clicked open her clutch and dropped her keys inside. "The play ends around nine, so I wouldn't expect us before ten."

Bertram cleared his throat. "Possibly eleven."

"Don't wait up." She threw her arms around Moira, tight.

Moira hugged her back and took the opportunity to glare at Bertram over her shoulder.

He quirked a brow, but he didn't smile. If he smiled, she might come down with the plague right on the spot.

"Lock the door and don't stay up all night," her aunt said.

"I won't. Have a good time."

Moira shut the door, clicking the lock three times. She settled the flowers into a vase in the kitchen and hauled herself upstairs.

Full dark settled around her as she sat at her desk, surrounded by textbooks that were open or needing to be opened. The location never changed, but the landscape changed depending on what she studied. The light from her laptop wasn't enough to beat back the dark so she switched on her desk lamp.

A loose paper fluttered to the top of her desk. Moira secured the errant scrap back to the corkboard over her work area. The stick-figure drawing Ansel had given her caught her eye. She stared at the drawing as she sat back down.

How could she tell Ansel she was going to homecoming with his brother? He'd been acting so strange lately. When he'd asked her to go to the movies, she'd said yes without hesitation because that was what they usually did for her birthday. The last time he asked it felt different, though. She got the sense Ansel might have wanted it to mean more than their usual movie, but he'd never said anything, not out loud, not seriously. If he had, maybe she wouldn't be in the position she was in now. If Ansel had asked her out, for real, she would have said yes. Now Aaron had asked her out. Was it possible to like them both? Because she did. Ansel was her best friend, but there was something about Aaron that drew her to him. Maybe she was making a big deal out of nothing and Ansel would be cool with her going out with his twin brother. Yeah, right. She leaned back, pressing her fingertips to her closed eyelids.

The next second she felt like she'd been struck by an especially strong arc of static electricity. She leaped out of her chair with such force it clattered over behind her. She was on her feet, twitching and jittery like she'd had one energy drink too many.

OUTSIDE—the thought reverberated through her brain, with a loud and insistent pounding that slowly faded.

She reached out with her dragon sense. "No, no, no, no, no."

Moira raced to the window and threw up the sash. Zephyr stood at the base of the same tree Ansel had hidden behind. The tree Zephyr would have had to have climbed to get into her bedroom and bite her.

From behind the tree, Zephyr waggled a hand full of talons at her.

Moira shut the window and rushed downstairs to the kitchen. She yanked open the backdoor and stuck her head outside. She started to wave Zephyr over but ended up holding up her hand to get him to stay where he was. He was way too broad to fit through the human-sized door. She slammed it shut and sprinted to the basement.

Without stopping Moira pounded down the stairs and headed straight for the cellar doors. They didn't use the doors much and, as a result, the lever lock was stuck in place. It took a couple of kicks to knock it loose. The doors squealed when she pushed them open, but she was in too much of a hurry to try and be quiet. She stuck her head and shoulders out. Nothing stirred. She waved Zephyr over and hurried to find something to grease the unused hinges with. A good dousing of oil and they were nearly soundless when she shut them behind Zephyr. He moved to an open space on the floor, standing hunched over so his head didn't hit the ceiling.

"What are you doing here?" she asked, her voice little more than a hiss.

"Did my message come through?" Zephyr's tail swept the floor behind him. He sat down curling it around himself. As long as he leaned forward and braced his forearms on his knees, he wouldn't bang his head.

"Your message?" Moira went to the middle of the basement and pulled a cord. A single, naked bulb lit up over her head. She hadn't needed the light to see earlier. Her night vision was excellent, a recent development she attributed to Zephyr's bite, along with her increased speed of healing.

"I tried to tell you I was here—outside." Zephyr's pupils narrowed with the light, but he didn't blink.

"I thought we agreed you wouldn't do that again."

"We agreed I would not project my feelings to you. I was letting you know I was here."

"It worked. One second I was fine, the next I felt like I'd been hit with a taser."

"Oh." Zephyr's brows drew down.

"Yeah." Moira rubbed her forehead. "Can you do it again?"

Yellow eyes flashed to hers.

"The message thing. We have to work on this link between us. Maybe if we practice, we'll get better at it."

Moira took a deep breath and closed her eyes, centering herself. She opened her eyes and nodded at Zephyr.

And then she was on her butt in the middle of the basement floor. Luckily, she didn't land on anything. "Okay, see, maybe you could send a quieter message. Every time you do that it knocks me off my feet." She started to stand, thought better of it, and stayed where she was. "Again."

Another jolt. "Stop, stop." She waved him off. "Maybe don't try to think words at me. Everything goes wonky when you try to talk to me like that. Let's just stick to feelings. What are you doing here anyway?"

"You were upset. Is it because Bertram has taken your aunt away?"

Moira couldn't stop her lips from curling up. "I'm pretty sure he's going to bring her back." Her smile faded. "No, that's not what's bothering me." Her eyes narrowed. "Hold on, I was pretty freaked out in the woods earlier this week and you didn't check on me then."

Zephyr's chin dipped and he brushed his snout. "I thought I should investigate this time."

Moira threw up her hands. "You can't just drop by, Zeph. What if someone saw you?"

"My camouflage and the dark kept me from being seen. And you are not upset with me."

Moira's eye narrowed. "Get out of my head."

"I am not in it. Perhaps you should practice keeping your feelings to yourself."

His calmness irritated her further.

"Good idea." Her hands clenched into fists on top of her thighs and she shut her eyes, tight.

She called up an image of a red brick wall. To either side, the limbs of the wall stretched into infinity. Likewise, the wall climbed upward into perpetuity. She imagined herself running a finger along the rough mortar between the blocks. It was cool to the touch.

Zephyr shifted in the silence. "So, what happened?"

Her eyes sprang open. The wall crumbled into a pile of brick dust. "Calm yourself."

She wanted to snap.

He would know that.

She thrust both hands through her hair.

For several minutes she tried to stop up her feelings with no results. She forced herself to relax, which worked about as well as it sounded. She meditated. Nothing worked. If she imagined a brick wall, she saw the line that connected them running under it, over it, through a hole right in the center. It was always there.

She let out a frustrated noise. "This isn't working. I'm sorry Zeph. I'm sorry you have to feel all the crap I feel. I can't control it." She wondered how awful it must be to have a teenager stuck in your head and realized she already knew how terrible it was.

"I am alone, Moira." When she looked up, Zephyr bent his head to meet her gaze. "But thanks to you I am not lonely." His words resonated through the basement and through whatever it was that bonded them together. She wondered what Zephyr gained from having bitten her. Maybe that was it. "We will find a way to manage." He blinked. "Are you going to tell me what happened?"

Moira let go of the worry she felt for not being able to keep her feelings to herself and drew up her knees, resting her forehead on them. "Aaron asked me to Homecoming. I said yes."

"Who is Aaron?"

"Aaron is Ansel's older brother."

"Ansel has a brother?"

Her head came up as she nodded. "They're twins."

"They look alike, but they are not similar?"

"No. Not really."

Zephyr shook his head. "Human biology is bizarre." Then he asked, "Do you want to talk about it?"

Moira's head fell forward to her knees once more.

The dragon heaved a sigh. "Let us not."

27

Weary of worrying about Homecoming, Moira ran upstairs and grabbed one of the bags of chips she'd bought earlier. She pulled open the top for Zephyr on her way back to the basement. He could do it himself, but he tended to shred the bags. Moira handed him the bag of chips, watching his snout disappear inside. The sides collapsed as he breathed in their spicy aroma. He closed his eyes, lifting his face free with a rumble of appreciation.

Moira turned over a milk crate and sat on it, thinking.

"What?" Zephyr asked. He plucked a single, large chip from the bag, pinched delicately between two talons. He tossed it into his mouth and grabbed another.

Moira laced her fingers together over one knee. "I was wondering—if we find a way for you to get back to where you came from, what happens to this connection between us? Does it just go away?"

Zephyr allowed the chip he was about to eat to fall back into the bag, so Moira knew he was giving her question serious thought. After a minute, he said, "I do not know."

"Maybe things would go back to normal," she said, but she didn't believe it. She wasn't worried about what the bite had done to her. She assumed her newfound abilities would fade. She would just have to get used to not healing as fast. Learn to deal with getting sick again. And never do any more magic. Her new skills would atrophy without Zephyr around to practice with, forgetting for the moment she wouldn't have had to learn everything she did if he hadn't bitten her in the first place. Over time she would forget what she had learned. But how was she supposed to forget Zephyr, or that dragons existed somewhere beyond the margins of maps? They thrived in another world. The one she was trying to help him get back to.

"Perhaps," he grunted, staring off into the basement, giving no indication of what he was thinking.

"You do want to go home, right?"

"I do not belong here," he said.

"But you hatched here. What do you know about where you come from?"

Zephyr started eating again. "I will have to wait and discover it for myself."

Moira didn't question him further. She would miss him. There was something about his big, lumbering presence she found reassuring. She liked talking to him about the books he was reading and watching him practice, that would never get boring. When the time came, she hoped she would have the chance to say goodbye.

Zephyr finished the bag of chips.

"Do you think your camouflage and the dark will keep a bag of chips from being seen if I send it with you?" Moira asked.

A low chuckle rolled out of him.

Moira couldn't hold back a smile.

"If I am in contact with the chips, I can camouflage them as well."

"Okay. Let me get you a bag to go." No one else was going to eat the spicy chips. Moira grabbed another bag and opened the cellar doors. She checked to make sure no one was around.

"See you tomorrow," Moira said as Zephyr stepped outside.

He rumbled a farewell and took off through her back yard. He stood about a foot taller than her now. He continued to grow, but nothing like he had after eating the fire rocks. As she watched, his head and neck melted into shadow, followed by his chest and arms, one hand holding the chips. Finally, the last of him, his long, flexible tail faded into the night. With Zephyr safely on his way, Moira pulled the cellar doors closed, threw the latch, and went upstairs to find something to eat. It was already a little after nine. She wondered how her aunt's date was going.

Finished, Moira opened the dishwasher to stand her plate inside. An electrical pulse shot through her, making her convulse and drop the porcelain disc. It clattered to the bottom of the machine.

HEL—

"Hel—hel what? Hello? What is going on?" she asked the question out loud, but thought it at the same time sending her confusion and frustration down the connection between her and Zephyr.

In return, she got nothing.

She ignored the word of the message and focused on the feeling she got when it came through.

It hadn't felt like a greeting.

Moira stuffed her feet into her shoes and ran out the back door.

✜

She stumbled more than once on her way into the woods. Full dark had fallen and no matter how good her night vision had become, she still tripped over well-hidden tree roots and uneven ground.

Moira zeroed in on Zephyr, but from what she could tell, she was headed to his meadow. She slowed as she approached unsure of what she would find. Maybe it was a test. Zephyr wanted to know how fast Moira could get to him if he needed help.

That was all, just a test.

Then she heard a thump, followed by a grunt.

A retch-inducing stench rolled over her.

Troll.

The smell stopped her in her tracks. She waited for her stomach to stop turning and slipped forward. *Crunch.* Chips littered the ground. She stepped over the rest and passed the tattered remains of the bag she'd sent with Zephyr.

In the middle of the meadow, Zephyr and a troll circled each other, both with swords drawn and dirty. Blood trickled from her dragon's nostrils. Zephyr favored his right leg. The troll was short, but broad, and held a hand to a gash in its side.

Moira slid to her right toward Zephyr's hideout.

If she could get to her bow and arrows—

She heard a wet snort and froze.

Another troll stood between her and where she needed to go.

With its back to her, it crossed its arms, watching. Was it waiting for its turn to have a go with Zephyr? The thought made her insides clench. She had to get to her bow.

Her movements slowed to a creep as she gave the second troll a wide birth through the trees. The fight raged on, but there was nothing she could do. Zephyr hissed and snapped at his opponent, the ground shaking. Finally, Moira slipped behind the rock pile and dove for her bow and quiver spilling the arrows.

"Quit playing. The captain wants it dead. Finish it," a rough voice said, the sound of steel grating against a stone.

Moira stuffed a handful of arrows into her quiver and leaped to the top of the rock pile.

Zephyr swayed where he stood, but he still held his sword aloft. He glared at the troll across from him. The troll wrapped both hands around its sword and charged.

Moira didn't think, just reacted. She released an arrow.

She missed.

But the troll stopped its charge.

For a second, no one moved.

A yell split the air as the troll she had skirted past roared and pulled an ax from over its shoulder.

"No," Zephyr shouted and turned toward her. "You should not be here."

Moira couldn't believe what she was hearing.

"You don't need help? I'll just head home then." She drew another arrow and fired at the troll wielding the ax, but it dodged her hastily shot missile and continued toward her.

"Get down!" Zephyr roared. "Now!"

Moira scurried behind the rock pile.

An arrow clattered against the stones where she had just stood.

Another troll.

One she hadn't seen.

Zephyr climbed the rocks and stood on top, claiming the high ground for himself.

She was supposed to be helping and now she was trapped.

An arrow struck the ground two feet from where she huddled. She scrambled away. Steel rang against steel.

Zephyr let out an ear-splitting roar that echoed in Moira's head. She covered her ears and squeezed her eyes shut tight.

When the battle cry faded, Moira opened her eyes. She had to do something. Fear raced through her, but it was outpaced by thoughts of what she would do next.

Moira readied another arrow and slipped downwind of Zephyr and the troll with the sword. She peeked over the rock wall, scanning. There, on the opposite side of the meadow. The third troll aimed and released an arrow. It sank into the ground where she had just been sitting.

This time Moira gathered her will and released it at the same time as she fired. Her arrow found the troll's eye, snapping its head back. It fell to the ground, dead.

Moira reloaded and fired at the troll with the ax, but it shifted at the last moment and the arrow struck it high up on the shoulder. It grunted and reached up to pull her arrow out before snapping it in two and tossing the broken pieces aside.

The troll with the sword took a swipe at Zephyr's ankles.

Her dragon jumped in the air, came down on the uneven pile of rocks, rolling and sliding into the meadow. He just managed to grab the point of his sword with his opposite hand in time to hold it up and block a two-handed overhead blow from his opponent's blade.

They struggled.

Moira came over the rock pile and fired, hitting the troll in the neck. It staggered back, clutching its throat.

It wheezed and sank to its knees.

Zephyr rolled to his side and shot up in front of her as the troll with the ax stalked forward.

Moira reached for another arrow and found nothing but air.

The troll swung its ax in a two-handed overhead blow.

Zephyr stopped it with his sword. The troll kicked him.

Moira leaned one way and then the other, dodging Zephyr's tail. It whistled as it went by.

From the corner of her eye, she saw the troll she hit in the throat slump over, dead. She skidded to its side and worked the hilt of the sword free from its fingers.

Zephyr blocked another swing of his opponent's ax. Their weapons grated as they slid against each other. The troll swung a fist, slamming into Zephyr's side. Zephyr grunted before he kneed it in the gut and the two separated.

Moira saw an opening, summoned her will, and tossed the sword.

Zephyr backed up a step, completed a half twist and grabbed the hilt of the blade out of the air with his free hand.

The troll bellowed his rage and began a vicious, whirling attack.

Zephyr blocked the swirling ax with both swords and fought back, but he was slowing down. She didn't know how long he'd been fighting. Her arrival seemed to have renewed his strength for a time, but she could see him struggling to keep up. She could feel his weariness.

Moira turned and sprinted to the first troll she shot. She grabbed an arrow from its quiver and raised her bow.

Across the meadow the troll used the handle of its ax to get inside of Zephyr's reach and poke him in the belly, causing him to double over. The troll raised its ax overhead.

She blew out a breath and focused. She fired.

The troll jerked to a stop, the ax tumbling out of its hands.

Zephyr sidestepped the troll as it fell forward, her arrow sticking out of the middle of its back. Zephyr gave the troll at his feet a long look. Then he turned toward Moira and toppled over onto his side.

28

Moira ran to Zephyr's side, skidding to a halt next to him.

His hot breath steamed in the night air.

"Are you all right?" she asked.

He grunted, slipping as he tried to get to his feet. "I will be."

"What happened?"

"Ambush," Zephyr said. "They were waiting. I should have been paying more attention."

Moira peered through the dark into the woods around them. "Are there any more?"

Zephyr went still as his eyes shot wide. "I do not know." He turned his big head, searching the meadow, his snout in the air. "We should go look."

Her hand tightened on her bow. "You're hurt. We wouldn't make it far." She swallowed. "I could go."

"No. We go together or not at all," Zephyr huffed. "They talked. They did not think I would be very much trouble. They were very nearly right. No. If there are any more trolls out there, they will have to regroup before they try again."

Moira's grip relaxed, but she did not set her bow aside. She bent low, trying to assess the damage to Zephyr's leg. A wave of guilt washed over her, making her breath catch.

She rocked back.

The guilt wasn't hers.

"Whoa, stop that. What are you sorry for?" she asked.

It reminded her of when Zephyr tried to cheer her up, but different. He wasn't projecting his feelings as he had before, but she was picking up on them all the same. For all her effort to build a wall between them, their bond was more intact than ever and functioning quite well.

Zephyr growled and Moira felt another rush of self-pity.

She laid a hand on his forearm, the scales smooth and bumpy at the same time underneath her palm. It wasn't her he was angry with.

"I was lazy," he said. "I did not use my camouflage this close to the meadow. When I realized—I barely got to the sword in time. I called out to you before I could stop myself." He shook his head. "I should not have put you in danger."

She frowned and glanced at the carnage around them. "Yes. You should have."

He sniffed. "I could have handled it."

Moira heard his words, but she felt the emotions behind them, and those said way more. "Zephyr, I'm your dragoneer. If you need my help, you have to promise me to call for it."

He wouldn't meet her eyes. "You are too important."

"You're important, too, you impossible dragon!" Moira dragged in a lungful of air and tried again. "Listen, we're in this together until we get you back home. The Librarian warned me Zephyr. I have to keep you safe, or terrible things will happen. I think I was wrong, trying to block the connection between us. You shouldn't be holding back either. If you need anything, you have to let me know. Now let's take a look at that leg."

Zephyr didn't say anything.

The waves of guilt eased as she found what caused him to favor his right side. A deep gash ran across his flank, the bleeding slowed to a sluggish trickle. Moira probed the rough edges of the wound with gentle fingertips. Zephyr hissed.

"If I thought I could find a needle that would make it through your tough hide I would say you need stitches."

"I will heal. Help me up."

"You need to take it easy."

"I need to rest."

Zephyr climbed to his feet, taking one sword with him. Moira got under his right arm helping him make his way over the rocks into the shelter of the overhang. He lay down and curled himself into a ball. Moira rechecked his wound. Blood oozed from the center, the edges ragged, but otherwise, the movement hadn't reopened the gash.

"What are we going to do about the bodies?" She couldn't move them herself and Zephyr was in no condition to help.

"Leave them," Zephyr rumbled. His eyelids drooping closed.

Moira stood over him a moment. She closed her own eyes and summoned whatever feelings of peace and harmony she could muster and passed them on to Zephyr.

He shuddered once and lay still, fast asleep.

❄

Whatever time it was when Moira crept in, she didn't have to worry about waking her aunt because she wasn't home yet.

Moira didn't know how she was able to sleep after leaving Zephyr, but she surprised herself by falling into a dreamless slumber.

Three more trolls. They'd fought three more trolls and won. Somehow. Something bothered her about these three more than their previous attackers, but she couldn't put her finger on what exactly. Perhaps she was just more disturbed by the fact that Zephyr had been injured.

Moira could do this. She could help Zephyr get back home. The sooner she saw him safely back to where he was from, the sooner she would never see another troll. She was less and less sure about sending him back to a place where every troll seemed to have it in for him though.

But Zephyr was right. He didn't belong there.

The thought made her sad and her movements slowed as she went downstairs and poured herself a cup of coffee.

"That'll stunt your growth," her aunt said from her place at the table.

"I'll risk it." She waved some cream over her cup before she tossed in a handful of sugar. She took a sip. "Mmmm. How was your date?"

"Fine, thank you." Her aunt sipped her coffee.

"Is that all? Just fine?"

"That's all." She shook out her newspaper and disappeared behind it.

Moira stretched up on her tiptoes to peek over the top. Her aunt ignored her, but Moira thought she looked a little sad around the eyes. She didn't say anything about seeing Bertram again, which was what Moira wanted, right? Was he heeding her advice about not asking her aunt out for a second date? Or were neither of them interested?

Moira wasn't sure if she was ready for an answer to any of those questions, so she let the matter drop. She had bigger things to worry about. She slurped the rest of her coffee down and called goodbye to her aunt on the way out the back door.

Sometime after she'd made it home the rain had started. It wasn't a deluge, but it was the kind of persistent wet that soaked everything through to its core. She wanted to check on Zephyr's leg and make sure his hidey-hole stayed dry. The wind picked up and it reminded her winter would come soon enough. For now, the small golden leaves of the honey locust trees swirled down with the rain.

Moira didn't see anyone on her way to the meadow. The bodies of the three trolls were lined up on the ground at the edge of the clearing.

Zephyr stood upwind. Moira went straight to his side. "How's the leg?"

"Better."

Moira looked. His scales were healed over, a slightly lighter shade of brownish-black than before. "Do all dragons heal so fast?"

He stretched the leg and pointed his three toes. "It depends, but yes, young dragons heal fast with enough rest and food."

Taking the hint, Moira unloaded the rest of the spicy chips and hot sauce into Zephyr's alcove, which remained dry.

"What do we do with them?" she asked.

"We will have to bury them as before."

As they stood over the bodies, Moira had a thought. "Does any of their stuff look familiar? Is there anything on them that might give us an idea of why they want you dead so bad?"

Zephyr's head jerked and she felt a surge of surprise. His tail whipped into the air behind him. "I did not think of this." He bent and started going over the first troll's armor. Moira saw it wasn't made of metal. Instead, the trolls wore clothes made of thick leather. In the light of day, each of their skin tones was different from the next. The troll who'd almost hit her with its arrows had a greenish tint to its skin. The one Zephyr had fought with was orange while the last and largest troll's skin, who had wielded the ax, was tinged purple.

Zephyr checked over their clothing and weapons but didn't find anything.

Disappointment.

"What they're wearing doesn't leave a lot of room for pockets," Moira said. "I didn't think we were going to find a calling card for whomever they worked for, but it was worth a shot." She squinted at the three bodies. "Do you think these three were more scouts?" she asked.

Zephyr sniffed. "I do not know. They were very well armed for scouts."

The sound of footsteps reached their ears, but neither moved. While Zephyr's gaze lingered on the dead bodies, Moira raised her head to watch Bertram as he approached the meadow. He did not look up. His hands fluttered at his sides, but he didn't raise his arms. He appeared to be having a conversation with himself. It must have been serious because he was glowering. She hoped it didn't have anything to do with her aunt. When he got close, he glanced up and saw Zephyr. He did a double-take. His eyes widened before his gaze dropped to the three bodies on the ground. Moira watched the blood drain from his face as he came to a stop.

"What happened?" he asked.

They told him the whole story, leaving out Zephyr's visit to her house and his calling her for help. If anything, Bertram grew even paler, his skin turning a sickly grey.

"You could have been killed," he said.

"But we weren't," Moira replied.

"You could have died," he repeated. Two bright spots of color flared to life over his cheekbones. "What were you thinking? Coming out here in the middle of the night?" He sounded more confused than anything, and he was acting stranger than normal.

Her eyes met Zephyr's in a sideways glance.

"I wanted to check on Zephyr. Good thing I did." She left it at that.

Bertram's throat worked as he swallowed. Then he nodded. "Yes. Good thing." His gaze went over the trolls again. "Is this all of them?"

Moira looked at Zephyr with a squint and he at her. "We think so?" Moira said.

Bertram stared at her and then Zephyr. "You think so? Do you mean to tell me you're not sure if one or more got away?"

"We were a little busy fighting at the time. And Zephyr was hurt. One could have gotten away. We're not sure," Moira said.

"They would have needed to regroup," Zephyr said.

Bertram covered his mouth with both hands, closed his eyes, and nodded.

"Do you think these were more scouts?" Moira asked.

Bertram didn't answer right away. First, he had to uncover his mouth. Then his eyes opened, going to the dead trolls on the ground. He didn't appear to be staring at them so much as through them. "Yes. Of course," Bertram said. He turned away. Moira could no longer make out his expression. He pushed both hands through his hair walking in the direction of the tent near the edge of the meadow. It blended in with the trees so well she forgot it was there. In a moment he returned with a shovel.

"If Zephyr doesn't mind helping..." Bertram's voice trailed off.

"Why do you have a shovel in your tent?" she asked.

"Sanitary precautions."

"Ah."

They moved off into the woods away from the meadow.

Zephyr took the shovel and began to dig.

"Hold on, Zeph." Moira turned to Bertram. "Shouldn't I be able to help?"

"I don't see why not. We can take turns with the shovel—"

"Not like that." She turned back to Zephyr. "You might want to move out of the way."

He did as she suggested and found a tree to scratch his back against.

Moira thought about what she wanted to do. This wasn't a pebble. And it wasn't an arrow. This was more than three cubic meters of earth she wanted to move, but she didn't doubt that it could be done. She focused on what she was about to do. She closed her eyes and raised a hand. Instead of releasing her will the way she would with an arrow, she tapped into the source and made a scooping motion with her hand at the same time. The rain neither helped nor hindered her. Rocks, leaf litter, and other detritus rolled and rumbled as roots separated and were pulled apart.

Moira opened her eyes.

A large pile of earth was mounded next to the hole from where it had been removed.

Bertram stared at the hole, turned toward her, and nodded.

She repeated the process three more times.

Zephyr and Bertram dragged the bodies into the hole.

Moira stood apart. Pins and needles raced down her arms. She shook them out and the sensation faded. She'd done it. And she wasn't too tired from moving all of the dirt out of the way to be able to push it back over the bodies once Bertram and Zephyr laid them in place. Zephyr took the shovel afterward and patted everything down, the rain turning the freshest dirt to mud.

Bertram frowned at the burial mound, throwing her glances now and then, nodding to himself. "Very good, Ms. Noble."

Moira didn't respond, but she was pleased he thought so. She stretched, the static fading from her limbs.

"If a troll did get away, it's time to work some more magic," Bertram told her back at the meadow. "Otherwise, Zephyr will have to move. He should probably move anyway."

Moira hadn't thought of having to relocate Zephyr. It made sense. If a troll had gotten away, others could be led straight back to him.

"Will more magic help? You said Ansel got through because he knew I was out here somewhere. Won't the trolls be able to get through if they know Zephyr is here?"

"This time you'll be more specific with your intentions. You know you're trying to turn trolls away."

Moira was willing to give it a shot if it helped keep Zephyr safe while they found a new place for him to stay. And because she'd done it before, tapping into her will didn't take as long. They were able to complete a quick circuit through the forest, Moira building on what was already there, making no mention of the presence in the woods she had awakened the first time through. They made plans to find a new place for Zephyr as soon as possible.

Back in the meadow, the rain continued to fall, but they started with drills. Moira practiced with the sword this time, dodging Zephyr's tail without fail. They moved together as a unit, in sync. Bertram stood under a tree out of the rain, watching. Always watching. They did not falter. Bertram stopped them with a wave of his hand. "Well, you both seem to have mastered that."

Moira did not look at Zephyr and in return, she could feel Zephyr not looking at her.

The last thing she expected was for Ansel to stalk into the meadow in the middle of the downpour.

29

The rain plastered Ansel's hair to his forehead making it darker, turning it brown. No sketchbook. He wouldn't want to get the pages wet.

"Good," Bertram said. "You two can do some sparring."

"Ansel," Moira said his name.

No response. He didn't say anything as he picked up the two practice swords and tossed one to Moira.

She snagged it out of the air and held out the hilt of the steel sword to Zephyr. Her dragon took it and walked to the edge of the meadow to practice on his own.

"We should talk," she said.

"About what?" Ansel asked. He turned his back on her.

Moira's throat tightened. She stared at his back, adjusting her grip on the practice sword.

"Begin," Bertram said.

Ansel attacked. Moira brought the wooden blade around quick. The two swords connected with a clatter.

"You might want to start slow and give yourself a chance to warm up," Bertram said.

Ansel either didn't hear him or he didn't care because he attacked again right away, pushing Moira back. She slipped on the wet grass and almost went down, recovered, and countered. The wooden blades clashed with ringing noises. Ansel lurched back to sidestep a blow. Moira advanced. He feinted left. She fell for it. The tip of Ansel's practice sword aimed for her belly. She twisted and the point grazed her, the edge of the wooden blade continuing to run along her side. If it had been a real sword, her best friend would have just disemboweled her. A flush of anger rose through her. Ansel used his momentum to sweep past. Moira's elbow connected with his midsection driving the breath out of him.

Zephyr stopped what he was doing and turned toward them.

"Remember you're not actually trying to kill each other," Bertram said.

Ansel grabbed his side and attacked again.

Moira blocked it and answered with an attack of her own. One second she was going up against Ansel, the next she was fighting a stranger. They went back and forth, hammering at each other again and again, silent except for the sound of their harsh breathing and their swords striking against one another. Finally, she'd had enough.

Moira knocked his wooden blade aside with a blow of her own. "What is going on?"

"What? Just thought I'd help you make up for missing last night since you'll miss next Friday, too. You know, because of Homecoming and all." Ansel didn't know when to stop, raising his sword again. Moira slapped it aside and advanced, pushing him back against the pile of rubble.

There was nowhere for either of them to go.

"How do you know about that?" she asked.

"How do you think?" Ansel made a cutting move, but it was sloppy.

She knocked his blade away.

Ansel lowered his sword, giving up. "Aaron couldn't wait to tell me about how you're going to Homecoming with him."

The tip of Moira's sword dipped toward the ground. "I was going to tell you."

Ansel frowned and shook his head, confused. "Since when do you go to Homecoming anyway?"

"Since someone asked me to, I guess."

"If you wanted to go, we could have gone together, you and me."

Moira sucked in a breath. "You didn't ask."

Ansel laughed, but he didn't smile. "Fine. I'm asking now. Moira Noble, will you go to Homecoming with me?"

She ground her teeth together. "I can't."

"You didn't even think about it."

"There's nothing to think about, Ansel. Aaron asked me, and I said yes. I can't back out on him just because you decide you don't want me to go with your brother."

Ansel pushed himself to his feet. "You don't know anything Moira. When his locker flooded, he could have picked any locker and he chose the one right next to yours. He only did it to mess with me. Trust me, you don't want to go with Aaron."

Moira stared at him.

Zephyr stepped forward.

Ansel's head jerked to the side. His eyes widened.

Moira lifted a hand. It was clear Ansel was upset. The hot breath of a dragon down his neck wouldn't calm him down any.

Zephyr stopped but held his ground.

Bertram stepped forward, arms crossed. "You're wrong, Mr. Idlewild," he said, one hand coming up to scratch his beard-covered chin. "If Ms. Noble didn't want to go with your brother, she would have told him no. But she didn't. She said yes."

Ansel's gaze flicked from Bertram to Zephyr, then back to Moira, the rain falling harder. The practice sword tumbled from his hand into the grass. He gave the three of them a wide berth, skirting the edge of the meadow before marching off into the woods. Bertram and Zephyr watched him go.

Moira let her sword fall to the ground. She couldn't quite face Bertram or Zephyr. She didn't want to follow Ansel, afraid they might say more to hurt each other than they already had. "I'm going to practice with the bow now."

She clambered over the rock pile before the wetness that sprang to her eyes could spill over. Out of sight of the others, she felt a drop fall from her lashes. When another traced the curve of her cheek, she tilted her head back. The rain hit her upturned face and mingled with the wetness already there. Her flush cooled within minutes, but the back of her neck still felt hot. When she tried to put on the guard to protect her forearm her hands shook. She swallowed past the lump in her throat and fought to regain some sort of composure. She should have told Ansel about Homecoming as soon as she saw him. By that reasoning, she should have called and told him last night.

Why hadn't she? Because she thought his feelings might be hurt. She thought Ansel might have some interest in her beyond friendship, though he'd never come out and said so. Did he ask her to Homecoming just now to keep her from going with his brother or did he ask because he truly wanted to go with her? Could it be both? What would she have said if he asked her before Aaron?

She would have said yes.

As soon as she thought the question, she knew the answer. If Ansel had gotten his act together and asked her to Homecoming she would have said yes. But he hadn't. Perhaps he'd been too busy with his art, and school, and helping Moira train, which he didn't have to do, but she couldn't make excuses for him. Such thoughts would drive her mad.

As hard as it was to believe that Ansel would ask her to Homecoming, it was harder to believe he would ask her to go back on her word to Aaron. Moira didn't make promises she didn't intend to keep. Ansel knew that, yet he asked anyway. Did he think so little of her character that he expected her to go back on her word?

Moira breathed deep, reaching to find some kind of calm, but found herself getting angry, like a fire banked inside her, a fleeting word or thought fanned the flames over and over. She stood. The rain had washed her face clean and her eyes no longer stung. She wiped away what moisture she could and rejoined Bertram and Zephyr.

Neither one had anything to say for which she was grateful.

Bertram stroked his beard, limiting any remarks he had to single words and grunts.

Zephyr paced back and forth, watching her hit her mark over and over until it came time for them to work side-by-side. Every time he swung with his sword, his tail flew the opposite way to act as a counterbalance and she dodged it. He didn't say anything either, but he knew what she was feeling.

She fired arrows into her target over and over until her arms sagged with fatigue. Her anger faded and numbness took its place. She suggested not training again until Monday after school and was surprised when Bertram and Zephyr agreed. Bertram muttered something about teaching an extra yoga class and Zephyr said he wanted to do some reading and asked for another book. She wasn't sure she believed either of them, but she nodded and left without saying more.

When she got home, she dug out a slip of paper she'd never thought she'd use and punched in seven digits she'd never thought she'd dial.

✻

"You're sure you don't want me to go with you?" her aunt asked.

"You have to work."

"I know, but we could go after."

"You'll be exhausted and no fun to shop with."

"You're not exactly a barrel full of monkeys to shop with either."

Moira smiled and hugged her aunt. "See—it's a good thing I'm going to look for a dress with Natalia."

Her aunt's hand sprouted a plastic card. She handed it over. "Nothing too outrageous and nothing too expensive."

"Of course not."

Someone knocked on the front door. Her aunt answered the summons, greeting Natalia and inviting her inside.

Moira made the introductions.

"We'll be back before dinner, Ms. Noble. My parents have plans and I have to get back so I can watch my little sister and brother."

Her aunt nodded. "Please, call me Paige."

Natalia's forehead furrowed, but she continued to smile. "I really can't. How about Ms. Paige? My parents insist on some formality, I don't know why, but it worked and I can't not do it."

Her aunt laughed. "That's fine. It was nice meeting you, Natalia. Have a good time."

Moira followed Natalia to her sensible four-door sedan and got into the passenger seat. It was no pickup truck, but she couldn't complain. Natalia turned out to be a defensive driver and they didn't talk much on the way to the mall. She pulled into a space outside the food court.

"Okay, help me remember where we parked. Also, I don't know about you, but I require sustenance before we try on a million dresses. I'm thinking smoothie," Natalia said.

"Sounds good." And it did, which surprised Moira. She wasn't a smoothie person, but then again, she wasn't supposed to be a Homecoming person either. She was trying all sorts of new things.

They went in, got a bunch of fruit blended into liquid form and meandered toward The Nines, a boutique Natalia thought would have the kind of formalwear they were interested in.

"So. Are you and Ansel going to Homecoming together?"

"What? No."

Natalia didn't say anything for a minute. "Does that mean you're going by yourself?"

Moira's mouth fell open. Before Aaron asked her to go, the thought of attending Homecoming had never crossed her mind. She would never have attempted something like it on her own. "No. I'm going with Aaron."

Natalia came to a sudden stop at the same time as her eyebrows shot up. "Whoa. I did not see that one coming. How long have you guys been together?

"What? We're not. We don't have to be dating or anything, do we? It's just a dance."

Natalia sipped her smoothie. "True. We can just get you a turtle-neck, then."

Moira stifled a laugh. "Maybe a burlap sack. I mean, why did we even bother to come shopping?"

Natalia pretended to think it over. "Ah, well, we're already here. Might as well get fancy."

Moira nodded. There was nothing wrong with getting dressed up to go to a dance, even if she was just going with Aaron as a friend. "Are you going with someone?" she asked.

Natalia took a long sip. "Yes. I am."

When she didn't volunteer any more information, Moira sipped her drink. If everyone thought, like Natalia, that she would be going to Homecoming with Ansel, then everyone was in for a surprise. The two passed by an assortment of shops, peering into the windows. A selection of goods and blank-faced mannequins posed back at them.

Moira opened her mouth, ready to crack and ask her who she was going with when Natalia heaved a heavy sigh. "I'm walking in the door with Charlie Barrett, but I'm really going with Jessica Walters. She's coming with Jason Cagle because we don't want people to know we're seeing each other. Not just yet anyway." She bit her lip.

Moira's eyes widened for a second, but only because she couldn't imagine what Natalia would have in common with Charlie Barrett. Then she remembered they worked on the school newspaper together. "Oh. Okay."

Natalia frowned. "You won't tell anyone? That Jess and I are," her voice lowered to a fraction of the volume it had been, "together."

"Please," Moira said and sucked on the end of her straw.

A slow smile spread across Natalia's features. "I knew I liked you." Her eyes widened. "Not like that, but, you know, I thought you would be discreet."

Moira shrugged. "No big deal."

Natalia huffed out a laugh. "Ha. Right. Not to you maybe. This town might be growing, but it still feels small. People think they're more accepting than they are. We're just not ready to fight that fight yet. Maybe when we're in college, but not now."

Moira understood. Perhaps not better than someone else, but she had an idea. She knew what it was like to have a secret. On your own, it was a burden. Having someone to share it with didn't make it any less burdensome, but it helped to not have to hide it all the time. She thought of Bertram, and Ansel, and Zephyr himself. Moira turned toward Natalia and waited for the other girl to turn her way. "I get it." That was all. She hoped it was enough.

Natalia turned back to stare at the shop window in front of them but Moira could see her reflection in the glass. She wasn't appraising the items on display. Her gaze was turned inward and Moira saw on her face the worry and the struggle to remain present like there was something else on her mind. "I'm sorry, you know. About your dad. I never got a chance to tell you that before."

The window display suddenly caught her interest, not that she saw any of it. "It's okay."

"You seem different. I know you've had some…issues. We all do, but I heard yours were pretty serious. I don't know what you're doing, but keep doing it."

Moira chewed the inside of her lip. Natalia was right. Once upon a time, her anxiety ruled her instead of the other way around. But if she'd never had that experience would she have been able to handle being bitten by a dragon?

"Thanks," she said.

Another minute passed. Finally, Natalia raised her cup and nudged Moira with her elbow. "C' mon. Let's try on every dress they have until we find the ones that'll knock our dates dead."

30

Moira didn't know what to expect Monday morning. Nerves made her stomach clench as she meandered the halls on the way to her locker between classes. Despite the shopping trip and the time off from training she'd had too much time to think about Ansel, what he'd said and what he hadn't.

She blinked and there he was, in the same hallway, his gaze skipping past, brushing past hers and moving along as if he hadn't seen her. But he did see her. She knew he did.

Moira came to a dead stop. Other students jostled their way around her.

Her eyes stung and the pain in her stomach moved up and settled in her chest. She blinked rapidly and forced her feet forward, one hard-won step after another. Whatever hope she had that they could talk was pushed aside. Maybe after the dance. Maybe then his eyes wouldn't skip over her like she wasn't there and he would speak to her again. However, she didn't want him to talk. No. She wanted him to listen. She would make him listen. Make him understand.

She blinked harder, certain she couldn't make him do anything. She didn't intend to nurse the pain. She wanted to forget all about it, but it was there and left alone, she knew it would turn into something else, anxiety or anger. In the girl's bathroom, she closed herself in a stall and cried hot, salty tears as quietly as she could. No one wanted to get caught having a good cry in the bathroom. Too many questions, or worse, assumptions. Afterward, she rinsed her face in cold water and was only a few minutes late to her next class.

She saw Aaron later in the day, but he wasn't alone. His gaze met hers over the head of whoever he was speaking with and he smiled. Moira didn't interrupt.

After school, she trained until she had blisters. Then she trained until they were broken and bloodied. The pain helped her focus. Overnight the welts healed. The next day she did it all over again.

Ansel didn't return to the meadow.

Bertram said little. He appeared more preoccupied than normal, but he was around to offer what guidance he could concerning dragons. Any thoughts he might have had about Ansel he kept to himself. When he did speak, they talked about finding a new place for Zephyr to stay. They all kept their eyes and ears open for any signs of trolls, but there were none.

Zephyr didn't use their connection to try and make her feel better, because she thought he knew he couldn't. She was glad he didn't try. On top of all her other emotions settled a fine layer of guilt like a cloud of dust. She couldn't control her feelings, and Zephyr could feel every one of them. He never said anything, but she would catch him watching her, and more than once he would rumble about the book he was reading or ask her to scratch a scale on his back he couldn't quite reach. These were all meant to pull her thoughts away from Ansel. They were small reprieves, but they were welcome.

Friday after school, Moira arrived home and handed her aunt her progress report from school with a hug, but not a word. Then she plodded upstairs to the bathroom. She shut the door, turned on the shower, sitting on the closed toilet lid.

The third stair from the top squeaked. "Moira?" her aunt called through the door.

She shook herself in an attempt to rid herself of the malaise that followed her everywhere she went. "Aunt Paige."

"You're doing well. Over half of your teachers think you're 'a pleasure to have in class.' Including your independent studies teacher." She let her statement hang in the air.

Moira nodded, though her aunt couldn't see her. "I think he was trying to be funny."

"Ah." The sound of paper rustling. "Good job, kiddo. What time did you say Aaron was picking you up?"

Moira told her and listened for the third stair to squeak again. Once it did, she got undressed and climbed under the spray. She made the water as hot as it would go and tried to force herself into feeling excited about the night to come. She started a mental list, ticking items off as she went.

Good grades, check.

Dress, check.

First high school dance ever, check.

With a date, check.

Aaron, check.

The boy who asked her to go with him. Not the boy who looked just like him, but now couldn't stand the sight of her.

Moira turned her back to the showerhead and leaned her side against the tiled wall. Tears fell from her lids, sliding down her cheeks unabated. Instead of forcing herself to be cheerful she gave herself permission to feel sad first. Unlike the first time at school, when she cried in the bathroom stall, this time her tears had nothing to do with the shock of being dismissed outright. Her shoulders shook with her sobs, but she tried to keep quiet. If Aunt Paige heard, she would want to know what was wrong and Moira didn't have the words to get it all out. But she did have the tears and she grieved for the loss of her friendship with Ansel.

The water cooled. Moira turned her face into the spray, hoping it would help erase some of the damage crying had done to her face. Her shower had a brisk finish, but by the end of it, she felt better. Well enough to be cautiously optimistic about the evening ahead instead of filled with a sense of dread.

Moira scooted into her bedroom and got herself ready. She stepped into her dress and drew it upward, slipping her arms through the capped sleeves, holding it close so she could draw the zipper up the side. The pleated bodice was a snug fit, but she could breathe. The longest points of the kerchief hem brushed her legs just below the knees. She did a quick twirl and the bottom of the dress ballooned upward with flair. Moira smiled. The dress was black as coal but for the jeweled details sewn into it, front and back. The accents flashed when the light hit them, throwing off colorful sparks.

Her aunt knocked and came in. "You look wonderful. A little too grown-up, but nice." She held up a fist full of bobby pins. "Ready for hair?"

"I think so."

Her aunt pinned up her hair in the back while somehow wrestling the remainder of her curls into submission and getting them to lie in an artful wave to one side.

"Makeup?"

"Uh—"

Her aunt put up a hand. "Be right back." She left and came back with an armful.

"You're fifteen and blessed with a good complexion. You don't need a ton of makeup, just a little something." She made Moira open her eyes wide so she could comb through her lashes with a wand dipped in inky mascara. The lip gloss she turned over and let Moira do for herself. The sugar-and-cream color went on smooth but made her lips feel sticky. Her aunt took both items and placed them in the clutch Moira was borrowing from her.

Her aunt stepped back, scrutinizing her appearance, loosely holding her by the upper arms. "Beautiful, but something's missing. You finish getting ready—I'll see if I can find it."

She left and Moira slipped her feet into a pair of black ballerina flats and picked up her wrap. Her aunt returned as Moira grabbed the clutch and opened it. Inside were the mascara and lip gloss, but also a shiny foil packet that made her eyes widen. "Aunt Paige? Why is there a condom in here?" Then she remembered the clutch was the one her aunt had used when she went out with Bertram and had a terrible thought—what if there had been two? She swallowed back the bile that rose in her throat with a grimace.

"I'm a nurse. If I haven't told you what a condom is for, I'm really not doing my job."

"Aunt Paige, I'm fifteen."

"I'm well aware. That fact keeps me up at night. I just want you to be safe and use protection. Let me be clear, I am in no way condoning underage sex, but do you think I could stop you?"

Moira exhaled a puff of air.

"Hey, you know what's super hot?" her aunt asked.

Moira glanced up with raised brows. They answered together. "Consent."

"On that note, I got you this," she held up a canister of pepper spray just like the one she kept on her keychain; the one she had taught Moira how to use. She wondered if her aunt took that on her date with Bertram, too, but she didn't ask, just tucked it into the clutch with everything else.

"And this." A fine chain trickled through her aunt's fingers. On the end was an infinity loop pendant in white gold with diamonds. "I saw this and thought it would go with whatever you might find to wear." She mimed a turning motion, and Moira presented her with her back. Her aunt fastened the clasp.

Moira gave the chain a gentle tug, and the pendant settled just below the hollow of her throat high above the sweetheart neckline of her dress. "Thank you. It's beautiful." She twisted to hug her aunt.

Her aunt squeezed her tight. Then she pulled away and bounced—physically bounced—up and down while clapping her hands together in silence. "Time for pictures."

Moira wanted to groan, but she couldn't in the face of such pure enthusiasm.

Her aunt went to get her camera and proceeded to take what Moira estimated to be about one million photographs.

Her face hurt from smiling when the doorbell rang.

31

Her aunt opened the door.

"Good evening, Miss Noble," Aaron said, stepping inside. He filled out the dark suit he wore. His firm, square jaw was clean-shaven and his normally tousled hair was combed down neatly. When they both got a good look at him, her aunt let out a low whistle.

Moira interpreted. "You look very nice."

Aaron tugged at his bowtie. It matched the dark silver waistcoat he wore under his black jacket. A pewter pocket square peeked out of the front of the coat. "Thank you. You look very nice also." He stared into her eyes as he said it, and Moira felt her stomach take a small dip. "I got you this." He held out a clear plastic container.

Moira took it and pried open the lid pulling out the fresh white roses bound in silvery ribbon—a wrist corsage. "It's beautiful, thank you." She slipped the lacey elastic loop over her left hand. "But I didn't—"

"Yes, you did," her aunt said. She'd slid over to the front hall closet and brought out a boutonniere made from a single fresh white rose.

Moira stepped in close to Aaron and pushed the large pin through the stem of the flower and into place on his lapel. She caught a woodsy scent on top of fresh soap and glanced up to find Aaron watching her. He smiled. Moira's stomach dipped again, this time harder.

"Picture time," her aunt said.

Moira could not suppress a groan.

When she was sure her face would crack from all the smiling, her aunt hugged her and told her to have a good time. Then she hugged Aaron and whispered something in his ear. Moira didn't hear what she said, but Aaron smiled as they parted. They made their escape.

A bright blue Chevrolet Chevelle crouched at the curb. The SuperSport 396 gave her the impression it was waiting to pounce. She knew what it was because Ansel was always helping his dad and brother work on it. Moira stopped on the sidewalk, admiring its top line.

"Dad let me borrow it for the night."

She reached for the passenger side door.

"Whoa." Aaron stilled her with a touch of his hand to her arm. "I know you are perfectly capable of opening this door by yourself, but I am going to do it because that is what a gentleman does. You're going to let me because that is what a lady does." He opened the door. "We can fake it for one night."

Moira smiled, said, "Thank you," and slid inside onto the wide bench seat covered in white leather.

Aaron made sure her dress was clear of the door before he pushed it closed and went around to slide behind the steering wheel. He twisted the key in the ignition, and the engine turned over with a throaty purr instead of the growl she expected. He grinned. "You look great. Sorry we didn't get a chance to talk all week."

"Glad you remembered to pick me up. Thought you might have changed your mind."

"Never. Just had to put the paper to bed, is all. Have you seen the new issue?"

"No, not yet."

They pulled away from the curb.

"Do you mind if we swing by my house? My mom wanted to take some pictures."

"Uh, sure." She'd been to his house before, at least once or twice a summer. "Is, um, Ansel around?"

Aaron kept his eyes on the road. "I don't think so. Haven't seen him much all week."

The Idlewilds lived in an older home to the north with a large garage and plenty of mature trees. Moira secretly coveted the weeping willow in their front yard and always took a turn on the tire swing hanging from its branches, but didn't want to try it in her dress.

Aaron pulled over at the end of the lane and came around the car to open Moira's door. Before her feet touched the ground, his mom spilled out the front door with a digital camera slung around her neck, waving. "Don't you look lovely? I won't keep you too long. Just want to grab a couple of photos."

"Hi, Mrs. Idlewild." Her bespecled eyes disappeared behind the camera and all Moira could see was the top of her permed head.

"You don't have to come inside, just stand by the car." She started snapping pictures right away and kept up a steady stream of chatter. "Dave had to work late, but I'll show him these when he gets home. We were so pleased when Aaron told us all over dinner that you were going to the dance together."

Moira's smile turned brittle. Was that how Ansel found out? He said Aaron all but rubbed his nose in it, but that wasn't the way it sounded.

"Come around to the front of the car and I'll take a couple more. You two look wonderful together."

Moira used the move to refresh her smile. She didn't know what had been said or how. She hadn't been there, but she was here now, and she had a choice to make. She could fret about what she had no control over or live in the moment and try to enjoy herself. It was a quick decision. She had gotten dressed up after all.

"Okay, I think that's it. You two are free to go."

Aaron went to his mom's side and gave her a quick hug and a kiss on the cheek. She straightened his already straight bow tie and said, "Have a good time. See you later. Not too late."

They piled back into the car, buckled up, and pulled away from the curb, waving as they left. "What time is your curfew, anyway?" Moira asked.

"Midnight."

"Mine's eleven."

Aaron flashed her a smile. "Your aunt reminded me."

They pulled into the school parking lot, but when Aaron turned off the car, he stayed behind the wheel. "Kick-off's not till seven. Technically, I don't have to show up until half-time." His thumb tapped the top of the steering wheel. "I want to show you something before we go to the dance."

Inside Aaron led her to the newspaper office. He let himself in, switched on a desk lamp and handed her the latest issue. "Hot off the presses," he said with a wink.

"You sure do know how to show a girl a good time," she said.

There were four pages to the paper, each dedicated to a theme, but she wanted to see the feature article on Ansel. It wasn't on the first page, so Moira opened the paper. Under a headline about Ansel the Artist, there wasn't just an article, but an original sketch taking up a quarter of the page. The subject of the drawing had her pulse skipping along a mile a minute. Her smile slipped away. In the middle of the school newspaper was a portrait of Zephyr.

Ansel had captured the likeness of her dragon in detail from the scales on his hide to the pores on his snout. He'd also captured a bit of whatever it was that made Zephyr the dragon he was. Something in the eyes. She wished she could appreciate it more. She would say it was very lifelike, which was the problem. Her hands shook, making the paper rustle in the quiet.

"I know. There's something about it," Aaron said.

Moira glanced up. Aaron stood next to her. She'd forgotten he was there.

"The first time I saw that piece, I had this visceral reaction to it. I can't explain it. I had to run it as soon as I saw it. Had to beg Ansel to let me. He didn't want to for some reason." He shook his head.

"Can I keep this?"

"Sure. Ready to go to the dance?"

Moira nodded and folded the newspaper as many times as it took to fit inside her clutch. She took shallow breaths, trying to regain some semblance of calm. What did she have to worry about? Zephyr's portrait was just a picture. No one knew Zephyr was real except her, Bertram, and Ansel. There was nothing she could do about the drawing now. She squared her shoulders, determined, more than ever, to have a good time. No use in worrying. The whole thing could turn out to be a non-event.

❈

They followed a thumping bass line to the gymnasium and found the place transformed. It was amazing what a ridiculous number of balloons and low lighting could do. Music blasted from the opposite end of the space. It might not have been anyone's favorite song, but it was loud and that more than made up for it.

Aaron drew Moira to the left inside the door with his fingertips at her wrist. He bent close to her ear so he wouldn't have to yell over the music. "Are you hungry?" he asked. The timbre of his voice so close to her ear sent a vibration down her spine. He leaned back to look at her.

She shook her head.

He smiled and grabbed her hand, tugging her along behind him to the dance floor where many bodies threw themselves about. He led her past couples that moved in tandem to the beat and the odd pair that swayed together no matter the tempo. Somewhere in the middle of it all, he let go of her hand and turned toward her. Both of his feet left the floor. He arched in mid-air and came down on one foot before he started jiggering in a way that made her think he had hurt himself when he landed. There was no scream of pain, though. He was grinning and his head bobbed in time with the music.

Moira stood rooted in place.

Natalia called out and waved from her spot on the dance floor a few couples away. She wasn't dancing. The dress she had picked was an off-the-shoulder, mermaid-style gown in a deep red that made it difficult to walk, let alone dance. Natalia stood in place and wiggled, but from the smile on her face, she was having a good time. She was surrounded by a group of people that included Jessica Weaver. Moira waved back and gave her a thumbs up. Natalia's greeting alerted others and shouts of welcome reached them over the music. Aaron's friends called out to him from all sides. When he turned away to shout back, Moira slipped away.

Dancing. Fast dancing. Not something she was comfortable doing in public. Of course, she knew they were going to a dance, she just didn't think—she stopped. She didn't think. Of course, Aaron would want to dance. Why would she have thought he wouldn't want to dance? She could've asked her aunt for some pointers or at least researched some steps online, watched some videos, been prepared. She guessed she'd been a bit preoccupied.

At the punchbowl, she was halfway through her first cup when Aaron caught up to her.

He raised his voice to compete with the music. "Is that a 'no' to dancing then?"

"No—" she held up a hand. "—I don't mean, 'no, I don't want to dance.' I just mean I'm not sure how to dance to this."

"Finally! Something you don't know how to do. C'mon." He took her cup and set it down, caught her hand in his, and led her over to one of the darker corners of the dance floor. He stopped at the edge of the crowd. "You'll love it—there aren't any rules. Just have a good time."

She rolled her eyes.

Aaron tugged on her hand. "Okay, you do have to move in some way. Beyond that, don't run into anyone and you should be okay. Feel the beat and go from there." He started to bounce on the balls of his feet in time with the music.

Moira tapped her toe and glanced around.

No one paid them any attention.

The music lapped at Moira's feet before it swam up her body. Her knees bent and her hips started to sway. Soon she moved with the music. Aaron grooved along beside her. They circled one another, each making the other laugh with a weird dance move, back and forth until a downshift in tempo stalled their movements. The DJ slid on a slow song. Around them, couples stepped in close to one another, some holding hands, others holding necks and waists.

Aaron drew her toward him with his left hand, but not into him the way other boys on the dance floor did. His right hand settled high up on her back just below her shoulder blade. Her left palm rested on top of his right shoulder

She snuck a glance upward. Aaron grinned. Moira's mouth stretched wide in return. This wasn't so bad. She had no trouble standing in one place and shuffling her feet, turning in one direction.

"I like this song," Aaron said.

Moira had never heard it before, so she made an effort to tune into the music. There was a solid bass riff with soaring vocals on top. She smiled and nodded. "Yeah."

Aaron didn't say anything more and Moira was content to be held and sway to the music. The song came to an end. Neither one moved away from the other. The tempo picked up. They continued as if it hadn't. Moira wondered if they would get dizzy from turning in the same direction for so long and if maybe they should turn the other way to unwind when another couple jostled them.

The couple said sorry and moved on. No longer caught up in dancing, Moira glanced around the crowded gymnasium.

Her gaze skipped over the other couples, skidded to a stop and bounced back to one in particular. One half of the pair across the dance floor looked an awful lot like her date. Ansel wore a suit similar to his brothers, only his tie and vest matched the color of his date's dress. She didn't recognize the girl, but she had long straight blonde hair and wore a tight, sparkly green sheath.

Aaron followed her gaze. "Huh. He came after all."

"What do you mean?"

"When I told my parents we were going to the dance together, Ansel got real quiet and said something about coming too, but I didn't think he had it in him."

Moira blinked and turned to Aaron. "Why would you think that?"

He stared at his brother. "It's not really his thing."

Across the dance floor, Ansel and his date held each close despite the upbeat tempo of the music.

"I guess I was wrong," Aaron said. He took her hand. "Do you want to go say hi?"

"No." Moira shook her head. "Let's dance."

They started moving again. Two more fast songs played before another slow one. As Aaron led Moira in circles again around the edge of the dance floor she glanced over his shoulder. Her eyes met Ansel's over the head of his date. Whoever she was, her head rested against his chest. Moira's chin inched upward. She refused to look away first. Another couple slid between them as Aaron turned them about the floor and Ansel was lost to sight.

Did she hope he was having a good time? She might not be able to say so yet, but she didn't wish him ill. She could never do that. Did he feel the same? Moira hoped he might. He would be surprised to find out she was having a good time. Aaron was a good dance partner. He'd been nothing but polite. They moved well together.

Until a sudden jolt shot through her with such ferocity, she jumped clear out of Aaron's arms.

One word rang in her head—*TROUBLE.*

32

"I have to go." Moira rushed away from the dance floor toward the exit.

"Wait—what?" Aaron called after her. "Where are you going? What just happened?"

"I need to go." She pushed open the gym door surprising a pair of students who jumped and sprang apart.

Aaron followed close behind.

Moira knew she was being rude, but she couldn't stop and explain. The psychic shout-out from her dragon, telling her there was 'trouble' had been filled with a sense of impending doom.

Aaron grabbed her hand and pulled her to a stop. "I thought we were having a good time. Did I do something wrong?"

Moira swung around to face him. "No, nothing, but I have to go. I'm sorry." She pulled away and Aaron dropped her hand as if burned.

Moira twisted away, ready to go when his next words stopped her.

"Do you need a ride? I could get you there fast. Give me a chance to open up the headers."

Here she was abandoning her date in the middle of the dance he'd invited her to with no explanation, and he wanted to know if she needed a ride. It would have been a lot easier to walk away if he hadn't offered. The corners of Moira's mouth lifted before they turned down in a grimace. She didn't want to leave her first dance this way. She tried to clear her expression but was afraid she couldn't hide it well enough, so when she turned back to Aaron, she stepped in close and pressed her cheek to his. "No, thank you. For what it's worth, I was having a great time."

She began to pull away, but Aaron's arm came up behind her and held her close. Her gaze clashed with his, and before Moira could ask what he was doing, Aaron leaned down and pressed his lips to hers.

She heard the door to the gym get thrown open, but she didn't think anything of it. Every thought flew right out of her head.

Aaron pulled away first. "Me, too," he said.

His face filled her vision as she took a step back.

He let her go.

She took one more step backward, trying to sear the moment in her memory so she could visit it again and again—Aaron in his bow tie and the way his mouth felt against hers. She wished she had more time to take in every detail, but she had to go. She raised her hand in a small wave, turned, and slipped away down the hall. Her hand went to her cheek. She didn't feel just warm, but feverish. Her fingertips drifted down to her lips. They were warm, too, with heat not entirely her own, but it was fading fast. Besides their increased temperature, they didn't feel any different. She was sure they didn't look any different. But she felt different.

She dropped her hand and headed to her locker, passing other couples on her way.

She finished spinning her combination as another jolt hit her, the same message as before. "I'm coming," she muttered aloud. Was Zephyr's message growing more intense? She couldn't tell, but she tried to let the anxiety and worry she felt flow down their connection so he would know she got it. Only one thing would spook Zephyr bad enough that he would risk trying to communicate with her in such a way when he knew what it did to her.

Moira kept extra clothing in her locker for training and emergencies. She didn't have time for a total wardrobe change, but she did grab a dark hooded sweatshirt that zipped down the front and hung up her wrap. Items got shuffled in and out of her clutch into the pockets of her hoodie. She didn't have another pair of shoes, so she was glad she wasn't wearing heels.

Moira hurried back past the gym. The DJ played a faster song set and a punchy rock tune accompanied her into the woods but fell quiet after several meters into the trees. She left the trail and concentrated on finding Zephyr. Her dragon-o-meter led her deep into the woods. Moira's sense of direction joined in. With a start, she realized where she was headed. She moved faster, branches and brambles scratching at her bare legs until she reached the base of the tallest hill for miles around.

The head of the trail leading to the peak was easy to find. Whatever pointed her in the direction she needed to go stopped.

"Zephyr." She breathed his name, no louder than a whisper, so soft she could barely hear it over the pounding of her own heart.

"Here," Zephyr said in a similarly hushed tone. He pulled away from the deepest shadows. In one hand, he held the sword, and in the other, her bow and quiver. All in all, not a good sign.

"Trolls?" she asked.

His answer ended in a hiss.

She slid the quiver onto her back and gripped the bow.

Zephyr took the lead. The trail was steep. Even without carrying anything heavier than her weapons, Moira was soon out of breath and conscious of how loud her breathing was. Zephyr's breath steamed out of him at an increased rate, but he moved without a sound. As they climbed, a storm blew in from out of nowhere. It started to rain and the sky flashed with lightning. They cut the last switchback and Zephyr tipped his head to the side and held up a hand. They crept forward in silence. Moira's heart pounded. She stuck close to Zephyr's left side.

From the corner of Moira's eye, she saw Zephyr's head jerk. His nostrils flared. She smelled it too; troll.

They stole forward until they could see into the clearing on top of the hill. With the clouds overhead there was no moonlight, but they didn't need it. A standing pillar of light stood in the air illuminating the space. In front of the static line of fiery white light was a man wearing a suit of armor and a cloak so long it brushed the ground when the wind whipped past. There was something familiar about him. She sucked in a breath. It was the man from her vision in the library. At his side was a troll. Across from them were two more trolls and a man.

Bertram.

Moira had her bow up and an arrow drawn in an instant.

The weight of Zephyr's hand on her shoulder stopped her from firing.

Her gaze met his. He released her shoulder and held up one talon-tipped digit.

Moira lowered her bow.

The armored man surveyed the top of the hill. Moira heard him clearly when he spoke. "This is the second time you've summoned me with nothing to show for it. Is there something you have to tell me? About why you haven't found the wyvern and killed it?" His voice was deep and modulated almost as if the whole encounter bored him. They could have been talking about the weather instead of murder. He stood at ease with his hands clasped behind his back. He had the same dark hair, cropped close to his skull as he had in her vision. His nose was crooked, his mouth a cruel slash. This close she got a better view of a strong, square jaw. Who was he?

"I told you, there were complications." Bertram shrugged. His shoulders brushed up against the two trolls on either side of him, they stood so close.

"You say the dragon killed the first troll I sent with you."

Bertram shrank backward and nodded.

"I sent more scouts—"

"You shouldn't have done that," Bertram said as he took a step forward. The trolls on either side of him pressed closer, crowding him.

"Silence! I sent more scouts and you say the dragon killed those as well. Then you summon me to say the dragon is half-grown. You asked for soldiers and I gave them to you." The man raised two gauntleted hands in the air. "And still you return empty-handed."

"I know. But the dragon—" Bertram began.

"But it's not just the dragon, is it? The dragon has help. You may have turned up with nothing, but one of my soldiers returned with an interesting tale. There's something you're not telling me. What is it?" The man's hands dropped to his sides.

Bertram kept his mouth closed.

"The dragon is an abomination and will be disposed of. The imp general is tired of waiting, as am I. Hold him."

The trolls on either side of Bertram obeyed and grabbed him by the arms. Did that make the man their commander? No, she thought back to what one of the other trolls had said when they ambushed Zephyr. This man was their captain.

Bertram struggled.

The captain of the trolls stepped forward and smashed Bertram across the face making his head snap to the side.

"What happened?" the captain asked.

Bertram spat a stream of blood before he answered. "Things changed."

"All you had to do was find the dragon and kill it. What aren't you telling me?"

Bertram glared at the other man. "You get this book out of my head, and I'll tell you whatever you want to know."

The captain laughed. It was an unpleasant noise that grated along Moira's nerves. "The book you asked for?"

"I never asked for this."

"No. You asked for power and I gave it to you. It's not my problem if you were too stupid to figure out how to use it. In exchange, I asked you to do one thing, and you failed." He stepped toward Bertram and raised his hands, close to, but not quite touching either side of his head. "You will wish you had told me." He pressed his thumbs into

Bertram's cheekbones and the rest of his fingers against his skull before the man lifted his face skyward and closed his eyes.

Overhead, thunder rumbled and lightning exploded in the clouds.

Bertram strained and thrashed, but the trolls on either side held him in place. His jaw clenched as he stared into his tormenter's upturned face.

Moira's hands clenched so tight her hands shook. Whoever this guy was he gave Bertram the book that was stuck in his head. And he sent a troll along with him to find and kill Zephyr. She had no doubt they would have succeeded if she hadn't gotten the fire rocks to him first. It sounded like Bertram would have let it happen, too. But he didn't. Instead, he'd pushed her out of the way when the troll came after her and made up a story about training her, waiting for the perfect time, playing both sides. Then he'd sent the trolls after Zephyr while he went out on a date with her aunt. Moira recalled his look of shock and the way the color had drained away from his face when he saw Zephyr alive and well the next morning. Again, Moira unknowingly foiled his plans by answering her dragon's call her help. Here she was, doing it again.

She jerked the bow up ready to fire, at the trolls or Bertram, she wasn't sure.

Zephyr held up a hand with a shake of his head.

She clenched her jaw and lowered the bow. She wanted to put a stop to what was happening, but there were too many variables.

In the clearing, the captain made an interested sound. "The book does take up quite a bit of space in your funny little brain, doesn't it? What aren't you telling me?"

Bertram grunted and clamped his eyes shut tight.

"No use trying to fight."

Bertram struggled, but he couldn't go anywhere, not with a troll on either side of him.

The captain's head snapped forward, his eyes opening to glare at Bertram. "A dragoneer—impossible!" For the first time, he sounded less sure of himself. "Who is it?"

Bertram screamed.

The man's lip curled in a sneer. "Stop struggling and show him to me."

Bertram's back curved and stiffened as if caught up in some kind of electric shock. Strung tight one instant, his body sagged in the next, his head dropping to the side, eyes open, glazed and unseeing.

The captain recoiled, wiping his hands on Bertram's coat.

"What is it?" The words were so guttural it took Moira a second to realize the largest troll next to the captain had spoken.

"An unforeseen complication. Nothing more. We take care of the dragoneer the same way we take care of the dragon." He drew a sword from his hip. "Hold him." He leveled the point straight at Bertram's heart and reared back.

This time Moira didn't hesitate; she fired before the captain could run Bertram through. The head of the arrow pierced the middle of his breastplate. The sword fell from his grasp. Both hands gripped the shaft sprouting from his armor. He gasped and sputtered, blood flying from his lips. His gaze turned to the shadows, his voice nothing but a rasp. "Find them. Kill them." He toppled sideways into the troll next to him, unmoving, his eyes closed. The troll lifted his captain, lurched toward the frozen column of light, stepped into it, and disappeared.

The remaining trolls did not waste time. They flung Bertram to the ground. The smaller of the two had no hair on his head and pulled out a long knife while the other unsheathed a double-headed ax.

Moira's second arrow hit the ax-handler in the shoulder. It jerked and shouted. Baldy got an arrow through the hand. It dropped the blade, howling.

Moira stepped into the clearing, another arrow nocked and ready to fire. "Get away from him."

They didn't budge. Their beady eyes squinted before they looked at each other and laughed.

Was it the dress?

The first troll pulled the arrow from its shoulder, snapping it in two. The other yanked the arrow from its palm and flicked the blood on Bertram before tossing it aside. Their laughter grew.

They never saw Zephyr coming.

One second he was beside her and the next he was rushing the larger troll. Their laughter died. Zephyr's sword met the troll's ax with a clang. The smaller troll crouched and growled over Bertram.

Moira glared. "I said, get away from him."

Light from the standing pillar glinted off the Troll's hairless scalp as it sprang toward her, faster than she thought possible. Moira fired. Her arrow hit the forward-moving troll square in the left eye, jerking it to a halt. It fell straight down to the ground, dead.

The other troll roared and advanced toward Bertram. Zephyr leaped in front of him and used the sword to intercept the troll's ax. Zephyr roared. His tail swept the ground and Moira jumped clear.

Zephyr was taller than the troll and just as wide. The sword he wielded would be full-size for a grown man, but for Zephyr, it was more of a short sword. Still effective, though. He used it to block another blow from the ax. Then he stepped in close and slashed at the troll connecting with its upper torso, leaving a long scratch.

Moira saw an opening and fired.

Distracted by Zephyr, the troll didn't have time to duck but shifted so the arrow missed and struck high up on its bicep. It roared, falling back, but not far enough. It stayed far from the edge of the cliff.

Zephyr followed, and Moira reloaded. She fired again. Her arrow hit the troll in the throat as it brought the ax around to bury in Zephyr's side. Zephyr slid out of reach letting the ax whistle by before stepping forward to bring the sword around in a two-handed swing. The troll's head flew from its shoulders.

The severed melon hadn't come to a rest before Moira leaped over the body of the other dead troll and ran to Bertram's side. She skidded to a halt and dropped to her knees beside him.

"Bertram!" She tapped him on the jaw.

He moaned and his eyelids fluttered. A thin stream of blood ran from his nose and ear. Unfocused, his eyes rolled around before his gaze settled on her and sharpened to a blazing point. His entire body convulsed as he strained to speak. "I'm sorry—I tried to help—tried to keep you secret—keep you safe—I just wanted this book out of my head." His breathing sped up.

Moira put a hand on his shoulder. "Calm down. It's okay."

"No—no, it's not." He gasped, his hand moving to his chest, just over his heart as his eyes rolled back in his head. His body jerked once before going still.

33

Zephyr came to stand by her side, wiping the blood from his sword. "How is he?"

"I'm not sure." She grabbed Bertram's wrist and closed her eyes, searching—not with her fingers, but with her whole being. Maybe he'd finally had that heart attack after all. When she felt the thrum of a pulse, the breath she was holding shuddered out of her. She opened her eyes and bent over him. There was a faint whooshing of air as his chest rose and fell. "He's breathing, but I can't do anything for him. Not here." She let go of his arm and stood.

"That's it Zephyr. That's your way home." Moira faced the pillar of light.

Zephyr turned to face the same way, but he didn't move toward the doorway.

"This is your chance. If you don't take it, I honestly don't know if I'll be able to find you another way back to where you came from," Moira said.

Zephyr's gaze went from the column of light to Moira and back again. "I don't know."

"Neither do I. I don't know what's waiting for you over there, but you said you can't stay here."

Zephyr nodded. "I cannot. I do not belong here."

He didn't, but that didn't mean she had to agree with him.

A tiny voice in the back of her head whispered *you could make a place for him*. She was sure of it. She had no idea how they would go about doing so, but they could find space for him somewhere. It might not be close, but they could look. They could find a way.

Zephyr's brows drew down into a line. "I have to go."

Sadness. Moira felt it surge through her. "I know."

He stepped toward the brilliant pillar and Moira felt like she'd been punched in the gut. The air rushed out of her as her shoulders rounded, curving around the hurt. She watched him walk to the light and stop. He turned back. Zephyr raised the hilt of his sword to his opposite shoulder in salute and dipped his head low in goodbye. He lowered the blade, turned, and stepped into the light.

Sparks flew from the column and for an instant, it blazed brighter. Moira shielded her eyes.

The night air whistled.

She recognized the sound a fraction of a second before pain lanced through her right arm and knocked her to the ground. Her bow clattered after her. An arrow sprouted from the top of her arm. First, it felt hot. Then it grew icy cold. The chill worried her more. She tried to lift her arm and the searing heat returned. She gasped and panted for breath.

A troll stepped into the clearing, smaller than the others had been. It picked its way toward her over the uneven ground and the departed bodies of its kind, pausing to stare down at Bertram.

There was nothing she could do from where she lay. If it decided to kill Bertram right in front of her, there was nothing she could do but look away.

"Hey," Moira called. "That was a crappy shot."

The troll's head cocked to the side.

"What were you aiming for? My heart? You missed. By a lot." Her pain fueled the words coming out of her mouth. "I could do better with my eyes closed, but I'd be willing to give you some pointers." Her voice sputtered in pain and fear, but she had to get the troll to come closer.

Its lip curled.

"Yeah, I've only been at this a couple of weeks, but I'm way better than you."

The troll stepped over Bertram and closer to her.

Moira's breath came faster and faster.

The troll stopped, looming over her.

Without a word it reached down and grabbed the shaft of the arrow and twisted. The shaft moved. Sparks flew across her vision. She screamed and flailed with her other arm, rolling and jerking on the ground. The troll smiled, squatting next to her. It reached out to take hold of the arrow's shaft again. Moira came up holding the can of pepper spray she'd removed from her aunt's clutch and stowed in her pocket.

She let the troll have it.

It screamed and jumped backward, hands flying to its face clawing and scratching as the capsaicin burned its mucous membranes.

Its cries ceased when it was stabbed from behind.

Moira gasped.

Zephyr stepped to the side, pulling his blade free from the troll. It slumped to the ground, dead.

Moira lay back against the earth, clutching her right side. "I could have finished it," she said.

Zephyr frowned down at her. "I have no doubt." He hovered over her. "How bad?"

"Why'd you come back Zeph? Because I got shot?" She asked the question to get it out of the way. If Zephyr only came back because she was hurt, then he would be on his way again as soon as she got better.

"I did not leave. Not really," he said.

"What do you mean? I saw you disappear."

"You are too stubborn, dragoneer," he said with a huff, exasperated.

"Tell me about it," she rolled her eyes. As long as she didn't have to do more than lie there, the pain stayed in her arm. "What happened?"

"I approached the light with thoughts of home and it returned me here."

Moira didn't say anything for a moment and then, "Huh."

"Yes."

"Interesting." She almost smiled.

"Indeed."

"So, you do kind of belong here."

Zephyr's yellow eyes turned heavenward. "It would appear so."

Moira's shoulder quivered and she let out a cry. "Stop. Stop. It hurts to laugh."

Zephyr jerked to attention, all business. "Then do not."

Moira closed her eyes. "Alright, what do we do here?"

Zephyr didn't say anything for a minute. Then he rumbled. "I have an idea."

"I am all ears."

"Use your magic to remove the arrow."

Moira's eyes popped open and she stared into the clouded sky above her. Could she do that to herself? She didn't have much to lose. "I'll give it a try, but I'm going to need your help. Can you take hold of the shaft? Gently. Don't pull, just hold on to it."

Zephyr grasped the shaft of the arrow down near her arm.

Moira's left hand came up to rest on his. She drew both comfort and reassurance from the contact before she closed her eyes and concentrated. Her arm hurt. And if she did what she was about to attempt to do, it would hurt a lot more. When the troll had twisted the shaft, it turned, which told her the arrowhead wasn't lodged in a bone. That was something, at least. She only had to deal with soft tissue. She gathered herself. She wasn't directing an arrow where to land, quite the opposite. Ready, she tapped into her will and pushed.

She grunted and guided Zephyr's hand back, slowly. She hissed, but she didn't try to fight the pain. It rolled over her spreading itself thin until her entire body radiated with a dull ache. The arrowhead lifted free and Moira relaxed her will. Zephyr pressed a hand to the open wound.

"Yes. Apply pressure. Thank you," she said.

Her arm, cool from the loss of blood, warmed with the pressure Zephyr applied.

She got concerned when her arm grew hot.

Moira blinked her eyes open. "Zephyr?"

Her dragon bent his head over her, eyes closed.

Her arm was on fire.

And then, it wasn't.

Zephyr leaned back and lifted his face to the sky.

Moira sat up with a groan and unzipped her sweater. She rolled the fabric down from her shoulder. Her arm was stiff and ached, but there was no open wound. A shiny pink line about an inch and a half in length ran across her skin where the arrow had sliced into her. She tugged the sweater the rest of the way off and fashioned it into a sling. With Zephyr's help, she tied it around herself. Her arm partially immobilized, she needed a hand from Zephyr to climb to her feet.

"We need to do something about that," Moira nodded to the pillar of light.

Zephyr looked from her to the lit doorway. "I think I know what it wants."

He dragged the nearest troll by its ankle toward the light. He laid it on the ground in front of the column. As he went to get the other dead trolls, plus a head, Moira watched the light pool and spread, absorbing the dead body. When all the pieces had been likewise absorbed, the standing column of light flickered and went out.

Overhead the skies cleared and the stars shone down.

Bertram hadn't moved. Moira checked his breathing. "Do you think you can carry him?" Moira asked.

Zephyr sheathed his sword. "He betrayed us."

Moira sucked in a breath. The betrayal stung them both. "But he helped us, too."

"Why?"

"I think because of me. That first time in the woods when the troll found us. They were working together, but he didn't expect to find anyone with you. He drew the line at killing another person."

"But he would have killed me."

"He would have tried." Moira peered up at Zephyr. "But he didn't."

"Because of you."

"And then he insisted on training me. Maybe because he was trying to pull a double-cross on whoever that guy was, the one I shot?"

"The captain of the trolls."

"I think so. Whoever he was, he gave Bertram the book, but it did something to him. All he wanted was to get rid of it. Bertram might not have helped us for the right reasons, but I don't know. Maybe it should count for something."

Zephyr stared down at Bertram for a full half a minute. She counted the seconds to herself. Then Zephyr blinked and raised his head with a sniff. "I never trusted him."

"I know," she said. It made no difference now, but Moira got the sense Zephyr had to say it out loud. She was happy to listen if it meant they could move on. "But I promised to help him if I could, remember? Can you carry him?"

A sigh rumbled out of him, but Zephyr bent and lifted Bertram over his shoulder in a fireman's carry. "Where to?"

34

Where to?

Great question.

They could take him to a hospital, but Moira wasn't sure they had the right type of doctors available to help.

They needed help.

HELP ME.

The notes in the library.

The thought that had niggled away at her finally fell into place.

"We've got to get down this hill." Moira got a solid grip on her bow and quiver, careful of her injured arm. They started down the hill together.

"Where are we going?" he asked.

"Back to school."

They picked their way downhill and moved through the woods to the rear of the high school near the loading docks. The big bay door was open. There weren't any cameras there that she knew of. A janitor swept the floors inside. They crouched out of sight in the dark, waiting. The janitor took a break. When he left, Moira rushed inside with Zephyr close behind, hurrying through the halls. Moira opened the double library doors so Zephyr could duck inside. It was dark in the stacks away from the windows. Most of the lights had been turned off to conserve energy. At a table surrounded by towering shelves of books on all four sides, Zephyr laid Bertram down. Moira set her bow and quiver aside.

Bertram lay still. Moira checked for a pulse. Satisfied he was still alive, she lifted her head and stared at the stacks of books around them.

Zephyr inspected the shelves, turning his head to read the titles.

"Librarian!"

Zephyr's head snapped around at her shout.

No one appeared.

"Where are you?" Her good arm flew up from her side as she turned in a circle seeking the mysterious Librarian. "Bertram asked you for help, didn't he? But you couldn't help him, could you?" She stopped turning and stood in front of a bookcase. "Or maybe you wouldn't."

She swept an entire shelf of books to the floor.

Zephyr winced. "Must we?"

"We must." She pushed another shelf full of books to the floor, a series of images flashing through her mind.

A troll standing over her with a cruel smile.

Zephyr stepping into the column of light.

Bertram slumped over, unconscious.

Her arrow sprouting from the middle of the captain's breastplate.

Ansel dancing with someone else.

Moira glanced down. Her feet were awash in a sea of books. "Librarian!"

Zephyr jumped and growled a warning.

Moira's head snapped around.

"He is dying." The Librarian stood at the head of Bertram's table dressed in his sharp black suit. "Do you have the book?"

Moira ground her teeth together. "What book?"

His brows knit together. "The physical copy of the book your friend has stuck in his head. The only way I can remove what has been placed in his mind is if I have somewhere for it to go. I told him that. More than once."

"No, I don't have the book," she said. She relaxed her jaw before she continued. "Neither does he. It disappeared after it got stuck in his head. Didn't he tell you that after he asked you for help? He's the one who left all those notes, isn't he?"

The Librarian inclined his head, the only indication he gave that she was right. His focus shifted to Bertram. "What has happened?" He frowned, causing a line to appear between his brows.

Moira swallowed. "Someone—a man—did this to him. Took his head in his hands and, I think, forced himself into Bertram's memories. Made Bertram show him things."

The Librarian scowled and stepped close to the table.

Zephyr growled a warning.

The Librarian faced the dragon with no problems. There was no hint of dragon-freeze about him. "I wish to examine him, not do him harm."

Zephyr glanced at Moira.

She nodded, but Zephyr didn't back away.

The Librarian laid the tips of all ten fingers around the crown of Bertram's head. Bertram didn't stir. The Librarian's eyes remained open, and, though she was prepared, she still flinched when the black of his pupils overtook the white sclera of his eye. "The book is intact. However, his mind can no longer carry the burden of it. He is dying. Without the book, there is nothing I can do." His eyes reverted to normal as he lifted his hands away.

"What? Can't you take the book out and put it in a blank one or something?"

"It's more complicated than that." The Librarian spread his hands. "Books have lives of their own. Especially this one." He nodded toward Bertram. "It wasn't just a copy. It was the original manuscript of *The Book of Wyverns*. An original can't be stuffed into any old blank book. It wouldn't fit. Every book has its own unique space. If you had focused on your training, we wouldn't be in this position."

"Excuse me? You mean, if I had dropped out of school." She couldn't believe what she was hearing. The Librarian blamed her for what happened to Bertram. Of course, Bertram was the one to tell her to keep up appearances and stick to a regular schedule as much as possible. "I protected Zephyr."

The Librarian's gaze turned to Zephyr looking him up and down. "Indeed."

"What happens if Bertram dies?"

The Librarian's eyes narrowed. "The book dies too. There's nothing I can do."

Moira didn't buy it. The Librarian, whoever or whatever he was, was the only being she knew of strong enough to help them. Even Bertram must have thought so if he left all those notes.

She closed her eyes and massaged her temples and tried to think.

The book needed space.

Maybe they could give the book what it needed.

She lowered her hand. "Would it be possible for you to transfer the book to someone else?"

The Librarian tilted his head, considering the question. "Yes. It's possible."

"Can you transfer it to me?"

Zephyr's head snapped up.

The Librarian's head tilted to the side as if we were giving her question serious thought. "The burden of any book is too great to carry for long unless one is willing to make concessions."

Moira stared at him. "Concessions. What kind of concessions?"

"Memories."

Zephyr shook his head. "I do not like this idea."

"I need my memories. I need to remember Zephyr. I need to remember everything that's happened. How could I function without my memories?" Moira asked.

"You would relinquish personal memories, not your muscle or procedural memories. For instance, you wouldn't remember the first time you rode a bicycle, but you would still, in fact, be able to ride a bicycle, presuming that's something you learned to do in the first place."

Moira's eyes narrowed. "Are you asking me if I can ride a bike?"

"Can you?"

Moira swallowed. "Do it."

The Librarian's eyes widened a fraction. Perhaps she'd managed to surprise him for once.

"No. It is too dangerous," Zephyr said.

"What happens to Bertram?" Moira asked.

"His mind will bear some scars, but in time he will be able to function quite the same as before."

Zephyr huffed.

"Zeph, I don't see another way. They're only memories." She swallowed the sudden lump in her throat. "I'll make more." She stepped around to the head of the table, tripping over a book to get there.

The Librarian lifted a brow.

"Sorry," Moira said, but she didn't know if she was apologizing to him or the books.

He dipped his head low and touched one hand to the top of Bertram's head before peering up at her with eyes gone completely black, devoid of any human quality.

Moira blocked the sight by closing her own eyes. Something brushed her temple. The touch was so light it could have been a lock of hair pulled free by the wind. To her surprise, she felt a real breeze stir. She kept her eyes shut tight. The air swirled around her legs. Then it rushed past her, making pages from the books she'd shoved to the floor rustle and flap. A whispered din of conversation joined the commotion. Hushed at first, the sound built until it was deafening. Noise and the sensation of being inside a blender were followed by sudden stillness and quiet.

The silence was so abrupt Moira wondered if she had been struck deaf.

"Moira?"

She gasped. She wasn't deaf, but whatever the Librarian did affected her equilibrium. The ground pitched and rolled beneath her though she was pretty sure she didn't move. She reached out a hand in search of something solid and felt the table under her palm. Even with her eyes closed, the room spun. She bent over double and dropped to her knees.

A hand was on her elbow an instant later. Zephyr tsked. "What have you done?"

Her eyelids fluttered. The light was too bright. She'd only shut her eyes for a minute, but it felt like they'd been closed for hours. She checked the clock on the wall. Hardly any time had passed. She shielded her eyes and squinted. All of the books she'd pushed from their shelves were back in place.

Bertram still lay flat out on the table. She looked closer. He hadn't moved, but he appeared different, more relaxed.

Moira grew steadier by the second. There was no pain. She expected she might have a headache, but other than her short bout of dizziness, she was fine. At least she thought so anyway.

The Librarian stood off to one side, tugging at the cuffs of his shirt. His eyes, normal once more, stared off into space, his expression thoughtful. There was something different about him, but she couldn't out her finger on it right then.

Zephyr said her name.

"I'm okay." She stood with Zephyr's help, wobbling once on the way up.

"What do we do now?" Zephyr asked.

Moira rolled her shoulders and winced. The left was fine, but the right was still stiff. SHe eased out of the makeshift sling and picked up her bow and quiver. "I need to make a phone call."

35

A week later Moira was in a visitor's chair next to a hospital bed where she'd sat quietly twice before. Bertram lay in the bed, unmoving and pale, his features relaxed. Someone had tucked the blanket up under his arms, leaving his hands out to rest at his sides. Her aunt couldn't tell her how he came to be in the hospital, but Moira knew. An anonymous phone call had been placed from inside the school saying there had been an accident in the library. No one saw what happened and no one was there when the paramedics discovered Bertram unconscious.

Questions abounded. What was Mr. Bertram doing in the library on Homecoming? Why was he on a table? What was wrong with him? Why wouldn't he wake up? Rumors followed. Most revolved around some sort of drug use. Moira heard them all. She knew what had happened and not even she could guess why his condition hadn't improved since he was brought in seven days ago. There was no reason for Bertram not to have regained consciousness, but he hadn't and the doctors were starting to worry.

Her aunt was starting to worry.

"Aunt Paige says I should talk to you. She thinks you might be able to hear me." Moira kept her voice low. Bertram didn't have a roommate, but she didn't want anything she said to go beyond the pale green walls. Bertram laid there. She glanced away.

"Let's see, what have you missed? I got shot with an arrow, but I'm fine. Healed up pretty quick. Aaron, you know, Ansel's twin brother? He was voted Homecoming Duke. Don't know if you're into that sort of thing." She paused, frowning. "Then he showed up for school on Monday morning with a black eye. No one knows what happened, but the next time I saw Ansel he had a split lip and bruised knuckles so I can hazard a guess. Speaking of Ansel, he's still not talking to me. Aaron asked me out. I'm supposed to meet up with him later tonight. Kind of a date type sort of thing."

Moira sat forward, her elbows on her knees. "Zephyr's doing well." She scooted closer to the bed. "But we're both still trying to understand." She sighed. "You must have got involved in something you thought would be good, but it went bad. I don't know how. Now I'm Zephyr's dragoneer." She sat up straight. "You were supposed to kill him, weren't you? But you couldn't. Zephyr changed the rules of the game when he bit me and you didn't want to play anymore, but you couldn't get out of it, could you? Not with the book stuck in your head. You needed it gone. What were you thinking? Did you think the captain of the trolls would help you? Not until he knew Zephyr was dead and probably not even then."

Moira didn't know why she asked him questions. It wasn't like he was going to answer. She kept talking because she hadn't talked to anyone about this except Zephyr and he was tired of hearing it. The dragon would never say that, but she could tell. "How surprised were you that morning when you saw me and Zephyr standing over the bodies of three dead trolls? You sent them to kill Zephyr when you thought for sure I wouldn't be around. And you were going to try the same thing again the night of the dance, but it didn't work out that way." She sat back and closed her eyes, pressing her fingertips to her closed lids. Instead of Zephyr being murdered by a band of trolls led by their captain, her dragon was alive and now she had a book stuck in her head.

The book didn't affect her physically in the same way, or as much, as she had seen it affect Bertram. It didn't cause her any problems at all until she tried to recall a specific moment from her past. Then her pulse would pound, her breath coming faster and faster. If she pushed it her vision went dark around the edges. Her mind would turn, skipping around, seeking alternative routes to what she wanted to know. When her thoughts were pulled away from the memories she couldn't recall, her vision cleared, and she could function again. Through this process, she found she retained her intellect, but couldn't remember where she'd gained any of it. Recent events were easier to recall than older memories. Everything from her childhood was a dark blur. She could still ride a bike. Since the Librarian had mentioned it, she'd hopped on her old Trek for a spin around the driveway when she'd seen it in the garage. Every time she tried to think about how she'd learned though, there was nothing but the blur.

As for the book itself, she had no impression of what might have been disclosed within its pages. She had no way to access the information and she didn't spontaneously know any more about dragons than she did before. As long as she didn't try to remember anything from too far back in her past, the book sat in her head and didn't cause her any trouble. She got headaches now and then, but not any worse than before the Librarian transferred the book to her.

The pain came when she realized that giving up her memories meant she'd lost her father all over again. She could only remember his face because she'd studied a picture of the two of them. What kept her from dissolving into a heaving, heaping mess, was that she didn't need the memories to know how much her dad had loved her. Her insides knew it to her bones and her head knew it, too. She hadn't stopped loving her father when he died and that kept her going even if she couldn't remember him.

"Zeph didn't want me to come." Moira sat forward again. "You said you were sorry. I believe you. I don't think you meant for any of this to happen, but it did. And I honestly believe you tried to help. You wanted the book out of your head; it's gone now. The Librarian got it out. So why haven't you woken up?"

No response.

Not that she expected one.

"What am I missing? You taught me so much, but you didn't teach me how to do any of this without you." Her hands curled into fists, but there was nothing to fight, not physically.

The only other person she could talk to about Zephyr wasn't speaking to her. Not having Bertram around didn't feel right. She missed him. Despite her connection with Zephyr, Moira felt more isolated and alone than ever.

There was a tap at the door. Moira sat back and sniffed, wiping her nose. Her aunt opened the door and slipped inside, closing it gently behind her. "Hey. How's it going?"

Moira raised her empty hands. "He's still out of it. I don't know if I'm doing any good here."

"Oh, honey." Her aunt stepped in close to Moira's chair and slipped her arm around her shoulders. "I didn't expect you to do anything. I just appreciate you being here. Harold would tell you that himself if he could." She let go and went around the bed to check on all the machines Bertram was connected to. When she was done, she took his hand and stared down at him.

"What happened?" Moira asked. "On your date."

"Nothing happened." She smiled a sad, little smile. Moira thought that might have been the problem; that nothing had happened. "I was nervous. You could probably tell. It was my first date in a long time. You know that. And he was, I don't know, distracted, maybe? But we had a good time. At least I thought we did." She smiled down at their hands.

"Would you do it again? Go out on another date with him?"

Her aunt gave it some serious thought, squinting down at the figure in the bed, perhaps trying to resolve what she was seeing with the last image she had of Bertram up and walking around. "You know, I think

I would. I enjoyed his company. Yes. I would go on another date with him." She squeezed his hand and let go. "Maybe just dinner though." She checked her watch. "Are you almost ready to go? I've got a few more patients to check on, but then I'll clock out and come back and get you. Sound good?"

Moira said it did and waited for her aunt to leave the room. When she was sure there was no way her aunt might overhear, she leaned in close. "Did you hear that? If you wake up, my aunt said she would go on another date with you."

No response. Moira heaved a sigh, stood, and stretched.

Whatever the captain of the trolls had done to Bertram, modern medical science was having a hard time fixing.

In which case, modern medical science might need some help.

Moira squinted at the machines and devices surrounding the bed. She couldn't. Could she? She'd never tried to work magic on a person before. If there was a line she wasn't supposed to cross, then exerting her will over another human being sounded like it should be that line. Thinking of using magic to make someone do something felt wrong. But maybe she wouldn't be making him do anything. When she considered what she knew, magic felt like the only course of action in this particular situation. Bertram's condition could be more fragile than she suspected and what she was thinking of doing could do more harm than good. But he could just as well die if she did nothing. What if she got it wrong and made him worse?

"Please, Lord, don't let me kill him." Moira laid her right hand over Bertram's left. His hand was cool but warmed quickly. She closed her eyes. And then she worked backward through time, calling up all the recent memories she could. Bertram stretched out on a table in the library. Bertram being carried over Zephyr's shoulder. Bertram in the woods. Bertram watching her and Ansel spar. Bertram teaching her yoga. With each image, she released a bit of her will, down and out through her fingertips where they rested on top of Bertram's hand. As she released her will she visualized a flash of light like a picture being taken. She made her memories a beacon for Bertram to follow, attempting to draw him away from wherever his mind lingered. She made it back to the night he came over for dinner.

A machine beeped. Moira didn't know which one made the noise, but she opened her eyes. She looked down at Bertram. No change. "Bertram?"

No answer. Then another beep.

She stepped back, raising her hands and pushing them through her hair. She didn't know what she was doing. Didn't know what she ought to try. "What did he do to you?"

Bertram's eyes moved beneath his eyelids, once, twice. Then they pitched and rolled like he was in the middle of a dream.

Moira stepped back up to the side of the bed, squeezed Bertram's hand, and kept trying. She went all the way back to the first day of freshman year and walking into Bertram's class. There he was, standing at the front of the class, at ease, ready to share his love of chemistry. He was smiling. He was happy.

Moira opened her eyes. "Come on, Mr. Bertram." She had no more memories of her own to use. The machine beeped again, but his eyelids had stopped twitching. She lifted her hand from his and turned away from the bed. Whatever she thought she was doing, didn't work. Her shoulders slumped. At least now she knew she had tried everything.

A rustle of fabric reached her ears and Moira raised her head.

"Ms. Noble?"

Acknowledgments

No one writes in a vacuum or, at least, they probably shouldn't. This story would not be what it is today without the help of many people. Several of those individuals are longtime members of the writing group Tuesdays With Story in Madison, WI, which I've been a member of for over ten years. To those who read my chapters time after time and commented, you have my gratitude.

To my very first readers: Janice McDonald, Jerry Peterson, John Schneller, Pat Edwards, Jessie Jones, Tracey Gemmel, August Crass, and Tracey Phillips, you have my thanks. Special thanks to Diane Boles for passing the manuscript on to my first young adult reader, Alex Seaborg.

A special thanks to my sister, Amanda Lahners, for not reading this until I needed her to.

Thank you to my husband. I could not do any of this without you. And to my kids, thanks for being you.

Finally, thank you to you, the reader. I don't know how this book came to be in your hands, but I hope you've enjoyed it. If so, please mention it to someone else. The truth is, independent books need people like you to help spread the word, either by writing a review or passing it on.

Thanks again.

About the Author

Amber Boudreau has a background in geology. In between household projects and parenting, she writes youth and adult fantasy. A native of northwest Indiana, she currently lives in Madison, Wisconsin with her husband and two children.

The Dragoneer is her debut novel.

She can be reached on Facebook, Instagram, or Twitter at **@AnAmberAuthor** or at **authoramberboudreau.com**.

Selected works from Our Catalogue

No Place
By Sam Swicegood

The Wizards on Walnut Street
By Sam Swicegood

The Dragoneer and the Pretender
—coming soon
By Amber Boudreau